THE SILK MERCHANT'S CONVENIENT WIFE

Elisabeth Hobbes

MILLS & BOON

First Published in Great Britain 2020
by Mills & Boon, an imprint of HarperCollins*Publishers*
1 London Bridge Street, London, SE1 9GF

© 2020 Claire Lackford

ISBN: 978-0-263-27719-7

MIX
Paper from
responsible sources
FSC™ C007454

This book is produced from independently certified FSC™ paper
to ensure responsible forest management.
For more information visit www.harpercollins.co.uk/green.

Printed and bound in Spain
by CPI, Barcelona

To Julia, without whom this book would be
a lot longer and more rambling. x

Prologue

1837

Δεν θα παντρευτώ ποτέ
I shall never marry

Jonathan Harcourt laid his pen down and looked at his words in satisfaction. The hand was untidy and the Greek lettering uneven but the language itself was accurate.

He added the date with a flourish.

twenty-eightth of August 1837

He crossed out the errant 't' with a frown. Nevertheless, it was an acceptable start for the first entry in his new journal—a rare gift from his father to a son about to embark on his journey to boarding school.

'I shall never marry.'

Jonathan said it out loud, having no fear of anyone hearing him. His parents' current icy argument was keeping them occupied downstairs, pointedly ignoring each other. He had no idea what Mother had done now to raise Father's ire. Presumably something insignificant which no rational person would consider worthy of more than a slight admonishment. Of course a husband had the right to chastise his wife, but Christopher Harcourt's silent disapproval could last for hours and turn the whole house into an Arctic of animosity.

There was the sound of both voices raised in a rapid cacophony that Jonathan tried to ignore. Jonathan ground his fists against his ears to try to block out the sound of sharp voices. It was either that or storm downstairs into the parlour and demand that Father stopped shouting. He knew better than to intervene, but Jonathan promised himself that one day, when he was older than twelve, Christopher Harcourt would pay for the misery he had caused.

There was the sound of the study door slamming, followed shortly afterwards by the sound of the front door slamming. Jonathan sat up. This was unusual. Normally matters were concluded by both parents retiring to their own, separate, bedrooms. He wondered which parent had stormed out into the night and whether they were now walking in the dark around the parkland behind Darbrough Court or along the bridle path into Chester-le-Street itself.

The question was answered shortly afterwards when Anne Harcourt crept into Jonathan's room, her silhouette in the door frame plunging it into shadows.

'Are you awake?'

There was no point Jonathan pretending he had managed to sleep through the noise now they knew he was old enough to listen and have his opinions.

'Yes. Are you all right, Mother?'

He should know better than to ask. Whenever he tried to comfort his mother she immediately leapt to his father's defence. Not this time, however. She glanced over her shoulder.

'No, Johnny, I'm not. But I will be soon. We both will be.' She walked around the darkened room. 'Are you packed and ready for tomorrow?'

Jonathan was due to leave at first light to begin his new life at St Peter's School in York. His uniform, books and a few other precious belongings were packed in the wooden trunk that stood, corded and labelled, at the end of his bed. His journal would go into his carrying case along with his purse of money and a couple of apples and slices of bread. The journey would be split into two parts. Jonathan would travel with the family coachman as far as Durham and from there he would take a public stagecoach to York where he would be welcomed by staff from St Peter's and taken to the school.

'I'm ready.'

His mother found him in the darkness and drew him into a hug. He was twelve and his father disapproved of shows of affection that he thought should have ended when Jonathan was first breeched. Jonathan couldn't recall ever seeing his parents touching, much less embracing. It felt almost like a rebellion for Anne to do it now and he wasn't entirely comfortable with it. He stiffened and she released him.

'Be ready for the carriage. Stepney will have everything waiting for you.'

She left and Jonathan settled back, trying to sleep.

Jonathan arrived in Durham, shivering and yawning in the watery, dawn light as planned. Autumn was making its appearance known even though it was only the twenty-ninth day of August. He bid farewell to Mr Stepney, his father's coachman, and stood at the coaching inn alone, determined not to be daunted by the bustle. Other passengers, horses and coachmen paid no attention to the undersized twelve-year-old until someone tapped him on the shoulder, causing him to jump.

A man dressed in a shabby cloak was smiling at him.

'Master Harcourt, heading to York? Come this way, please.'

He didn't look like an employee of the stagecoach company, but as he had called Jonathan by name, Jonathan obediently followed as the man dragged the heavy trunk around the corner. He expected to find a coach waiting, but instead came face to face with his mother sitting on a trunk similar to Jonathan's own. She was dressed in a plain blue travelling cloak and bonnet he had never seen before with a black veil covering the upper part of her face.

'Are you coming to York with me?'

'No.' She stood and brushed her cloak down purposefully. 'And you are not going there either.'

She pointed to the mail coach that stood with a pair of horses ready across the street. 'We're taking this instead. Make haste.'

The messenger had begun loading their two trunks on to the roof of the coach and securing them. Mrs Harcourt climbed inside and Jonathan followed. They were not the only passengers. An old man sat with his legs sprawled in the seat opposite but moved them grudgingly in the presence of a lady.

'Where are we going?' he asked.

Mrs Harcourt looked at him. 'Not now. We're stopping again soon and then I'll tell you.'

Jonathan never learned the name of the first town they arrived in. The trunks were transferred to an open wagon and Jonathan found himself sitting on hard boards beside his mother.

His mother said nothing until the whip cracked and the wagon gave a slow lurch into movement. Only then did she seem to relax.

'Mother, now please explain what is happening,' Jonathan urged.

'I have left Darbrough Court. I have left your father and my marriage.'

Jonathan reached for her hand, remembering at the last moment that contact was strictly discouraged by his father. The implications of his mother's words sunk in and he took her fingers anyway. If what she said was true, his father's commands no longer mattered. She met his eyes and, for the first time in years, Jonathan saw hope, not defeat, staring back at him. Jonathan's scalp prickled in fear and anticipation. He was expected at St Peter's in two days. What would happen when he did not arrive? More to the point, what would happen when his father discovered his mother's absence? She must have guessed his thoughts.

'Your father thinks I am visiting a friend from

my school days. He won't expect me back for a week. I very much doubt he will care in any case. This is the start of a new life for both of us, Johnny.'

And what a new life it was. After three further changes of coach and two nights in travelling inns, they arrived in a small town at mid-afternoon. The narrow streets of terraced houses seemed to close in around them as they stopped outside a tall, single-fronted, three-storeyed house in the middle of a row of eight.

Jonathan frowned. This couldn't be right? Darbrough Court had six grand rooms on the ground floor alone and four bedrooms. It had stood in large grounds with rose gardens and a lake. His mother looked at him apologetically.

'This is all I can afford with the annuity my parents left me and that is only because the landlord was generous to an old acquaintance. But it's ours and we're safe from your father here. As far as everyone here is concerned, I'm a widow and we have had to leave our home, forced out by an unfeeling heir to the estate.'

A man was swaddled in a dark cloak beside the door. He handed Mrs Harcourt the keys and together she and Jonathan dragged their trunks inside. The house was sparsely furnished: a parlour and kitchen on the ground floor, a scullery behind that with a door leading to the yard and a privy shared between all eight houses. On the second floor were two bedrooms and on the third was a single room with long, low windows at front and back.

'It's a weaver's cottage,' she said as she came to stand beside him. 'No boarding school and no luxuries, but we'll be safe and we can be happy. This is Macclesfield. It's a town of silk.'

A thrill went through Jonathan. The description sounded exotic and romantic, but grey skies huddled over row after row of grey-slate rooftops and the grey mill that loomed on the hills appeared to enclose the town within a wall. It felt like anything but silk.

The first month was bliss. They remained undetected by Mr Harcourt and gradually Jonathan stopped looking over his shoulder, waiting for the hand of his father to descend. Conscious of taking him from the school he had been set to attend, Mrs Harcourt taught Jonathan herself as best she could. They pored over French and Latin together by lamplight. She sang as she worked with Kitty, their one maid. She learned to do laundry and cook meals, much to Jonathan's astonishment. She even taught Jonathan how to sew, joking that when he eventually married, his wife would find it a welcome surprise. Jonathan said nothing. He'd already decided long ago never to marry and saw no reason to change his mind. Why would he when marriage was such a joyless, unpleasant experience?

'We have a queen on the throne now, Johnny.' She laughed. 'A woman can do anything she sets her mind to.'

'Then I shall earn and support us,' Jonathan told her. 'I'm old enough now.'

He set out the next morning and found work delivering messages around Macclesfield, competing with other lads for the penny errands. The other boys mocked his accent and what they saw as encroachment on their territory from a toffee-nosed boy, but Jonathan was quick on his feet and soon learned his way around the backstreets and alleys of the town. He learned to play down his background and play up his accent and the amusement it generated when he asked for *bread* or which *way* to go. A cheeky request with a grin often earned him a tip simply for being a novelty. His life was a far cry from the lessons he should have been having at his school in York, but he relished this freedom.

It was on his third week of walking the streets with parcels and letters when his life changed for ever. He was bearing a message from the haberdasher to Mr Edward Langdon, Esquire, at Langdon's Mill on the edge of town. The red-brick building seemed to grow even bigger as Jonathan walked closer, following the path along the river. This mill was somehow more welcoming than the ones closer to the centre of town which stood like sentinels or the grey edifice on the hillside. From a distance the rattle of machinery was thunderous. He knocked on the door of the mill offices with a loud thump and kicked his feet against the cobbles while he waited. The door opened and Jonathan was greeted unexpectedly by Mr Langdon himself.

Jonathan stared in surprise, not expecting to see the mill owner. He knew Mr Langdon by sight, having seen him at a distance promenading around the centre of Macclesfield on Sunday afternoons. He was a bachelor in his early forties and Jonathan had heard his name spoken around Macclesfield by women wondering in frustration why he ignored all their daughters. There were rumours of scandal in his past, but wealth, it seemed, wiped out any indiscretion when it came to marriage. Another reason for Jonathan to hold the institution in contempt.

Jonathan held out the note silently.

'You'll want paying, I suppose,' Mr Langdon said.

'Aye, sir,' Jonathan agreed. Then, unexpectedly, he found himself adding, 'No.'

Langdon peered down at him. He had softly drawn-back gingery hair that was beginning to grey at the temples and a pointed chin that gave him the demeanour of a fox. It was a handsomely interesting face, made remarkable by a pair of wire-rimmed spectacles balanced on the end of a straight nose. He peered over the top of them and Jonathan felt the examination of the older man's blue eyes on him. His confidence deflated a little.

'I mean, yes, I want paying for this, please, sir. But I want a job.'

The idea came to him in a rush. The imposing mill with three storeys of windows and high iron gates was daunting, but the location by the river had caught Jonathan's eye. The machines continued to bellow mysteriously from inside and his curiosity prickled. Mr Langdon made silk, Jonathan knew, but he had no idea how or what went on behind the high doors.

'You appear to already be in possession of a job. You're a messenger boy,' Mr Langdon said. He turned to go, dismissing Jonathan.

'I want a better one.' Jonathan called. 'I'm better than the job I have. I want a job here.'

His voice took him by surprise. Where had this boldness come from? It caught Mr Langdon's attention, however, because he turned back.

'You look familiar. Have I seen you before?' Mr Langdon asked.

Jonathan bowed his head. Now was the time to be humble and polite; something he should have done from the start. 'No. I only moved here from near Durham recently.'

Mr Langdon regarded him with proper interest for the first time, peering closer at Jonathan.

'Do I rent a house to your mother, boy? On Back Paradise Street?'

Jonathan had never wondered who his landlord was. Mrs Harcourt had only spoken of 'an acquaintance'.

'I do live there. My name is Jonathan Harcourt.'

Mr Langdon bit his knuckle. Jonathan tensed, holding his breath while Mr Langdon scrutinised him further.

'You should have come to me first rather than wasting shoe leather running around the streets with errands. Yes, I can find you work.'

'Not in the mill, if you please,' Jonathan said. 'Not on the machines. Here. In your office. I can read and write. In Latin, too. I'm good with numbers.' He decided not to mention his Greek, which he still laboriously practised in his journal each Sunday night.

Mr Langdon seemed to find this amusing.

'You'll start in the mill, not the offices,' he said firmly. 'Two years there. Once I've seen what you can offer me, we'll discuss what I can offer you.'

'One year,' Jonathan answered.

Mr Langdon laughed. 'Eighteen months. And you'll work in every area, learning what we do here.'

Jonathan agreed readily. He held out a hand to Mr Langdon, who laughed once again and shook it. 'I predict you have an interesting future ahead of you, young Master Harcourt. Do give my regards to your mother when you go home tonight.'

And that was the start of what would become a long-lasting friendship.

Jonathan worked in the mill for the first ten of his eighteen months, moving from floor to floor, learning how to thread the silks for the Jacquard cards, plan patterns and operate the looms. After that, Mr Langdon promoted him to tallying the orders and the bales of silk and then to ordering the silks themselves. By the time three years had passed, Jonathan was overseeing the spinning floor.

At the end of another year he was working in Mr Langdon's office as Mr Langdon's underclerk, dealing with clients and working on designs for the damask cloths. By the time Jonathan was nineteen he was working as a full clerk, responsible for choosing the apprentices from the workhouse.

In Edward Langdon Jonathan found a friend and companion who nurtured his love of learnin and eventually opened his own house and library to the eager boy.

When Mrs Harcourt grew sick and succumbed to a tumour, Jonathan discovered that she had been saving his wages for years, somehow working miracles with what he gave her to provide food and clothing. There were also assorted pieces of jewellery that, once valued, meant the grieving young man was heir to a considerable amount of money.

On the afternoon of Jonathan's twenty-fourth birthday Edward Langdon invited his protégé into the office for a drink.

'I have a proposal,' Jonathan said. 'I want to invest in the mill. Would you consider selling me some shares?'

'I'm more than happy for you to invest,' Edward said, pouring two glasses of whisky from the crystal decanter he kept in his office. 'But I have another proposal. Join me as a partner.'

'You want me to be your partner?' Jonathan asked incredulously,.

'Junior partner, Jonathan. I'll still have the major share.' Edward held the glass to his nose and inhaled with a long, satisfactory sniff. 'Why

You've worked for me and with me and

n your worth to me tenfold over the past

Jonathan's throat tightened. Whatever worth he had been to Edward, the older man had been a mentor, friend, brother and father to Jonathan.

'Thank you,' he said, finding his voice choking. 'I accept.'

'In that case, let's drink a toast.' Edward raised his glass.

'To Langdon and Harcourt.'

Chapter One

1850

Aurelia Upford was cleaning the windows of the first floor when the man strode up the gravel driveway to the front door. She paused and peered through the pane she had just cleaned.

Since the family had returned two weeks previously there had been no visitors to the house. Hardly surprising given that Sir Robert Upford and his family had been absent for five years, but just as well given the accumulated grime of five years' neglect that would take a dozen servants to clear. She put her cloth down and wiped her hands on the white apron she had borrowed from the scullery, glad to have an excuse to pause for a little while. The sun was setting behind the man. From the purposeful way he walked she imagined him to be relatively young. It was that sense of purpose that made her stomach coil with anxiety, but as he grew closer to the house he slowed and began staring intently to his left.

Aurelia smiled. Her sister, Cassandra, was cropping rose bushes in the overgrown knot garden to the left of the doorway. Of course she was, thought Aurelia with a shade of exasperation. Cassandra would not think to help her sisters or mother or the few servants they could afford by donning a cap and apron and cleaning the house. She would value amusing herself in the garden as an equally important form of work, despite the fact that it was late August and the garden could wait until spring.

Cassandra was clearly the reason the man had stopped walking, but it gave Aurelia the perfect opportunity to examine him a little closer. He wore a light wool overcoat, open to reveal a well-fitting double-breasted frock coat, accompanied by a fawn-coloured top hat. His face was cast into silhouette by the sun, but the long locks that peeked from beneath the brim and settled around his collar were cast into flames around his head, giving the impression he was on fire or wearing a halo as well as a hat.

He was tall and broad shouldered and held himself well. Aurelia assumed he must have come to see her father, but he looked unlike any of the usual creditors who came calling and threatening

Sir Robert to pay the gambling debts that had afflicted the family for so long. This thought pulled her from her reverie as anger twisted her stomach. She watched the visitor shake his head and move on past Cassandra, who had either not noticed or more likely pretended not to notice. He knocked on the door and Aurelia counted to twelve in her head before it was answered. She resumed cleaning the windows, wishing they could afford at least one more maid or boy to help in the task. She scrunched the cloth and began scrubbing at the cobwebs, anger lending her vigour.

Not more than five minutes passed before Aurelia's younger sister, Theodora, bounded up the stairs out of breath. Aurelia looked at her younger sister affectionately. Though seventeen, Theodora still conducted herself like a twelve-year-old at times, rushing around the house and stomping as she walked as if she were a boy.

Aurelia bit her lip. Dora didn't know about Father's debts and Aurelia hoped she never would.

'Do you know where Father is?' Dora asked.

'Probably out walking the grounds with the dogs, trying to catch rabbits,' Aurelia said with a shrug. 'Send the page boy to find him.'

Dora wrung her hands together. 'He went already without finding anyone else. Now there is a man sitting in Mother's morning room alone, waiting for someone to attend to him. Can you believe the silly boy let him in, then wandered off! What he'll think of us I don't know.'

'Didn't you go speak to him?'

'On my own!' Dora looked horrified. 'Mother would be furious.'

Aurelia frowned. Sending a seventeen-year-old into a room with a strange man would be indecent, but so was leaving a guest alone. The family had returned to the Cheshire house after five years' absence living in Oxfordshire, and creating a bad impression on local society was the last thing Sir Robert needed, especially after the scandal Aurelia had narrowly avoided. She would have to go keep the visitor company herself until Mother arrived.

'Who is this man anyway?'

'I heard him say he's from the mill. Langdon and Harcourt's,' Dora said. 'I don't know who he is, though. Who do you think he might be?'

Aurelia smiled. 'I imagine that as he has come to the front door, not the tradesman's entrance, he might be Mr Harcourt or Mr Langdon, wouldn't you say?'

Dora grinned. 'That's why you're the clever one! I suppose he must be. Anyway, please come quickly. I'm going to tell Mother now.' She strode along the corridor and hammered on her mother's bedroom door. Aurelia watched with affection. Dora was just as clever as she was herself. She picked up her bucket and cloth and walked downstairs to take them to the scullery, wondering what business a mill owner could have with a baronet. Leaving them on the landing would most likely result in Dora knocking them over. She would have to risk impropriety and go speak to the visitor herself.

As she was about to go into the scullery, a voice called her.

'Miss! No one has taken my coat!'

The man was not secreted in the parlour any longer, but standing in the entrance hall, looking at her, his broad shoulders tensed. His full lips were pressed into a tight line and he seemed irritated at being left waiting. He was holding out his overcoat and hat towards her. Aurelia was about to give him a sharp answer for speaking to her so rudely until she remembered she was carrying a bucket of water and wearing an apron, with strands of hair coming down and floating around her cheeks. Mistaking her for a kitchen maid was understandable.

Wanting to spare him any further embarrassment, Aurelia put down her bucket and held her hands out. His lips curved into a smile, softening his air of disapproval. It always took Aurelia by surprise how soft men's lips could be. She felt hers prickle and had to stop herself reaching up to touch them. As he laid the coat and hat in her waiting arms she caught a brief scent of cologne of some sort. It was warm and sweet, but with a lingering woodiness. Very masculine.

Immediately Aurelia spiralled back four months to her last, happy meeting with Arthur before everything had gone wrong. He had smelled different, of tobacco and brandy and sandalwood, but there had been the same hint of saltiness and depth that she decided must be the male body itself.

Not now, she commanded herself, pushing the memory down to the bottom of her heart where it belonged. She could not think of the man she had almost married without tears of anger and humiliation threatening to spring to her eyes. It had taken the move back to Cheshire to help her crawl out of the pit of despair, but the initial pain had lessened. Now Aurelia allowed herself one indulgence a day in the form of a walk by the river where she could weep or rant at her misfortune as much as she liked. Revealing any emotion in front of a stranger would be unthinkable.

She hung the coat and hat on the stand beside the front door very close to the parlour door that the man had just come out of. When she turned back around the visitor's eyes were on her. He frowned, stepping forward with his hand raised as if he intended to touch her.

'Sir!' she said in a shocked voice. From his polite manner she would not have put him as the type of man who would attempt to fumble with a servant in the absence of her mistress. She stepped back out of reach and he dropped his hand abruptly, brows shooting upwards in horror.

'I wasn't…! I mean to say… Are you unwell? Should I call someone?'

Aurelia put her hands to her cheeks. She was obviously not as in command of herself as she had believed if he thought her to be ill. She had passed a grave judgement on him with no foundation. His concern for a stranger—and a parlour-maid at that—touched her more than she would have thought. She shook her head.

'No, thank you.'

They stared at each other as if they were opponents in a game of chess, each waiting for the other to move first. He was younger than she thought a mill owner should be. In Aurelia's mind all businessmen should be serious old men with paunches and whiskers. They shouldn't be clean shaven and attractive with startlingly blue eyes. They shouldn't have an easy smile like the one that was starting to return to this man's face now he had assured himself she was not about to faint or fit.

'Are you sure you don't need help?' he asked. His voice was quite deep, but had a trace of an odd accent about it that gave it a pleasant lilt. Or maybe it was the words of concern themselves that made it appealing.

'No, thank you. Sir Robert or Lady Upford will be with you as soon as possible,' Aurelia said.

Aurelia lifted her bucket and made her way to the scullery, feeling only a little remorse that the visitor would believe Sir Robert would employ a servant rude enough to forget a *sir* at the end of a sentence.

She checked whether anyone had asked Mrs Peters, the housekeeper, to prepare afternoon tea. Of course no one had. Hiding her frustration at her lackadaisical family, Aurelia decided against joining the visitor and went to her bedroom. After the case of mistaken identity she could hardly now appear as Sir Robert's daughter without causing both of them embarrassment. Besides, if Cassandra could choose to amuse herself with flowers and gardens, then Aurelia saw no reason why she couldn't spend some time pleasing herself, too.

She knelt beside the bed and reached underneath until her fingers settled on the handle of a case. She pulled it out, sat in her favourite reading chair by the window and opened it.

What today? she asked herself she gazed at the books inside. Her guilty secret. Her hand settled on Ovid's *Medicamina Faciei Femineae* and she pulled that out, taking her Latin dictionary with it. Mother would be furious if she realised Aurelia had still kept her Latin books. If she knew what some of the subject matter was, she would have a genuine fit of the vapours.

She had read three pages, struggling over the translation and wondering whether grinding hart's horn into honey would improve her complexion enough to justify the inconvenience to the buck, when Dora burst through the door without even knocking.

'Mother says you need to come downstairs straight away!'

Aurelia shut the book with an audible snap and slipped it under the damask cushion that she was resting against. Dora knew about her reading and Aurelia was reasonably sure her sister would not betray her to their parents, but her instinct was always to hide the fact that she continued to study even long after her parents had told her such subjects were not suitable for a young lady.

'Mother is fretting. Father hasn't returned yet and she is now having to entertain Mr Harcourt—that's his name, by the way, you guessed right—by herself. She wants us to join her.'

Aurelia sighed gently. Her mother was an excellent hostess—a great part of the reason Sir Robert had married her, Aurelia suspected—and she had no need to have any company, being adept at talking at length to whomever she happened to sit opposite. This was entirely about taking the opportunity to parade her three daughters to a gentleman visitor.

'I'll come down shortly,' she said. 'I need to rearrange my hair.'

Dora left and Aurelia ran a comb over her dark locks, smoothing them back under her broad ribbon. She washed her face in the basin and as an afterthought dabbed a drop of eau de cologne behind each ear, taking her time in the hope that her father would have returned and taken the visitor to his study.

Sadly, this was not the case. By the time she got downstairs she collided with her mother in the parlour doorway before she could even enter.

'There you are,' Lady Upford hissed. 'We've been waiting for you and the tea hasn't arrived. That silly girl is taking her time about bringing the tray, Aurelia, would you see to it please.'

'Let me go see where Sally is,' she said.

Lady Upford tugged her sleeve and lowered her voice. 'When you do join us, Aurelia, please be mindful of what topics you choose to raise. I don't want Mr Harcourt to think I raised a bluestocking or liberal!'

Aurelia nodded. Over her mother's shoulder she could see Mr Harcourt was standing by the fireplace conversing with Cassandra, who was tossing her hair until her ringlets bobbed enticingly. He was giving her a charming smile and paying her all the attention in the room. Of course he would. Every man fell into raptures over Aurelia's older sister and they made a fine pair together. With her dainty features, warm brown eyes and chestnut locks that curled at the mere sight of a hot iron, Cassandra was stunningly beautiful. Mr Harcourt was tall and broad shouldered, though he did not appear overly muscular in the way a man who laboured physically would be. His hair was a sandy brown, cut long at the sides, with a wave across the forehead that covered the tips of his ears. He was clean-shaven with neatly trimmed sideburns. His blue eyes sparkled as he listened to Cassandra.

Altogether he was a good-looking man. Aurelia's skin prickled and she noticed the unexpected sensation with fascination. Her heart had been so firmly broken that she had determined to harden it before she let it heal and become vulnerable again. She was done with good-looking men who thought they could charm a woman with an easy smile, so to feel her body rebelling against what her mind had decreed was odd.

'I won't say anything,' she promised. She left the room quickly, hearing her mother begin to praise Cassandra's paintings as she left. Sally was halfway from the kitchen carrying a tray when Aurelia intercepted her.

'Let me help,' she said kindly. The young girl

bobbed an anxious curtsy, almost dropping the teacups as she did so.

'No, miss, I couldn't let you do that. It isn't proper.'

'Proper be dashed,' Aurelia said. 'I'm not standing on ceremony when we have a visitor and those cakes look so delicious.'

She lifted the cake stand and led the way back into the parlour.

Cassandra and Dora were now sitting on the long low sofa before the window while her mother sat in a chair opposite the fire and Mr Harcourt sat opposite her.

'The tea is here,' Aurelia said, placing the stand of cakes on the small table. Her mother thanked her and ordered Sally to pour the tea. Mr Harcourt was examining a book of sketches of Greek vases: the ones that the girls had been expressly forbidden to look at due to the scurrilous subject matter. He looked up when Aurelia spoke. His eyes grew wide as they met Aurelia's and he quickly closed the book so she couldn't see the contents. He nodded his thanks and accepted a cup of tea from Sally, but when Aurelia sat down on the sofa between her sisters, his handsome face took on an expression of utter bemusement. Aurelia wanted to laugh out loud.

'And here is my middle daughter at last,' Lady Upford said as Aurelia arranged her skirts. Mr

Harcourt's eyes widened. He glanced towards the cake stand, then to Sally who was still pouring tea, then back to Aurelia.

He rose and crossed the room to take Aurelia's hand. She smiled at him and pretended it was the first time they had met. What else could a lady do—after all, the mistake was not entirely on his part. She could have explained her identity when they first met and had compounded the confusion further by entering the room with the maid.

'I am charmed to make your acquaintance, Miss Aurelia,' he said. He had the grace to look abashed. 'Please allow me to introduce myself. My name is Jonathan Harcourt.'

She gave him her hand and he kissed it lightly, just skimming his lips across the back and causing the small hairs to flutter. His eyes held hers and she thought she saw a flicker of humour in them that made her want to smile back.

'How nice to meet you, Mr Harcourt. I do hope you weren't waiting long without company.'

Lady Upford turned to Mr Harcourt and gave him an apologetic smile.

'Aurelia organises servants so well. We have returned to the area after a long absence and when we left we did not think it fair to keep our staff on at half-pay so let them all go. Now we have discovered they have found employment elsewhere and we have had to employ entirely new staff. I must say the quality isn't what it was. You must return to visit us in a month or so, Mr Harcourt. By then we should have managed to find a full complement of adequate staff so we can show you how Sir Robert likes his household to be run.'

Lady Upford continued to chatter. Mr Harcourt was listening politely, even though the goings-on of the domestic arrangements of a house which he had not entered more than ten minutes earlier could be of no interest to him at all. Mr Harcourt glanced over at Aurelia and his eyes crinkled enticingly. Aurelia had the urge to make a remark to him about the maid who had received him at the door and see how he reacted, but this would then open her up to questions from her mother and sisters and she did not want that. After the scandal she had narrowly escaped with Arthur she wanted to be under no scrutiny.

Mr Harcourt finished his tea and stood to stretch his legs. He walked about the room, making appropriately admiring comments about the paintings, then stood at the fireplace, looking barely more at ease than he had when waiting in the hallway. Presently Cassandra went to the piano and began playing a gentle air. Aurelia and Dora sat silently drinking their tea and listening as their mother tried to discover as much about Mr Harcourt as she could.

'Are you a married man, Mr Harcourt?'

Aurelia nearly dropped her teacup at such an intrusive question. Mr Harcourt was standing half in profile to her and she saw his jaw tighten. His eyes flickered briefly to the corner of the room where Cassandra had paused playing to turn the page. Aurelia held her breath, realising that she was keen to discover the answer herself.

'I'm not and I'm perfectly content with that state,' Mr Harcourt answered in a more agreeable tone than the question merited. 'Despite what fanciful female writers might have the world believe, not every single man is in want of a wife.'

Aurelia bit her lip so she didn't smile. Her mother looked blank. She was not a reader and clearly had no idea what or whom Mr Harcourt was referring to.

'Harcourt of Harcourt and Langdon's Mill, you say,' she asked.

'Langdon and Harcourt's,' he corrected. 'I'm very much the junior partner. Mr Langdon was unable to join me today in person owing to a slight cold.'

His eyes flickered to the carriage clock on the mantelpiece. 'Do you have any idea when Sir Robert may return?' he asked. 'I know I breached etiquette terribly by calling unannounced and I would not want to keep you here if you are busy. I know how difficult it is moving into a new house and how much time that takes.'

Aurelia eyed him with a little more interest. His accent was unusual, now she considered it, not like the other members of the Cheshire town that she had heard since moving back. He was not local and presumably as much of a stranger now to the area as they had been when they moved away. A dull pain spread through her as she wished she could be back in Oxford.

The raucous sound of dogs barking broke through the genteel atmosphere as the door slammed and the sound of claws on the marble floor indicated Sir Robert had returned from his walk.

'Artemis, down! Mercury! Hermes, leave that umbrella!' Sir Robert's booming voice echoed through the hall, penetrating the genteel atmosphere of the parlour. 'Diana, to me!'

It was not only Sir Robert's children who took their names from the classical world. Aurelia counted herself lucky he kept his more outlandish names for his dogs. There was a clatter of something being knocked over and Sir Robert rang the gong in the hallway loudly to summon his butler. Quickly Aurelia rushed to the door and attracted his attention.

'Father, we have a visitor,' she said.

Sir Robert followed his daughter into the room, still dressed in his walking clothes and sturdy boots with the dogs sniffing at his heels. Immediately Lady Upford began to shriek in protest at four Irish Setters rolling on the carpet leaving ginger hair everywhere. Mr Harcourt looked appalled at the uproar. Aurelia and her sisters began to separate them and drag them from the room and out around the front of the house.

Aurelia lingered long enough to hear Mr Harcourt's measured voice saying, 'I'm terribly sorry for trespassing on your time without an appointment, Sir Robert. I am your nearest neighbour in a matter of speaking. My call is for social purposes, though I hope you and I may have the opportunity to conduct business in the future.'

Aurelia paused in the doorway to listen for her father's answer.

'Do come with me and we'll go somewhere a little more private and quieter,' Sir Robert said. 'This confounded noise is dreadful.'

The sisters looked at each other in amusement; it had been perfectly quiet until their father and his hounds appeared and ruined it.

'What do you think he wanted?' Cassandra asked. Aurelia fixed her hand on Diana's collar. The bitch was coming into heat and making every attempt to escape to satisfy her urges. Aurelia felt sympathetic and half-considered letting her slip free for an hour of fun.

'I can't say,' she replied, 'but if Mr Harcourt is hoping Father might invest in his silk trade he is going to be sadly disappointed when he discovers how little money we have.'

His impudence at calling with no appointment had been surprisingly effective, though. Sir Robert would have been unlikely to see him formally if at all possible, as he was determined to have little contact with society.

Cassandra laughed bitterly. 'A full complement of servants!' she said, mimicking their mother's tone. 'What rot! Eight servants are all Father says we can afford for the time being.'

They succeeded in putting the dogs back in their kennels. Aurelia lingered, petting them for a few moments, then returned to the house. The dogs had knocked the table askew so she spent a few minutes of rearranging ornaments, knowing the disarray would annoy her if she left it. When she heard Mr Harcourt's voice she lifted his hat and coat from the stand, catching again the scent that had tickled her senses the first time. Mr Harcourt exited her father's study a couple of steps ahead of Sir Robert. The men were laughing together, but Mr Harcourt paused when he saw Aurelia waiting and his brows lifted. She gave him a serene smile.

'Aurelia, what are you doing?' her father asked.

'I heard your guest's voice so thought I would find his coat for him,' she said in an innocent voice. 'I was here so it saves summoning the housemaid.'

She handed the garments to Mr Harcourt whose lips twitched into a quick, unexpected smile. He had nice lips, full and wide, and his smile was infectious. That she could look at a man so attractive without the least stirring in her heart was proof it was terminally broken. She acknowledged his thanks with a curtsy and watched him leave.

'Are you looking to catch a husband, my dear?' Sir Robert said, kissing her cheek. 'If you are, then I can ease your mind and tell you Mr Harcourt is unmarried. Rich, too.'

'No, I'm not,' Aurelia snapped. 'After the fiasco with Arthur I intend to remain a spinster for ever.'

She knew mentioning Arthur's name would quieten her father down. He hated the very mention of the wretch's name and it served him right that Aurelia should throw it in his face after his own tactless comment.

'That's good, my dear. I'd be stretched to find a dowry for any of you at present even if there was anyone of our position asking for your hand,' Sir Robert said. He pressed her hand and Aurelia tried not to feel bitter that his not-so-secret vice had put them in such dire financial straits.

Sir Robert began looking around the entrance hall. 'Now, what the devil became of my dogs?'

He wandered away, whistling and calling the

names of the hounds. Aurelia watched him go, then returned to the blessedly peaceful sanctuary of her room and her translation of Ovid's facial remedies for women. Purely theoretical, naturally, for what did she care how youthful her skin looked if she never intended to attract another man in her life?

Chapter Two

'Good grief, Edward!' Jonathan exclaimed as he walked into the study of Langdon's home. 'You owe me a large glass of something strong for agreeing to visit Sir Robert alone.'

Edward looked up from the book of engravings he had been peering at and gave a faintly questioning smile.

'I should send you next time,' Jonathan continued. 'You'd be more appreciative of Sir Robert's collection of pornographic Greek vases and Lady Upford would be less likely to try inflict her daughters on you as prospective wives.'

'Did she do that?' Edward asked. 'I recall she was a silly but formidable woman when the family lived here before, but I wondered if time might have mellowed her. Not that I ever met her, of course. I would never be admitted into her circle. Trade and gentry don't mix in their eyes.'

'Consider yourself fortunate,' Jonathan said. He passed a hand over his brow in an exaggerated manner. He spent hours each day in the stifling rooms of the factory amid the deafening noise of the machines, yet the half-hour he had spent in Lady Upford's company had given Jonathan more of a headache than the most wearing day amid the looms. The atmosphere in the room had been claustrophobic and the incessant chattering of Lady Upford and the presence of three young ladies was daunting to a man used to the solitude of his own spacious house.

'I imagine she needs to be formidable to keep a rein on her husband. If that man wasn't a member of the aristocracy, I would go as far as to call him a buffoon,' Jonathan said. 'He shambled around the room, tried to ply me with whisky, asked if I preferred to play cards or backgammon and then offered me a pup should his bitch fall pregnant.'

Edward chuckled and Jonathan was glad to see his friend showing some signs of animation. He had been very withdrawn and serious since coming down with the cold he had been unable to shift for almost a month.

'I'd go as far as to call him a buffoon anyway in that case,' Edward said. 'Did you manage to broach the matter of the land sale?'

Jonathan shook his head ruefully. 'I presented my case as a social visit, so unfortunately not.

He has invited me back to discuss the matter in a morning rather than afternoon when he says he will be more able to concentrate on matters of business. I wonder if he drinks to excess.'

His jaw tightened, remembering the decline his own father would descend into after too many spirits. All regrets that he had left a house as grand as Siddon Hall behind him vanished. He poured Edward a small glass of port and handed it to him with an impatient sigh.

'We do need that land if we are to expand and adopt efficiencies. I've made an appointment to see him in a week which should give me long enough to develop some resilience to him and his wife.'

'And his daughters?' Edward asked. 'Did they also require a suit of armour to encounter?'

Jonathan sat back in the chair and gazed into the fireplace, bringing the girls to mind. The eldest had been breathtakingly beautiful and the youngest amusingly boyish in her manner, but it had been the middle one who commanded his memory the most. The girl he had appallingly mistaken for a servant when he'd accosted her to take his coat and hat. Alternately cringing and laughing, he explained his error to Edward, who chortled.

'I remember the girls. Of course they were all much younger when they left. I did wonder if they would grow into beauties like their mother or if they would be cursed with their father's looks and temperament.'

'The oldest two certainly have their mother's looks,' Jonathan said. 'As to whether they have more sense than their father I could not say after spending so little time in their company. I'd hazard a guess that even the dogs I saw have more sense than him.'

Edward stared at him for what felt like an inordinate amount of time. 'And did you find yourself feeling anything towards these girls?' he asked.

Jonathan frowned. He wasn't sure what he was expected to feel. They had been pleasant company. The eldest had sparkled with life and gaiety, but he'd been glad when she began to play the piano as he had been struggling to think what he could possibly say to entertain her. The middle one had been more diverting owing to being the only one in the house who appeared capable of doing anything and given the fact that they now shared an unusual secret. Her eyes had gleamed with mischievousness. The youngest was barely a year out of being a schoolgirl.

'They are all very beautiful,' he admitted. 'And they are just as accomplished and well brought up as any young lady of their class and situation might be. They would be pleasant enough to spend an evening with, I am sure.'

'And any longer than an evening? Would you consider any of them as wives?' Edward asked.

Jonathan stood and began pacing round the room. The old question. The old vexing subject that he had made his feelings clear about over and over since reaching manhood. Whenever his circumstances had changed the threat of wedlock loomed as various fathers or mothers paraded their daughters before him. He and Edward had often laughed about how the ranks of unmarried had transferred their arrows from the older target to the younger man as soon as the two men had gone into partnership. Now to hear Edward making the suggestion struck a chord that was atonal and unsettling.

'You know I have no intention of marrying anyone. You and I are a pair of confirmed old bachelors, after all, and you've always known I intended to follow in your footsteps.'

He stopped before the fire and tapped his fingers on the mantelpiece. Edward placed his glass on the small table at his side. He stoked the fire, thrusting the point of the poker deep into the glowing coals.

'I was perhaps wrong to ever encourage you in that respect,' Edward murmured, turning to Jonathan with a bleak expression on his face.

Jonathan raised his eyebrows in surprise. This was a side that Jonathan had never seen before.

'You're talking nonsense. You are perfectly happy being unmarried and so am I.'

'I have my reasons for never having married,' Edward said, staring into the flames. 'And I hazard a guess they are different to yours. But I have known love and affection in my younger days—and affection in my older years. You have shied away even from those. Have you ever even known a woman?'

Jonathan folded his arms. 'I shall not dignify that with a response.

It was an admission in itself and Edward clearly saw it. He gave Jonathan a faint smile. 'You should consider taking a wife, even if one of these particular girls doesn't appeal to you. Now, if you will excuse me, I shall retire for the evening with memories of a past I can treasure. Will you be able to say the same at my age?'

He left the room. Jonathan saw himself out, Edward's words echoing through his mind.

Nothing more was said of the matter when the two men met in the mill offices the following morning and all talk regarding the Upford family concentrated on whether or not the baronet could be persuaded to sell the land needed.

By the time the day of Jonathan's appointment came around he was determined to succeed, whatever the cost. The sky was cloudless and the morning mist had cleared, leaving a warm autumn day of the kind Jonathan particularly liked. Rather than going along the road through the town and round the long way, he walked down the narrow lane behind the factory to the river. He broke of a tall stem of grass and used it as a switch to knock the tops off other grasses, sending the tufts flying. By the time he reached the river bank his trouser hems were damp and he was regretting his decision.

He looked at the Bollin, which was the natural boundary between his property and Sir Robert's land. The river was narrow here and meandered gently through the flat countryside. That idleness of the flow was half the source of Jonathan's problem. There was nothing but fields at the edge of the parkland on Sir Robert's side and most of them were not even being used for grazing at the moment. Surely Sir Robert would be happy to sell off the parcel that Edward and Jonathan needed.

He was so absorbed in his speculation that he did not notice he was no longer alone until a colossal splashing broke his contemplation.

'Caesar! Get out of there, you beast!'

He looked around to see the hind legs and feathery tail of a dog plunging into the river and paddling away, then he was hailed by a female voice. The middle Upford daughter, Miss Aurelia, was striding towards the opposite bank from across the field. She was carrying a dog's leash looped around one black-gloved hand.

'Oh, Mr Harcourt, I did not expect to encounter you again so soon,' she said breathlessly. 'Is it deep?' She gestured to the water and pulled her mouth to one side.

'In places, but it would only come to my thighs here,' Jonathan answered. Miss Upford stared intently at the part of his anatomy he had named and he felt a slight awkwardness at being examined.

'That's a relief. Mother would be devastated if Caesar came to harm.'

They both looked towards the dog—a King Charles Spaniel—which was swimming in joyous circles and looking far from in peril.

'Good morning, Miss Upford,' Jonathan said, finally recalling his manners and tipping his hat.

She dipped a curtsy and they stood looking at each other across the water. Her manner was not unfriendly but she did not seem particularly pleased to have met him.

'I could say the same,' he replied. 'This is a lonely place to be walking.'

'I like solitude,' she said crisply. 'Contrary to what society would have you believe, not all young ladies crave attention and company.'

She was wearing a walking dress the colour of ripe damsons. A matching capelet nipped in at her waist, emphasising the narrowness in contrast to her wide skirts. Her outfit was completed by a straw hat with a veil pulled over the top half of her face. She was currently peering at him from beneath with her chin tilted up. The effect was alluring, though she could only have dressed for herself if her walk was taking her to the boundary of her father's estate and she had thought not to encounter anyone.

'Then I should apologise for disturbing your peace,' Jonathan said. 'It gives me the opportunity to make another apology, however. I must crave your pardon for the dreadful mistake I made when I first encountered you. Will you forgive me?'

'It was understandable given the circumstances.' Miss Upford acknowledged his apology with a graceful tilt of her head. 'Now, we know why I am walking through a field of wet grass,' she said, gesturing at the spaniel who scrabbled out on to the bank beside her. 'But why are you here?'

He indicated the mill buildings which could just be seen over the treetops. 'This land belongs to the mill. I'm speculating how best to develop it.'

Miss Upford seized the dog deftly by the collar, doing her best to avoid the shower that erupted as he shook himself. 'Heel, you silly boy! Mother refuses to let him go out with Father's dogs.'

She fixed the leash to Caesar's collar, then

lifted her veil and gave Jonathan an interested look. 'Oh, how do you plan to use the land?'

'That very much depends on your father,' Jonathan said. He drew out his watch and opened the cover. 'In fact, I am due for an appointment with him at ten. Would you permit me to accompany you back to the house?'

She looked at him through narrowed eyes before answering.

'Yes, you may.' She hardly seemed overjoyed at the prospect, but then added, 'If you walk a short way down to where the river turns, it becomes narrow. You could probably step over easily.'

He could undoubtedly, but something rose inside Jonathan. Pride, or a need to impress Miss Upford. Perhaps simply a wish to change her steely expression to something less severe. He took a few steps backwards, then took a running jump and landed on the opposite bank gracefully beside Miss Upford. Immediately Caesar began snarling and straining at the leash towards Jonathan, trying to leap at him. Jonathan stepped back, one boot sinking into a patch of mud.

'Oh, do behave, you wretch!' Miss Upford snapped, pulling vigorously until the dog subsided. It took Jonathan a moment to realise she wasn't commanding him and he was in the process of standing up straighter. Their eyes met and she gave Jonathan an apologetic look with eyes the colour of coffee. They were fascinatingly dark, rimmed with short, thick lashes beneath straight brows and Jonathan could have spent the morning counting the individual flecks of caramel that speckled them.

Now he was closer to her he saw the rims were a little red and came to the conclusion she had been crying at some point. He remembered how downcast she had looked when she had taken his coat and hat in the hallway and how he had thought she was becoming ill. He had a terrible recollection of his mother, red eyed and weeping before she left Jonathan's father. A stab of pity went through him and he wondered what could have made her so sad she chose to come to such a solitary place with the unruly Caesar. He almost had the urge to take her hand and squeeze it in an attempt to offer comfort.

The idea took him by surprise. Perhaps Edward was right and he had spent too long avoiding the company of women if something so simple could draw such an odd impulsive sympathy from him. He gestured in the direction of the path back towards the house, but Miss Upford shook her head.

'I wanted to walk along the river. Do you mind?'

Jonathan shook his head and they walked side by side along the bank, doing their best to avoid the longest of the grass. Jonathan considered offering her an arm, but she seemed perfectly happy walking independently and pulling the dog on the leash to stop him diving in. Her manner was remarkably efficient and a far cry from the other young ladies Jonathan had encountered.

'Why were you carrying a bucket and wearing an apron?' he asked.

'The task needed to be done. As Mother explained, we aren't a complete household yet. I see no point in expecting someone else to take a task on if I can do it without much inconvenience to myself.'

'I commend your approach to life,' Jonathan said, tipping the brim of his hat and finding he truly meant it. As they reached the bend in the river he slowed down.

'This is the reason I am coming to speak to your father,' he said. He gestured to the bend in the Bollin which narrowed as it flowed in a narrow horseshoe through the mill grounds. 'You see, everything on this side of the river belongs to your father and I would like to purchase the land where the loop of the river goes into mine.'

Miss Upford looked at him inquisitively. 'What would you possibly do with one more field?' she asked in wonderment.

'My mill is powered by water,' Jonathan explained. 'A single wheel drives the shaft that powers the looms. Over time the river has silted up and narrowed, meaning the wheel turns slowly.'

'So it is the river you need, not the land,' Miss Upford said. 'You could divert the flow into a straighter line and the water will flow faster.'

'Well done, that's absolutely right.' Jonathan smiled approvingly and Miss Upford's elegant brows came together.

'It's a very simple concept to grasp, Mr Harcourt. Even a woman is able to understand such a thing.'

Jonathan floundered. 'I wasn't implying you couldn't, I hope.'

She gave him another frosty smile, but there had been a flicker of surprise in her intelligent brown eyes that Jonathan had liked.

'It's both the river and the land I want,' he said, hoping to break the atmosphere that had suddenly descended. 'I don't have the space to expand at the moment as I'd like to. I have plans, you see.'

He left the idea dangling, but she didn't ask him to elaborate so he walked on in silence and soon they reached the bridge across the Bollin and the road that led either back to Macclesfield or to Sir Robert's house. Miss Upford drew the leash tighter and drew her veil down, but not before Jonathan saw that her eyes were a little less red than when they had met.

'Perhaps you should make your own way to the house,' she suggested, glancing towards the double gates of the house. 'I'll walk on a little further towards the town before I turn back.'

So she did not want to be seen with him, Jonathan thought. Would her father disapprove of her walking out with a man without a chaperon? He bowed, trying not to mind that their conversation was at an end. As she walked away he called after her.

'Miss Upford?'

She looked back over her shoulder, giving Jonathan an excellent view of her slender neck, straight back and narrow waist.

'Why does your mother refuse to let Caesar walk with the other dogs?' he asked.

She gave a full smile; the first he had seen. It lit her face and her eyes glowed with mischief that was apparent even beneath her veil.

'He has ambitions above his station. He tries either to fight or to mount them, depending on their sex.'

Jonathan concealed a grin at the image of the boisterous King Charles trying to reach the relevant part of the towering Setters.

'It's good to have ambitions,' he remarked, which received an even more brilliant smile that vanished almost immediately. Either she thought such humour was too ribald a subject or she was deliberately trying to maintain a frosty demeanour, but as she walked swiftly away he was sure he saw her shoulders shaking with laughter.

Chapter Three

Sir Robert received Jonathan in the same office they had spoken in on his previous visit, but Jonathan noted that, now business was being done, the baronet sat behind his desk and looked down at Jonathan, who sat on a comfortable but markedly lower chair at the other side of the expanse of oak.

After a few preliminaries regarding the weather, Sir Robert said, 'I believe you arrived at the gates with my daughter. What are you doing with Aurelia?'

Jonathan explained the circumstances in which they had met, hoping to assure Sir Robert that it had been entirely coincidental. That explained her insistence in leaving him to walk alone. Did the baronet suspect he had compromised the girl? he wondered.

'I was surveying the river and the back of the mill,' he explained with a smile. 'Which brings me on to my purpose here today, if you will permit me to begin.'

He outlined his plans and named what he considered a generous price. 'Siddon Hall is my ancestral home,' Sir Robert said sternly. 'Six generations of Upfords have lived here and my forefathers built it with the sweat from their brows and the blood from their swords.' He stood and walked to the crest carved into the oak panelling above the fireplace, staring upwards. 'Now you expect me to relinquish part of that estate so that you can grow rich yourself! Do you think I have no pride in my heritage, young man, because you yourself have humble beginnings?'

Jonathan forced a smile on to his face and clenched his jaw. It was on the tip of his tongue to remark that if Sir Robert cared so much about his land why had he been an absentee landlord for so many years and why had he left his property in such a state that his own daughters were forced to garden and play housemaid? Moreover, the land was being used for no purpose. He held his tongue, knowing that to say something so rash would put an end to any possible negotiation and suspecting this was a clumsy opening gambit to encourage him to raise the price. Something which he had no intention of doing.

'I believe our price is fair for the land,' he said. 'However, if you yourself have plans to use it I would not dream of standing in your way, Sir Robert. I shall not take any more of your time and shall bid you good morning.'

He stood and gave a polite bow before turning for the door.

'Wait,' Sir Robert commanded. 'I should, perhaps, explain my reasons.'

'If you wish,' Jonathan said pleasantly, returning to his chair.

Sir Robert's eyes were full of cunning. They were similar to Miss Aurelia's, but lacking in the bright intelligence of hers at the riverside.

'I have concerns besides sentimentality,' Sir Robert said wistfully. 'I have not been blessed with a son and, when I die, the Upford baronetcy will pass to a distant nephew. My income from the land is the only means I have for providing dowries for my three daughters.'

He returned to his chair and shook his head sadly. 'I worry greatly about their futures as they are all yet unmarried.'

He gave Jonathan a penetrating stare. 'As you are yourself, I believe.'

Jonathan nodded cautiously as a creeping sense of nausea began to creep over him.

'If I knew that at least one of my daughters was provided for, I would feel easier about selling off their inheritance,' Sir Robert said. 'If only

I could be sure that at least one of them was secure in her future...'

He tailed off and stared out of the window. Jonathan said nothing. If Sir Robert was intending what Jonathan suspected he was, then in turn Jonathan would make him say the words himself.

Sir Robert beckoned Jonathan to join him at the window. The three Misses Upford were walking around the grounds. Miss Aurelia had rid herself of Caesar and was walking arm in arm with her older sister. They made a graceful pair as their full skirts swayed from side to side in unison as they walked and Jonathan could not ignore the slight fluttering in his heart at the sight of them. They were very beautiful, he acknowledged to himself, though Cassandra had the edge with her slender figure and delicate features.

If he was married to one of these women, would it be so terrible after all?

'I am reluctant to lose my ancestral home.' Sir Robert sighed in what Jonathan thought was an overly theatrical manner as if he were in a melodrama. 'If the land were part of my daughter's marriage settlement, I dare say I could come to agreeable terms.'

Jonathan hid his surprise well. Sir Robert was not only intending to saddle Jonathan with an unwanted wife, but also to still extract the money from him. Really, he had to admire the man's cheek. He could no longer bear to suffer the baronet's clumsy hints.

'Do you suggest I should take one of your daughters in lieu of the price?'

Sir Robert went red and began to bluster.

'You know nothing of me,' Jonathan interrupted. He glanced again at the girls and remembered how insistent Miss Aurelia had been that they were not seen together. 'Why would you be so eager to give me one of your daughters in marriage?'

'I've seen the street where you live,' Sir Robert said. 'It's a grand enough place for a man of your class. I dare say you could keep my daughter in the manner she has been raised in. Even though your origins are much humbler.'

Jonathan said nothing. He was not sure whether this was a compliment or censure. An aristocrat such as Sir Robert saw the entitlement to a grand house and surroundings as his birthright, but many in his position resented men of Jonathan's social class for daring to create their own wealth. He noted that Sir Robert had clearly been investigating him, indicating his interest had been piqued at their first meeting.

Jonathan's home was a town house a few streets away from the mill in a respectable street with a small square and garden. It was on the same plan as Edward's house: double fronted and three storeyed, with a private garden and privy. It was bigger than the house in which he had lived until his mother's death, yet considerably smaller than the house they had fled from when leaving Durham.

Jonathan bit his tongue. If Sir Robert knew of the grand house set in waterside grounds near Durham that Jonathan and his mother had left he would not be quite so quick to judge. He also knew the rumours that Sir Robert was more in need of money than he was letting on.

'Likes a game of cards or two, so I've heard,' the factory foreman had said and grinned when he had overheard Jonathan and Edward discussing the morning's appointments. He had received a cold response, but Edward later admitted the baronet was known to be incautious when it came to naming his stakes.

'I may have made my money through trade,' Jonathan said proudly, 'but every penny has been honestly earned and I have no doubt in the slightest I could provide everything your daughter would need.'

Everything apart from affection, he thought wryly. His marriage would be as much of a business deal as if he were ordering the purchase of a thousand spools of silk thread. Growing impatient of skirting around matters, he put his hands together and looked at Sir Robert over the top of the desk.

'My wife will bear no title, nor will my children, but they will never want for anything. Moreover, they will, in turn, inherit a considerable fortune. But let me make it quite clear that the woman in question does not have to be your daughter.'

He sat back and folded his arms, content to wait until Sir Robert made his next move. The reason for Sir Robert's apparent failure at the card tables became clear because not more than a minute had passed before he thrust his chair backwards, his face red, and leapt to his feet.

'I hope you did not mistake my intention,' Sir Robert said. 'You must forgive a father's concern—after all, it is only natural I want to ensure my dear girls are settled in good homes. I've seen your current home and I also know the street where you spent your youth. You've climbed high, Mr Harcourt, and I believe you could climb higher still. I could help you with that. Allow me to invite you to dinner on Thursday evening. We neighbours should get to know each other better and you may find you are more inclined to accept my proposal after meeting my daughters again. I shall look over the figures you have suggested and see if they are a fair recompense for losing the land.'

Jonathan accepted, keen to be gone from Sir Robert's presence. As he made his way down the long driveway, tipping his hat to the sisters who were walking through the overgrown knot garden, he mused that the least appealing part of the whole process might be gaining Sir Robert as a relation!

'Contemptuous man,' Jonathan raged to Edward as he strode about the office. 'Thinks to barter his daughters to a complete stranger in return for ready cash. He knows nothing of me and neither do they.'

He thought back to his father, domineering, cold and unpleasant. How fortunate he had been a son, not a daughter, because no doubt that man would have done similar. His conscience began to whisper to him; he had escaped from unpleasant circumstances, perhaps in marrying one of the girls at least one of them would be able to escape themselves.

'I think you should consider it,' Edward said quietly. With a hand that was shaking, he laid down his pen and closed the ledger.

'What!' Jonathan exclaimed. 'Don't begin that nonsense again. I'm perfectly happy as I am. Marriage is not for me.'

'Listen for a moment,' Edward said. 'I was lucky to have found you. You've been almost a son to me and I could not have imagined a better one if you were my natural child. You worked your time in the factory and you know the business better than I do now. We've grown it together, but I am painfully aware that I will not be growing it with you for much longer. And when I go, the business is entirely yours. Apart from some personal effects and gifts to old friends, my personal property and my shares in Langdon and Harcourt will pass to you alone.'

He paused and waited while Jonathan took his words in. Jonathan had always known there was no one else to whom Edward was close, but the implications had not struck him before. Sole ownership of Langdon and Harcourt. He'd be a rich man. Influential in the neighbourhood. John Brocklehurst had become Macclesfield's Member of Parliament thanks to his silk manufacturing company. What was to say Jonathan couldn't attain such heights? Langdon and Harcourt was not on the scale of Brocklehurst's venture, but there was no reason it couldn't aspire to be. Edward coughed, bringing Jonathan back to reality.

'I cannot guarantee that you will be as fortunate as I was to find a protégé as capable as you were and I want to discuss this with you.'

Edward closed his eyes and when he opened them Jonathan was dismayed to see they were filmy and moist.

'When I say I will not be with you for ever, I mean I shall not be with you for long,' Edward said. He looked at Jonathan and there were now tears brimming in his eyes. 'The doctors say I have a little over a year at most. Fifteen months if the saints smile on me or as little as six if they do not.'

Jonathan leapt to his feet and grasped his old friend by the hands.

'This must be a joke,' he said. His own voice was becoming reedy in desperation for it not to be true. 'You're jesting with me.'

Edward coughed again. 'My lungs are ruined. The doctor says that the fibres are in my lungs. My breathing will grow weaker and more difficult until I breathe no more.

Jonathan hung his head. He didn't want it to be true, but at the same time what Edward was saying was horribly familiar. Lung problems were a hazard brought on after years of working in the mills among the dust and the fibres so tiny they were barely visible, but which infiltrated the workers' bodies with every breath.

'What can I do to help? There must be something to treat you, we have money.'

Edward cut him off with a wave of his hand. 'My dear Jonathan, I've made my peace,' he said. 'For a long time I have anticipated this. Do you think this cold is merely a cold? I struggle more every day to breathe. What you can do for me is let me die knowing that my factory and our work is in safe hands with you and that you will have an heir yourself who in turn can take responsibility for the business.'

'Marriage almost destroyed my mother,' Jonathan said.

'Your father did that. You are not your father.'

Jonathan clenched his fists. No, he wasn't, but what if a wife transformed him into such a man? His father had appeared to despise his mother to the point of insanity, while still wanting to possess her and rule every moment of her life, from the clothes she wore to the way she dressed her hair and the visitors she had. There was no one who made him feel like that. If he could forbid any passion from growing, he would never repeat those mistakes.

'You're thinking of it,' Edward said. 'I can tell.'

Jonathan nodded. The land he needed would be his, Sir Robert's daughter would surely have a better life with him and he would be satisfying Edward's final wish. He did not need to have an intimate, romantic marriage. Merely provide a better home than the one he had been brought up in.

'Don't grieve for me,' Edward said, taking his hands. 'Honour my name by ensuring my business thrives and living a life happier than the one I was able to.'

'I'll...consider it,' Jonathan answered.

Late that night when sleep eluded him, Jonathan clambered from his bed and lit the oil lamp on his bedside table. He drew out his diary and read back the previous entries, all still in Greek as he had never given up that habit from his first journal. It made for dry and depressing reading. He had written of business. Of life in the factory. Of the new maid and cook he had employed— he wondered then whether any of them had once worked for Sir Robert's household. There was nothing in there about him. He did nothing. He had nothing beyond the house and his business and Edward.

And now Edward was dying and then Jonathan would be alone.

He sincerely wanted to fulfil Edward's last request. He would have done anything immediately if only it had not involved such personal sacrifice to him and forced him into the state which he had no wish to be in. All the same the baser urges of his body had reacted to the presence of the girls, especially the delicately pretty Aurelia whose melancholy had aroused his protective spirit.

A shudder of desire that ran the length of his

body, through every extremity, reminded him he was a man with a man's needs. He had never resorted to the methods that other young bachelors did to relieve himself of those yearnings by visiting one of the establishments in Manchester that he had heard about, but he did feel, naturally, those urges.

Restlessly, he wandered around the house. He had begun the process of purchasing it shortly before the death of his mother and she had never lived there. The empty rooms were barely furnished and the house was far too big for a single man to live in. For two people living together it was perfectly spacious and it was possible he would not encounter a wife too much. He would spend the majority of his day in the mill and need only spend evenings and nights in the company of his wife.

He returned to the bedroom and as he walked ideas began to swirl around his head. The house was big and could easily be divided into two. In fact, that had been one of the attractions when Jonathan chose it—that his mother might live under his roof almost independently. Any wife would be able to have her own apartment. Jonathan would only need to meet her for mealtimes. And at night.

He had reached his bedroom and stopped in the doorway to look at his bed. The sheets were crumpled from sleep, but he slept there alone. Getting an heir would require intercourse and at that thought he grew hot. He was twenty-five and still a virgin. Edward had been right: he had spared no time in his life for love or romance and even less to explore and satisfy the cravings he felt. He might as well have joined the priesthood instead of knocking on Edward's door all those years ago.

He climbed back into bed and drew the sheets up, listening to the silence. He was lonely. He admitted it to himself now. The brief conversation with Aurelia Upford had given him more happiness than he would have expected. Maybe marriage would suit him slightly better than he thought.

He rolled on to his belly and crooked his arm beneath the pillow, trying to find a more comfortable position, but sleep still eluded him. He knew that he had already made his decision and wasn't sure who he was providing these excuses for.

Sighing, Jonathan clambered from the bed, returned to his study and picked up a pen. In his journal he listed all the reasons he could think of for the marriage beyond the land and satisfying Edward's strange whim. He laid his pen down after three. Her beauty, her family connections and her accomplishments were all he could think of. But how many men married for less than that and lived perfectly tolerable lives? He stared at the blank page for a long time before decisively writing as many reasons as he could why agreeing to Sir Robert's terms would be sensible. Finally he added a single sentence beneath the column.

Tomorrow evening I shall propose to Miss Cassandra Upford.

Chapter Four

'I should prepare you for something exciting,' Lady Upford said as Aurelia and Cassandra stood before her for the customary inspection before a dinner with guests. 'There is a strong possibility that Mr Harcourt will ask for your hand in marriage this evening, Cassandra.'

Cassandra and Aurelia exchanged a glance of surprise. Aurelia's heart stopped. She had suspected that Mr Harcourt's invitation to dinner had been yet another attempt to push him towards the girls, but had not realised matters had progressed so far.

'But I barely know him and he barely knows me,' Cassandra said. 'Why, I haven't spoken more than a dozen words to him.'

Aurelia turned her head away to hide the blush that had risen to her neck. She had spoken a lot more to Mr Harcourt than that and hoped her parents did not know the extent of their conversation by the river.

'Why does that matter?' Lady Upford said. 'Your father and I had only spoken twice before our marriage. As the eldest, you are most likely to receive the honour and it would be a good match for you.'

'I won't do it,' Cassandra said. 'You can't make me marry him. He is no one.'

'Of course I cannot force you but if he asks you should accept,' their mother said. 'Goodness knows there is even less society here than I remember. You are in danger of becoming an old maid.'

'It was not my choice to move here from Oxford,' Cassandra said, her voice rising to a wail. She threw her fan across the room. Aurelia deftly caught it before it landed amid a display of carnations and upended the vase.

'You took me away from society and buried me in the countryside. I have danced with the sons of earls and now you want to marry me to a tradesman!'

Aurelia listened, aghast. She had never heard her sister speak to anybody with such frankness. Their mother looked close to swooning. Aurelia's scalp prickled at Cassandra's blatant snobbery. Cassandra could most likely have any man she wanted and not wanting to marry a man she didn't know was one matter, but calling Mr Harcourt a tradesman was deeply unfair. He owned a successful business and Aurelia knew he had ambitions. She recalled the determined look on his face when he had told her of his plans for the riverside fields. His enthusiasm had lit his face, giving him a boyish air that had been infinitely more appealing than when he had sat solemnly in the drawing room.

'I'd marry him,' she blurted without thinking.

'You?' Cassandra asked incredulously.

Aurelia stood trembling, wishing she hadn't spoken.

'What makes you believe that Mr Harcourt would consider you as a wife?' Lady Upford asked, turning her attention to Aurelia. 'Aside from That Unfortunate Incident, which we do not mention, every time a man has shown the slightest interest you managed to drive him away with your talk of political affairs and your unwomanly insistence on reading newspapers. A man does not want a wife who thinks herself his intellectual equal, but a woman capable of running his establishment as he commands and raising his children.'

Aurelia bit her tongue. When had her mother ever been subservient to her husband? She ruled him and chided him constantly, although she certainly made no pretence of being intellectual in the slightest.

'Mr Harcourt may not want me,' Aurelia said, 'but Cassandra clearly does not want him and you would not be so unfeeling as to force her into a marriage she would hate.'

Cassandra nodded, but looked a little less defiant. Aurelia handed back the fan and linked arms with her sister.

'Yes, perhaps Lia should marry him. After all, it's her scandal that has forced us back here into a house we can't afford to keep,' Lady Upford mused.

Aurelia reddened. 'Perhaps neither of us should marry him. I'm sure a man as rich as Mr Harcourt could find a wife in any place he chose to look,' she snapped.

Lady Upford shot her an angry look. 'We will have no more talk of this now. I can hear our guests arriving.'

She swept out of her room with her head high. Aurelia ran to the window and looked out. Mr Harcourt wasn't on foot this time, but in a two-wheeled pony chaise driven by a coachman. She tried to get a glimpse of him as he descended and came to the front door, but only saw his back and the top of a silk top hat as he helped Mr Langdon from the seat.

'Would you really marry him?' Cassandra whispered to her. 'Even without a title?'

Aurelia tore her gaze from the window. 'I don't much care who I marry and Mother is right. We could have stayed in Oxford if it wasn't for me.'

Cassandra hugged her tightly. 'Mother shouldn't have said that. It was cruel and not true. That wretch was at fault, not you.'

Aurelia hugged her sister back. She accepted it was due to her that they had returned from Oxfordshire, but the reason they could not afford to keep the house on the rambling Cheshire estate was her father's doing, not hers. 'At least Mr Harcourt lives close by so we would still see each other. But I think you should consider accepting him. How likely are you really to catch an earl living here?'

'I suppose you're right,' Cassandra said. 'I'll consider it, but I'm making no promises.'

That was the best answer Aurelia could expect, but she hoped Cassandra would see sense and not ruin her chance of marriage.

Dinner was less contentious than Aurelia had feared. Among the servants her mother had acquired was an excellent cook and Sir Robert's wine cellar was always well stocked—usually beyond his means. Mr Harcourt was seated between Lady Upford and Cassandra, while Aurelia was beside Mr Langdon. Throughout dinner Aurelia watched closely for signs that Cassandra was warming to the idea of marriage or that Mr Harcourt had fallen in love so quickly that his head was turned, but she saw nothing.

Mr Langdon was older than his business partner. He would have been a large and handsome man once, but now he was painfully thin with a sallow complexion and reddened lips that made him look severe. He was nothing of the sort and proved to be a fountain of local gossip, with eyes that flashed when something amused him. He kept Aurelia entertained all evening and even raised a smile from Cassandra.

'You are not married, I believe,' Lady Upford asked at one point. Aurelia and Cassandra exchanged an embarrassed glance.

'I have never met a woman capable of inducing me to enter that state.'

'You have never been in love?' Cassandra asked.

Mr Langdon let out a heartfelt sigh. 'I did not say that. I had the great misfortune to fall in love only after the object of my affection had been claimed by another.'

Aurelia toyed with her napkin, head bowed. Talk was verging uncomfortably close to her own heartbreak.

'I imagine that is a common scenario and many people marry anyway,' she said.

'I believe so. However, I determined not to add myself to those ranks. Marrying any poor girl simply for the sake of it would not have been kind to either of us.'

'Of course, as a man you can support yourself, living independently in a manner one of our sex would not be able to,' Dora supplied.

'At least, not until we are allowed the same opportunities for education,' Aurelia added.

'Time for dessert, I think,' Lady Upford said loudly, throwing a hard stare at Dora and ringing her silver bell vigorously for the servants to return to the room.

Aurelia gave her sister a surreptitious wink. Nothing was designed to signal a change of subject as quickly as the topic of female education. She glanced across the table and noticed that Mr Harcourt had leaned forward and was watching her intently with a thoughtful expression. She could not tell at all whether he approved or disapproved of what the girls had raised and it intrigued her to try find out.

When Sir Robert and Mr Harcourt retired to Sir Robert's study, Mr Langdon excused himself, saying that his chest required him to take a hot steam bath before retiring for the night.

'Tell Benson he can put Samuel and the chaise away,' Mr Harcourt told him. 'I'll walk home shortly.'

Mr Langdon's eyes flickered in the direction of the women who were standing together before the two men clasped hands and bid each other goodnight. Aurelia suspected his excuse was merely that and he was leaving Mr Harcourt to do what Lady Upford had predicted.

Lady Upford, Cassandra and Dora went into the drawing room to take coffee. Aurelia excused herself to attend to nature's call. As she passed through the entrance hall, she noticed the door to her father's study was ajar. Unable to resist, she crept closer and heard Mr Harcourt speaking.

'Sir Robert, you have the land that I need and I have the money that rumour suggests you are desperate for. You are the one insisting your daughter is part of the bargain, not I. I am more than happy to leave her out of matters entirely and deal solely in terms of the property and payment. I do not particularly want a wife, although I admit one would be advantageous to me.'

He didn't want a wife. The marriage proposal Lady Upford had been so confident of was little more beyond a business arrangement. Her parents must have discussed it after Mr Harcourt's previous visit, which was why Lady Upford had been so certain of it being offered. Aurelia pressed her ear to the door and listened, incensed by what her father was suggesting. And yet why not? It made sense he would take any opportunity to find one of the girls a husband. But knowing how dire his financial position was and how great his debts were, she could not believe he was willing to risk Mr Harcourt turning down his proposal and walking away.

'The only way you will obtain that land is if it is part of a marriage settlement,' Sir Robert said. 'Those terms are not open to negotiation.'

Aurelia wanted to scream in frustration. Of course Father would gamble on Mr Harcourt accepting his terms. It was his love of a wager that had put the family into the financial position they were currently struggling with. He should accept whatever offer Mr Harcourt had made for the land without playing a silly game.

'Which leaves us only one detail to discuss,' Sir Robert said. 'Which of the girls will it be? My wife spoke to both my daughters and prepared them to expect your question. Naturally as Cassandra is the elder...'

The door handle turned and Aurelia jumped back abruptly, not wanting to be caught eavesdropping. She attended to the demands of her bladder and as she came down the stairs, she once again heard her father's voice and the study door opened.

'I will find my daughter as soon as I can and give her the happy news.'

She couldn't be found there and had no time to warn Cassandra. Aurelia hastily fled into the morning parlour, which was the closest room. She heard her mother's voice.

'If you would care to wait in the morning parlour, Mr Harcourt, I shall send her to join you.'

Aurelia's stomach lurched. Mr Harcourt was going to be joining her in here while he waited for Cassandra.

She sat down at the piano in the corner. She enjoyed playing the instrument, though she had never quite persuaded the fingers of both hands to behave in unison with as much expertise as she would have liked. She lifted the lid and shuffled the music on the stand as an excuse for her presence there, then began to softly play scales. The door creaked open and she heard the soft footsteps on the oak floor go silent as Mr Harcourt trod on to the Persian rug that covered the floor.

'Miss Upford!' he said in surprise. 'I was not expecting to see anyone in here. I don't think your mother knew you were here.'

He spoke warmly and seemed pleased to see her. Aurelia smiled back. He swung his hands at his sides, looking nervous, then gestured towards the piano.

'Did I interrupt your practice? Please, play something for me.'

He was a pleasant man and no doubt Cassandra would be happy with him. She herself would be very glad to have Mr Harcourt as a brother.

'I play badly,' she admitted. She placed her left hand on the keys and performed a clumsy scale. He grinned, then straightened his face and murmured a compliment.

'You don't have to say that,' Aurelia said. 'I know young ladies are supposed to devote themselves to learning the instrument, but I have always preferred to spend my time in other ways.'

'Doing what? Besides walking dogs,' Mr Harcourt asked.

Aurelia bit her lip. His eyes had shown definite interest and his face was appealing. It felt more as if he was genuinely interested than just making passing conversation. She was about to tell him of her studies with Latin and Greek until she remembered her mother's warning. A man did not want a bookish wife or a bluestocking, but Mr Harcourt was not a potential husband for her. Even so, she thought it best not to reveal this at that point.

'Oh, the usual things,' she said breezily. 'Painting, flower arranging, dancing. Cassandra paints better than any of us.'

She gestured around the room to where a few

of her sister's watercolours stood framed on the top of the tables and the piano.

'Very nice,' Mr Harcourt said, glancing at them. He seemed anxious, pacing around the room, awaiting whatever her sister was about to say. Aurelia felt sorry for him. Had Sir Robert given any indication Cassandra might refuse? Presumably the delay in producing Cassandra was because she was having to be persuaded to appear.

'I've never tried playing,' Mr Harcourt said. 'Perhaps you could explain the rudiments.'

'If you want to learn how to place one finger beside the other,' Aurelia said with a gentle laugh. She gathered her skirts and moved to one end of the piano stool. After a hesitation, Mr Harcourt came and sat beside Aurelia at the piano. His leg brushed against her skirts. She barely felt it beneath the layers of petticoats, but being so close to a man was unsettling and a little exciting. She bit the inside of her lip, reminding herself that not only had she sworn never to become attached to a man after Arthur, but that this one belonged to her sister.

She began showing him the scale of C, watching him place his fingers on the keys as she instructed, one finger at a time above hers on the length of the key. Her hands were always cold and she could feel heat radiating from his. He had nice hands, she thought, long tapered fingers with well-shaped nails. A few scratches and callouses indicated he worked as well as being a man of leisure. 'That's good,' she said encouragingly. 'Try it again by yourself.'

She smiled round at him and was taken aback to find him staring intently at her. She drew her hand away from the keys. Mr Harcourt looked away immediately, then spoke quietly.

'Miss Upford, there is something I should like to speak to you about.'

His face became grave. Did he imagine she would be displeased at his coming to ask for Cassandra's hand? Had they breached etiquette too greatly by allowing their hands to almost touch?

'Do you recall when we met before I told you of my plans for the development of the mill? I have been speaking to your father this evening and…'

But he got no further because loud and rapid footsteps came echoing down the stairs and through the hall, then both Sir Robert and Lady Upford entered the room. Mr Harcourt sprang from the piano stool and Aurelia shifted even further into the corner.

'Mr Harcourt,' Sir Robert said, 'I apologise for the delay. I cannot find my daughter anywhere.'

Lady Upford gave a small cry. 'Why, she's here already,' she said, gesturing at Aurelia. 'Look, they've already found each other.'

She crossed the room and gave Aurelia a beaming smile. 'Aurelia, Mr Harcourt has something he would like to ask you.'

Aurelia felt herself grow cold. This was wrong. It was Cassandra he wanted to marry. She was the eldest daughter. It was right he should marry her. She looked from her mother to her father and finally to Mr Harcourt, whose face was more serious than she had seen it before. He walked slowly back towards her, as if each foot was encased in lead. He stopped in front of her and fixed her with a look so intense that it sent shivers hurtling up and down her spine and turned her legs to jelly. He blinked and pushed back a lock of hair that had fallen across his forehead.

'Miss Aurelia,' he said. 'Will you do me the honour of becoming my wife?'

Chapter Five

Aurelia became aware everyone in the room was waiting for an answer. She looked towards her mother, whose brows were knotted together. Lady Upford made a discreet but sharp gesture towards Mr Harcourt with her forefinger.

'I...'

Her throat had seized and she felt a hammering in her chest. Not the joy she had experienced when Arthur had proposed, but nor was it dread at the thought of becoming the wife of the man who was standing before her, now wearing an expression of anxiety on his face.

'You look faint. Do you need some water? A chair? Wine?'

He held a hand out as if fearing she might fall to the ground and need to be caught. His concern was touching and Aurelia felt mortified that her response had been so dramatic. The hammering had been caused by surprise at being the one he had asked. Cassandra must have held firm in her refusal after all.

'No. Nothing. I'm sorry.' She gave him a weak smile. 'I was taken aback. I never expected you would ask me such a thing. Of me, I mean.'

Mr Harcourt lowered his hand. 'If you need time to consider your answer, I can leave you now.'

He bowed and turned to go. Aurelia stepped forward. 'Mr Harcourt? Wait.'

There was no point in making the decision alone when the person she needed to discuss it with was about to leave the room.

He stopped and stood rigid. When he turned back his eyes were questioning but there was a hint of a smile playing about his lips. Aurelia was reminded of the eagerness in his manner when he had walked with her by the river. She looked at her parents.

'I would like to speak to Mr Harcourt in private.'

'Without a chaperon?' Lady Upford said. 'Sir Robert, what do you say?'

Her father looked as if he was about to deny the request, but Mr Harcourt forestalled any protest by offering his arm graciously to Lady Upford and gently steering her towards the door, passing her on to the arm of Sir Robert.

'I commend your consideration, Lady Upford,' he said in a creamy voice. 'Let me assure you your daughter will be perfectly safe in my care and, should she feel faint again, I will not hesitate to call you.'

Aurelia watched in disbelief as her parents were escorted out of their own room. Mr Harcourt closed the door quietly and then they were alone.

For a moment neither of them spoke. The sense of ease which had grown between them as they had played piano together had vanished.

Mr Harcourt spoke first. 'Would you care for a drink, Miss Upford?'

She nodded. He walked to the table where a variety of decanters and glasses stood, poured two measures of something and handed one to Aurelia. She sniffed it and blinked as the fumes tickled her nose and made the back of her throat burn.

'What is it?'

'Brandy. For medicinal purposes in this case. You looked as if you need something strong.'

'Is that why you are drinking it, too?' she asked boldly. He made a noise in his throat that was half-snort, half-laugh, and raised his glass to his lips.

'As you say.'

Aurelia turned the heavy glass around in her hand, examining the amber liquid. If her father knew what she was about to drink, he would be furious. Although he enjoyed having a glass or two himself, it was not something he thought ladies should drink. Mr Harcourt obviously thought differently, however. Emboldened by the thought that her future husband encouraged it, she took a tiny sip. She had had no idea what it would taste like, but hadn't expected anything quite so rich or warming. She pulled a face and wrinkled her nose and it was only after that when she realised she had already thought of Mr Harcourt as her future husband. Cautiously she took another sip and was gratified to see Mr Harcourt seemed to approve.

'That's better,' he said. 'You have a little more colour in your cheeks now.'

He smiled and Aurelia relaxed a little. Or perhaps that was the brandy working its magic as it wound down through her belly and warmed her. They sat opposite each other, saying nothing for a few minutes, sipping at their brandy. It was a comfortable silence and Aurelia felt more at peace than she would have expected given the circumstances. She doubted Cassandra would have been able to maintain her composure and felt relief that her father had obviously dissuaded Mr Harcourt from asking for her hand.

'I'm sorry my proposal was such a shock for you to hear,' he said.

Aurelia nodded. Her eyes darted to the door, knowing that they would only have a few minutes before her parents returned. She walked to the fire and sat down in one of the chairs, gesturing for Mr Harcourt to join her. He took the low chair opposite her and leaned forward. He rested his arms on his knees and looked at her expectantly. Aurelia took a deep breath.

'I overheard you and my father speaking his study a short while ago. I assume he came up with this scheme himself?'

Mr Harcourt gave her a sharp look. 'Overheard accidentally or intentionally?'

'Accidentally.' Aurelia flushed. 'At least, at first it was, but when I heard what you were discussing I didn't leave the hallway as quickly as I should have.'

He smiled and tried to hide it behind a cough but failed.

'Was it my father's idea that you ask for my hand?' she repeated. She looked at him questioningly and he nodded slowly.

'In lieu of payment or just to reduce the amount?' she asked. She thought better of the question and held her hand up. 'No, don't tell me. I'd rather not know my value.'

Mr Harcourt flushed and looked angry, though whether at her brazenness or the thought he had been trapped into the marriage.

'You may not be aware, but my father is heavily in debt,' she said.

'I had heard rumours to that effect,' Mr Harcourt admitted. 'Obviously I don't lower myself to listen to gossip.'

'I dare say if you had waited a little longer he may have become keener to sell and you would have got the land eventually,' Aurelia said, raising an eyebrow. 'You may still wish to bet upon that happening and save yourself the necessity of marriage.'

He gave her a long look that made her simultaneously shiver and grow warm inside.

'I should be frank with you, Miss Upford. I do not particularly want a wife. Marriage is not an institution I ever planned to enter—however, I am continually told a man in my position should marry. There are other considerations besides my need for your father's land that I have to take into account. Events seem to be conspiring to provide a solution to all my needs in one action.'

He looked grave and Aurelia's heart fluttered in sympathy. 'Will you tell me your other reasons?'

He shook his head. 'You must pardon me if I don't share those with you now.'

It seemed fair. After all, she had her own reasons for being tempted to accept. She wondered if his hopes had formerly been wrecked as hers had. Oddly enough, by sharing his reservations he had given her more inclination to accept knowing he was not entering willingly into it.

'Do you love me, Mr Harcourt?' she asked. 'Please, before you answer, do me the courtesy of answering honestly.'

He blinked and took another sip of his brandy before standing and placing it on the mantelpiece. He did everything meticulously slowly and Aurelia was gratified to see he was taking her question seriously. He turned back to face her and remained standing. His eyes moved over her. She realised he was assessing her physically and bristled, although she had done that herself on a number of occasions.

'No. I don't. I don't believe that love happens at first glance.' He gave her a cautious smile. 'I do find your company pleasant.'

'Thank you,' she said. Some of the tension trickled from her shoulders and she sat a little easier. 'If you had told me you did, then I would have refused your offer immediately.'

'Really?'

Now he seemed genuinely surprised. Did he think himself such a catch that he didn't consider such a thing possible? Had he also heard rumours about her past and considered Aurelia would be desperate to marry any man who would rescue her from her infamy? She hoped not. She stood and put her glass beside his.

'If you had said you loved me, then nothing would have induced me to accept your proposal. I do not want much from a marriage, but I demand honesty.'

His eyes widened. 'Then you are considering accepting?' he asked.

Aurelia walked to the window and parted the heavy damask curtains to looked out. The moon was a thick crescent and she could make out the line of trees at the boundary to the formal gardens. Beyond that were the fields and river, and beyond that lay the mill. It stood in darkness, although the lights of Macclesfield flickered in the distance beyond and around it. To move from this house to the town would not be so great a change.

'I am considering it,' she admitted.

Mr Harcourt joined her at the window, staring out as she did. He was taller than she was by some measure and broad shouldered. He held himself well, but that might have been tension as the tendons in his neck were tight. Now she had noticed it, Aurelia's eyes kept sliding back to his throat and the sharp jaw that cast it into shadow. His finely shaped lips were a firm, determined line. Despite everything she felt a little tug of attraction towards him, followed immediately by a greater rush of anger towards her father for placing both of them in this position.

Mr Harcourt put his hands behind his back and stared out across the gardens towards his mill.

'When we met by the river you spoke of expanding your grounds and needing my father's land to do that. What will you do with it?' Aurelia asked.

'Will that have a bearing on your decision?' Mr Harcourt raised his brows and Aurelia was reminded of her mother's words. She should refrain from showing interest or intelligence in case she put her suitor off.

'I'm just curious whether your end justifies the lengths you are prepared to go to.'

'I need the river more than the land, but I'm considering building a house for the apprentices to live in. The children come from the workhouse and I think that I could feed and clothe them cheaper than the fee we pay for their upkeep there. Better, too.'

His eyes took on a faraway look and his tone became enthusiastic. 'I want a schoolroom and a garden. The boys can be taught to read and write.'

'And the girls?' Aurelia asked. His enthusiasm was infectious and she found herself picturing a riverside house with children playing at the end of the working day. Mr Harcourt beamed at her and at that moment she could have married him on the spot.

'Oh, of course the girls can learn useful skills. Sewing and cooking and suchlike.'

'Or reading and writing,' Aurelia said under her breath. He jerked his head round and frowned as if he had only half-heard. Just as well, she thought. Any attempts to advance the education of girls would have to be done by degrees after they were wed.

'Mr Harcourt. I commend your ambition,' she said. 'Will you permit me to be frank myself? Although society is harsher on a single woman than her unmarried brothers, I am perfectly happy being unmarried, too. That is something we have in common. I see many advantages for you. What are mine?'

He said nothing. A man of little words, or maybe he could think of no advantage. She decided his house would be peaceful if nothing else. His next words made her wonder if he could have a career as a mind reader in the music halls.

'You may remember when we met by the river you told me you like solitude and your own space. Marrying me will give you that, Miss Upford. I'm a busy man and work long hours. My home isn't as large as Siddon Hall, but you will have your own bedchamber and sitting room. You will be mistress of your own establishment. I have fewer servants, but you won't be expected to carry buckets and clean windows.'

They grinned at each other, allied by the shared memory, and Aurelia felt that this was a man she could happily share a house with. He would be a good companion and she would have all the time she wished to read and study. He took her hand and she permitted him to keep hold of it. The thrill that rolled in her belly at being touched took her by surprise.

'Miss Upford. I should warn you that my marriage needs to be a marriage in the full meaning of the word.' He released her hand, adjusted his cuffs and twisted the stud of his cufflink round and round as if uneasy. 'I need an heir and I will obviously need to make certain marital demands of you. If you find that idea too unpleasant, then please tell me now and the matter will be at an end.'

He walked away and stood by the fire, staring into the flames in a tactful manner. Such frank speech was unexpected, yet welcome. Aurelia looked at him from a distance, imagining what would need to happen between them. She'd been kissed, of course, and more thoroughly than she should have permitted, but her romance with Arthur had never extended to anything more physical. She remembered Mr Harcourt's fingers beside hers on their piano. The shapely elegant digits as they played precisely. To have them touching her intimately would be curious. Feeling his broad-framed body pressing down on hers was an intriguing thought, but not an unpleasant one. It was at this point she realised that although she intended never to love again, she had no distaste at the prospect of lovemaking.

'I can accept your terms, Mr Harcourt,' she said. 'Although I would prefer to spend my nights alone.'

He looked at her and smiled. 'I would not have suggested anything other than that. I will leave you alone to live your life. You may do as you wish. My house will be at your disposal and, once I have an heir, if you so wish I will not disturb you again in that respect.'

He came back to her now and they faced each other. Mr Harcourt held himself straight.

'Miss Upford,' he asked. 'Will you consent to become my wife?'

Aurelia bit her lip.

'Yes, Mr Harcourt. I will.'

Chapter Six

The wedding day came around with unseemly rapidity. The banns were read and a little over a month to the day Jonathan found himself waiting at the Upford family church on a mild late September morning with only Edward at his side. The remaining congregation consisted of Miss Upford's sisters and mother and an elderly uncle. Both Jonathan and Miss Upford had been firm in their insistence that the ceremony was as quiet as possible.

Jonathan stood by the altar, watching the small figure make her way down the short aisle on the arm of Sir Robert. Her face was covered by a long lace veil and a wide skirt of white masses of ruched silk made her already slender figure look even smaller. Jonathan couldn't quite believe she was going to be his wife in a matter of minutes.

'What are you thinking?' Edward asked.

'That perhaps I should have offered her a bolt of our silk to make her dress,' Jonathan answered. 'I considered it, but thought it might be too intimate a wedding gift.'

'Too intimate for your wife?'

Jonathan gave a curt nod. It had reminded him too closely of his father's preference for choosing his mother's clothes and manner of dress. His mother had dressed in drab colours because his father had thought gaiety was unseemly. Jonathan was determined to exercise no such control over his own wife.

'I think she would find that unnecessary. Miss Upford and I both see this as a transaction of convenience and neither of us is expecting or wishing for romance. All our private intimacy will be purely to create the son you wish us to have.'

Edward looked chastened. 'I hope you will discover there is more joy to be had than at a business meeting, Jonathan,' he murmured.

There was no more time to speak because Miss Upford was drawing close: a ghostly figure wearing a dress with delicate embroidered flowers picked out in white-silk thread on white cut silk that were barely visible. Jonathan faced his bride and lifted back her veil. He looked into her eyes and was pleased to see there was no obvious sign of fear or regret or sadness. If she had shown any indication that she was regretting her decision,

Jonathan would have walked from the church without a word. Her face showed little emotion at all and they regarded each other seriously.

'Good morning, Mr Harcourt,' she murmured. The same greeting she had given him on the handful of times they had met between the night of his proposal and today.

'Good morning, Miss Upford,' he replied. Feeling this occasion demanded something more, he added, 'You look very pretty.'

Her lips twitched into a smile and her dark lashes fluttered rapidly. Despite his reservations he was filled with confidence that he had made the right decision. There was a discreet cough beside him. The priest was waiting to begin.

The ceremony was brief and ran with the smoothness of the finest oiled machine. If they were actors on the stage, they could not have been more perfect. The only point at which Jonathan faltered was when he was required to promise to love Miss Upford. He glanced from the priest to her and found her brown eyes staring back at him frankly. He was lying in a house of God in front of witnesses. Moreover, his bride was about to make the same lie. He quickly delved into his mind to see if there was any feeling towards Miss Upford that would not make his declaration heresy and seized upon the moment they had shared in the morning parlour when they had sat side by side at the piano and she had guided his hands over the keys.

He had felt fondly towards her then, and at that moment he had been secure in his belief that changing his mind at the last minute and asking for her hand instead of Miss Cassandra Upford's was the right decision. Yes, he liked her well enough that the lie would pass before his maker. He gave Miss Upford another smile that must have taken her by surprise because her eyes widened and her lips parted in a way that was very appealing. He rattled off the vows without any further hesitation.

The remainder of the ceremony passed without incident and before long Jonathan was slipping a slim gold band on to Miss Upford's finger. Her hand was small and cold, and almost lost in his palm. As she curled her fingers over, the almond-shaped nails brushed against Jonathan's wrist at the base of his palm. A bolt of heat shot along the length of his arm, catching him unawares as a sudden desire filled him. He swallowed, aware of the sudden burst of perspiration that washed over his back that had been brought on by the most innocent of touches. What would it be like to become even more intimate when at last they were husband and wife alone in the marriage bed for the first time? There was joy to be had, as Edward had said.

He looked up from their joint hands into his wife's face and it felt as though he was seeing her anew. And she was beautiful. Her pale throat rose from the low-fronted bodice of her dress and made him think of a swan's neck, shapely and slender. The modest pleating of silk concealed her décolletage from view while managing to give the impression her breasts were full and rounded beneath. Tiny pearl buttons ran in a line down to her slender waist. He desired her very much and hoped that his yearning was not visible on his face.

When the priest told him he might kiss his new wife, Jonathan hesitated before taking Miss Upford's face—no, *Mrs Harcourt's* face—in one hand and tilting it back. She never took her eyes from his, but kept them fixed on him, clear and open with the lustrous lashes framing the dark orbs. As Jonathan pressed his mouth against hers, his wife responded by pushing them into a bud and yielding to his touch.

Already exhilarated by the unfamiliar sensation of desire for her that had begun to crest, Jonathan spread his fingers across her cheekbone and parted his lips further. The heat of her breath skimmed over his lips, sending him spiralling into raptures. It only lasted a moment before he recollected where he was and that his bride was unlikely to be feeling the same spreading of passion that he was. He dropped his hand and pulled himself away, standing to face her. Watching the colour rise to her cheeks and transform them from rosy to deep scarlet, he could barely keep his mind from straying to the evening that would come and the night he would spend in his wife's bed. If a kiss could do such things to him, what would anything more intimate reduce him to?

They signed the register and returned to the house on foot, walking the short distance down the lane from the church to the grounds where neighbours of the Upfords and workers from Jonathan's mill lined the road to congratulate him and shout words of encouragement to the couple. Jonathan and Aurelia walked arm in arm and that would have been pleasant if they had been alone, but there was no time to speak privately because they were required to thank the well-wishers and catch the posies of flowers thrown by the small girls whose deft fingers usually spent the days threading spools of silk through the Jacquard pattern cards.

The only snatched moment when Jonathan felt even remotely close to his new wife was when the turning to the river walk came into view.

'It's a pity you didn't bring Caesar with you,' Jonathan remarked. 'He'd have enjoyed retrieving the flowers.'

'He's so ill-behaved he'd have torn them to

pieces and the girls would have cried,' Aurelia pointed out, her eyes brightening. 'If he hadn't tried to chase the church cat up the steeple, that is. He's safely shut in Mother's dressing room where he can't get into mischief. He sits in the window seat, pining for his lost love like a four-legged Romeo.'

Her face suddenly fell and she looked at the bunches of wildflowers held in her gloved hands. Jonathan was mystified what had brought on the change until he remembered their conversation about the dog. Caesar had been aiming above his station in life, trying to mount the prized Irish Setters. He wondered if his new wife had made the comparison between the dog and her husband, both aiming for a match with a woman above them.

Sir Robert and Lady Upford had ordered a wedding breakfast of lavish proportions, but the celebration was a sedate affair. If there had been more guests, Jonathan and his bride might have attempted to pretend that the union was a love match and held hands or whispered sweet words between coy looks. However, as the close family was fully aware of the circumstances and the smattering of neighbours that had been invited were more interested in the feast, they felt no need.

Besides, Jonathan reflected, how many wedding celebrations involved the newlywed husband joining his father-in-law and business partner to sign documents transferring the sale of land?

Jonathan, Edward and Sir Robert stood uneasily, whisky in hand, as each of their respective solicitors added their signature as witness. The occasion seemed as solemn as when Jonathan and Mrs Harcourt had signed the marriage register, although his new bride was a touch more agreeable than her father, who clapped Jonathan on the back and suggested a quick game or two of cards before returning to the party.

When Jonathan politely declined, Sir Robert smiled knowingly.

'Keen to be off, of course,' he said. 'Mr Langdon, would you excuse us for a moment? I would have words with my new son-in-law that are for his ears only.'

Edward excused himself and Jonathan waited in suspense, hoping this was not to be a father-like man-to-man talk about the intimacy of the marital bed.

He needn't have worried.

'You're in possession of the property and my daughter now, Mr Harcourt,' Sir Robert said. 'I trust you will take care of both as you should.'

Jonathan held his hand out to the baronet and gave him a firm look.

'I guarantee you will find both as well looked after as you could hope.'

'She's a good girl, if a little headstrong at times,' Sir Robert murmured. It was the first instance of fatherly concern Jonathan had seen and he returned to the party feeling warmer towards his father-in-law.

Miss Theodora Upford was massacring Bach on the piano when Jonathan entered the room and the conversations had grown louder to compensate. He could not see his wife immediately, but eventually spotted her sitting in an alcove with Edward, both holding flutes of champagne. Evidently they had retired there for some peace. The chair was a fussy piece of furniture; a double 'love chair' with each seat facing the other across a low rail that rose behind each sitter to create a back. Edward was leaning across the divider, speaking to Aurelia who leaned in confidentially, her face bright with interest. Jonathan wished he possessed his friend's easy charm. For a man who professed to have no interest in the fair sex, he was enviably confident in their company.

Jonathan began to walk towards them, but before he could arrive, Miss Cassandra Upford stepped into his path. She was dressed in rose-pink satin and had silk white and pink roses woven into her hair. No one should overshadow the bride on her wedding day, but Miss Upford seemed to be edging as close to the line as possible. He was glad that he had chosen the quieter of the sisters, even though he still felt a stab of conscience that he had committed a terrible social faux pas by overlooking the elder, unmarried daughter.

'I wanted to tell you how happy I am that you are marrying Aurelia,' Miss Upford said, giving him a becoming smile that made her cheeks dimple. Her brows knotted suddenly and she reminded him of Aurelia, whose manner was altogether more serious. 'You will take care of her, won't you? I love her dearly and she deserves to be happy.'

Jonathan glanced towards his wife, who was staring in his direction with an odd expression on her face. Although she was leaning in to Edward so he could speak to her, it was clear to Jonathan that she was watching the conversation between her husband and sister.

'Miss Upford,' he said stiffly, 'I am aware you know the circumstances of our marriage. Your sister and I do not love each other and she is as aware of my feelings towards her as I am of hers towards me. I made vows today and I intend to keep them. I promise you I will do my upmost to see our marriage is happy and successful.'

Miss Upford smiled again. She slid her eyes towards Aurelia. 'Good. I think that is more im-

portant to Aurelia than any vows of heartfelt de-
votion you could make. I'm so glad you are to be
my brother, Mr Harcourt. Would you permit me
to send you a sketch of Aurelia as a wedding gift
to you? I am by no means proficient, but I can
capture a likeness well.'

Jonathan had seen her watercolours and knew
the modesty was feigned. She was very good. He
threw out some compliments about the pieces of
her work he had seen and thanked her for the gift.
She held her hand out to him expectantly and Jonathan kissed it. She turned over her shoulder and
gave Aurelia a warm smile and sashayed away.
Jonathan resumed his attempt to reach his bride.
From the troubled expression she had not been
happy about his being waylaid by her sister.

Chapter Seven

Edward stood as Jonathan arrived and offered Jonathan his seat.

'You must forgive me for capturing your prize for at least a short while, Jonathan. I have been explaining to Mrs Harcourt that her principal task as your wife is to ensure you take time for dining out and amusement.'

Jonathan struggled to think of the former Miss Upford as Mrs Harcourt, though he could not yet bring himself to call her by her name.

'I don't believe that was one of the vows she made,' he joked.

Edward turned back to Aurelia and bowed over her hand. 'Yet another failing of the institution of marriage! Nevertheless, Mrs Harcourt, you and I shall begin our conspiracy now. I shall invite you both to dine with me a fortnight from now and you shall participate by agreeing.'

He secured her promise, then left the couple alone.

'What was Edward talking to you about?' Jonathan asked, taking his place beside his wife.

Jonathan sat in the seat Edward had vacated. The chair was a clever piece of design now he thought about it as it gave him an excellent view of his wife who twisted to face him. It displayed an elegant three-quarter silhouette with a line that swept from the glossy rolls of her hair gathered above the creamy neck he had admired in the church and down through her torso to the waist that seemed impossibly tiny. He longed to trace his finger along the line and wondered what the shape would look like sketched in charcoal and picked out on silk.

'Only what he told you,' Aurelia answered. She looked at him sharply. 'What was my sister saying to you?'

Jonathan confirmed his suspicions that she had not been happy to see them together.

'She was giving me her wishes that we will be happy together,' he replied. He did not add her strange comment about Aurelia deserving happiness.

Lady Upford glided over and insisted the couple should cut the towering cake and begin to make their preparations to depart. While Aurelia passed slivers out to the guests, Lady Upford gave instructions to the waiting butler to make sure the second layer was well wrapped and stored. Traditionally this would be eaten at the christening of the couple's first child. Neither Jonathan nor his bride mentioned this, but both eyed the thickly iced slab of fruit cake thoughtfully.

Aurelia left the party in the company of her sisters. Edward strolled over to Jonathan. He cocked his head in the direction of the departing women. He had the misty-eyed look of a man who had taken full advantage of the champagne Sir Robert had so liberally provided. He looked hearty and if it wasn't for the wheezing that followed each time he spoke, Jonathan would have suspected his illness to be mild.

'I hope you won't consider this too much of a sacrifice, Jonathan. Perhaps I should not have forced your hand, but I think you made the right choice.'

Jonathan grimaced. 'It's done now and I dare say we'll be able to tolerate each other.'

Mrs Harcourt returned a short while later dressed in the same walking dress she had worn when Jonathan had met her at the river. Her change of outfit signalled that she was ready to leave. Sir Robert had offered the couple his own covered carriage and pair of horse to take them to Jonathan's house. To Jonathan's surprise, Aurelia had refused the offer, saying her husband's chaise and pony would be adequate.

'I am leaving this house and life behind me,' she had explained. 'I should begin my new life with the facilities at my disposal.'

Jonathan had felt a burst of admiration for her, reminded a little of the independent spirit his mother had shown. In the end Jonathan had brokered a compromise. Sir Robert's second vehicle, an open-topped pony cart, had taken Mrs Harcourt's possessions to the house under the supervision of Annie, the lady's maid Aurelia swore she could not live without. Now, sitting together in the pony chaise, Jonathan wondered if his wife was regretting her choice. There was only one seat and she was forced to sit close beside him with her dress creased and pushed against his body. Jonathan's senses felt unusually heightened, which he put down to the champagne he had drunk, because the slightest movement caused their limbs to brush and the scent of her rosewater perfume made his head reel and his nerves spark like a tinderbox.

'I'm sorry we could not arrange a honeymoon tour,' he said as they jolted along the cobbled streets. 'With affairs being arranged so quickly I could not spare the time I would like. At another time we could travel together when I have more leisure at my disposal.'

Aurelia smiled at him. 'I'd like that. I have never travelled very far.'

'We could tour the south of the country if you would like,' Jonathan suggested. 'We could visit Oxford. I've never seen the city and I'm sure you would like to return to see acquaintances you made while you lived there.'

'No,' she said firmly. Jonathan wrinkled his brow. She bit her lip. 'There is no one in particular I would like to visit in that area. Anywhere else you choose I am happy to visit, but I would rather avoid Oxford.'

She turned her face and looked out of the window until they arrived at the house. Jonathan sat in silence, wondering at the strange intent of his bride to leave everything behind her.

By the time they arrived at Jonathan's house, Aurelia seemed to have recovered her equilibrium. He helped her down from the chaise and wondered briefly whether he should offer to carry her over the threshold in the traditional manner, but after the way she had withdrawn from him he thought better of it. Instead he knocked and, when Harris, his manservant, opened the door, he held a hand out to allow her to pass inside.

'Welcome to your new home, Mrs Harcourt.'

'Thank you, Mr Harcourt,' she answered seriously, bobbing him a small curtsy. She paused to stare around at the flowerbeds on either side of the double-fronted house before passing in front of Jonathan into the hallway.

Jonathan showed her around the house that was now hers and presented the small staff: Mrs Barnes, the cook-cum-housekeeper; Sarah, the all-duty maid; and Harris, Jonathan's manservant. The property was substantially smaller than the one she had just left and he looked for signs on her face that she was dissatisfied but she appeared pleased with everything and everyone. As he led her through the double parlour, dining room and past his study he felt a justifiable sense of pride and confidence growing inside him. He had worked for this and there was nothing in his life he should not feel able to accomplish. His business would continue to be a success and he knew he was equal to the task of ensuring his marriage would be likewise.

It was only when he led Aurelia to the first floor that he had cause to hesitate. The staircase led upwards through the centre of the house and the banisters turned either way, with a suite of rooms on the left and right.

'My rooms are to the left,' he explained, gesturing to the pair of doors belonging to his bed and dressing rooms. 'Yours are to the right.'

Mrs Harcourt turned left and walked around the landing, one hand trailing on the banister. Jonathan thought for a moment she was intending to enter his room and the frisson of excitement that set the hairs on his neck standing upright took him by surprise. That would come later and it struck him he hadn't discussed whether he would come to her or she to him. She continued past, however, and stopped in front of the large window above the front door. Jonathan joined her and looked out. He liked this view. The house looked out on to a small, grassy square where a nursemaid and her charge were enjoying the sunshine and throwing crumbs of rusk to a flock of pigeons. The child was no more than four and giggling loudly enough to be heard inside.

'Albertina Millicent Healy,' he said. 'She lives on the other side of the square.

Aurelia smiled. 'What a dreadful name, poor child!'

Jonathan suppressed a snort. He'd often thought the same.

'It isn't one I'd choose.'

He felt Aurelia stiffen beside him and could have kicked himself for mentioning the child he would one day have. The child she would have to give him.

'Let me show you your rooms,' he said. 'I hope you will find them to your satisfaction.'

'I'm sure everything will be perfect,' she answered. She lingered on the threshold as he held the door open. 'I shall see you for dinner. Good-bye, Mr Harcourt, for now.'

She slipped backwards into the room, peering at him as she closed the door.

He would come to her room, he decided. She belonged in the more feminine domain and when he lay in his own bed afterwards he would not be imagining her at his side.

Dinner was a quiet affair. The day had exhausted Jonathan. He would usually enjoy this time of peace in an informal manner dressed in his shirtsleeves with a tray at the fireside. Now, with a wife to accommodate, he felt duty bound to eat at the dining table wearing his wedding suit. He stared down the length of the table at Aurelia, who sat at the far end. If his bride was tired, she showed no outward signs. Her eyes glowed and in the hour they had been apart, her hair had been reworked into a low bun at the nape of her neck by Annie. It suited her wearing it low, with waves framing her face and softening it. When she wore it up her cheekbones were somehow pulled back, giving her a more severe demeanour. She had changed from the walking dress she had arrived in into a blue-satin gown with a scooped collar and tight sleeves. Jonathan, in his tight cravat and best waistcoat, felt uncomfortably formal for the time of night and wondered if his bride felt the same. And he did not know best how to ask her. He had no idea how to talk to her beyond brief exchanges concerning the soup.

Was it always going to be this uneasy? He hoped not, for the idea of spending the next forty years sitting opposite a silent woman made his heart sink.

As Aurelia toyed with her spoon, pushing the frothy lemon syllabub around the dish, Jonathan could bear the silence no longer. The marriage had been his idea so he should be the one to make the effort. He laid his spoon on the edge of the dish and, when she glanced in his direction, he smiled.

'Thank you for today,' he said. 'I must admit I was a trifle nervous when I arrived at the church, but seeing you smile at me put me at ease. I hope you haven't found it too arduous.'

'Only a little,' she admitted. She lowered her eyelashes and scooped a little of the pudding on to her spoon. 'I do find occasions with a great number of people quite overbearing at times. And I am a little tired.'

She lifted the spoon to her mouth. Jonathan watched, unable to tear his eyes away from the full, red lips as they closed around the spoon and licked away the cream.

'Are you happy with your rooms?' he asked.

'Very.' She smiled. 'You have excellent taste, Mr Harcourt.'

'I can claim no credit for that. Some of the pieces of furniture belonged to my mother,' Jonathan explained. He frowned. Perhaps she would object to using a dead woman's possessions, especially the one who would have been her mother-in-law. 'I hope you don't mind me using them for you. If there's anything you'd like to change, of course you must tell me at once.'

'No, everything is perfect, she said. 'In that case I should compliment your mother's taste.' She raised her eyes to meet his. 'Those were to have been her rooms, weren't they?' she asked.

Jonathan nodded. He had explained the event of her death to Aurelia, although not the circumstances under which they had moved to Macclesfield in the first place. One day if they somehow grew close enough he would, but not now.

'It's getting late,' he said. 'I think, unless you have any objection, I will retire for the night.'

Silence coalesced in the air between them. Jonathan held his breath, knowing that both of them would be thinking of what would happen once they made their way upstairs. He noticed Aurelia's fingers tighten over her spoon, the almond-shaped nails going white with a slight pressure. She placed it down neatly on the side of her dish.

'I have no objection,' she said quietly, not meeting his eye.

Jonathan pushed his chair back and helped Aurelia rise from hers. He walked behind her up the stairs, feeling the anticipation growing with each step. On the landing he paused.

'I shall come to your room shortly,' he said.

She nodded. He bowed and made his way to his bedroom where he undressed and doused his face in cold water. It had to be done. It wasn't that he did not want to make love to Aurelia. He very much did and the thought of finally satisfying the urges that had built within him for so long came as a relief. It was more the idea of laying claim to her when he knew she would doubtless find it uncomfortable and felt no emotional attachment to him. Some men would not mind. Some boasted freely of the women they visited for sexual gratification in return for payment, never wondering how willing their partners truly were. Jonathan had never been able to summon the nerve or inclination to indulge in what he suspected was a joyless transaction for both.

He summoned Aurelia's face before him and tried to picture some of the times they had spent together, content in each other's company. He liked her and she had said she liked him also. That would have to be enough.

He rinsed his teeth, dressed in his nightshirt and dressing gown and picked up his well-thumbed volume of *Waverley*. He read for fifteen minutes to give his bride the necessary time to make whatever preparations she was making, then closed the book, stood and straightened his dressing gown with the air of a knight preparing for battle.

It was time to visit his wife and there was no sense prolonging what was sure to be an excruciating encounter for both of them any longer than absolutely necessary.

Chapter Eight

~~~~~~~~~~~~~~~~~~~

Aurelia sat in front of the mirror on her dressing table and peered at the woman who stared back at her. She barely recognised the face whose rosy cheeks and bright eyes suggested an excitement she did not feel.

All she felt was relief to be alone and in her nightgown. Her feet had been squeezed into narrow silk shoes and her stays laced tighter than she preferred in order to squeeze into the impossibly small-waisted wedding gown. Now she was freed from both those cages her back and feet ached with unfamiliar freedom. She wanted to climb into bed, snuff the candle and sleep, but she could not do that. Her husband—and she knew those words would take a long time to become ordinary— would be here shortly and, after the wedding day was done, the wedding night would begin.

She understood the…particulars of how babies were created. Growing up around as many dogs as Sir Robert's household held, she had enough experience of them engaging in the reproductive act though she had a suspicion that humans lay face to face. She ran her fingers over the rows and rows of ruffles of her nightgown, more elaborate than the plain linen she usually wore. Her stomach filled with a thousand sharp-winged moths, beating to escape. Would Mr Harcourt expect her to remove it so he could see her naked? Would he want to remove it himself? She had no idea what was customary. Would he come to her room dressed as he had been at dinner, or wearing his own nightclothes? And should he be naked, too? Too many questions and knowing they would shortly be answered did not help in the slightest.

She drank a glass of water to calm her nerves, wishing it was the brandy he had offered to fortify her with on the night he had proposed.

This is what you wanted, she reminded herself.

Mr Harcourt had made it clear on the night of his proposal that a physical relationship was a part of the marriage he wanted. In fact, Aurelia's main purpose as Mrs Harcourt—if not her sole purpose—was to provide him with a son. She had known that and gone into the marriage with open eyes and it was too late to change her mind.

When a knock came at the door she took one last glance in the mirror at the girl she had been, knowing that the next time she looked into those eyes a woman would be staring back at her.

'Come in.'

She stood in the middle of the room in the spot where the light from the candle caught her. The doorknob turned slowly and it seemed like eternity passed before the door edged open and Mr Harcourt came in. He closed it behind him quietly and stood with his back to the door, facing Aurelia.

He was clad in a long dressing gown of deep rich blue with a pattern of paisleys worked in black so that as he took a step closer to Aurelia the pattern came and went according to whether the light shone on it or not. Aurelia was so caught up in admiring the garment that she entirely forgot to look at the man inside it until he spoke.

'Good evening, Mrs Harcourt. I trust you are well and everything is to your satisfaction?'

He glanced around and Aurelia smiled warmly.

'Everything is perfect,' she said. 'I could not have wished for a nicer room.'

She meant it sincerely. The well-proportioned bedrooms held ample furniture and the walls were decorated with paper depicting flowers and peacocks on a sunny yellow background. The size and furnishings would have been enough to keep her happy, but the door that lead to an adjoining sitting room had been the perfect discovery.

'I'm sure I will be very happy living here,' she

said and Mr Harcourt smiled again. He took another step towards her, but still did not touch her.

'You look very beautiful,' he said, looking up so that his eyes met hers for the first time.

She recognised the light in them as desire, having seen it plainly on Arthur's face on so many occasions. Unlike Arthur, Mr Harcourt was entitled to and expected to claim her. He seemed hesitant to begin taking his rights and, oddly, this meant Aurelia was finding herself more anxious and eager to begin.

He looked around once more. 'You have a lot of books,' he said, gesturing to the shelf which was already full of volumes. Only half of what she owned.

'I like to read,' she said, almost apologetically. Then she remembered she was married and Mr Harcourt did not care what she did. She did not have to apologise.

'I like to read, too,' he said. 'Histories, accounts of travelling, biographies...'

He tailed off and his serious expression returned. She wondered why he was hesitating and whether now he had seen her in her nightgown he was regretting that he had married her instead of the more beautiful Cassandra.

'You look very handsome, Mr Harcourt,' she said.

He blinked in surprise and Aurelia felt the heat rushing to her cheeks. What had possessed her to say something so forward? Her husband looked pleased, however, and he took another step forward until now he was close enough that she could smell the cologne he wore.

He reached a hand out and placed it on her shoulder. She remained motionless and, seeing that she did not protest, he extended his fingers up the side of her neck on her bare skin. She remembered him doing similar at the altar, which reminded her again of their kiss and the way her lips had responded to the pressure of his. Of how she had not wanted him to stop when he had drawn back.

'Are you…? Do you…? I mean…'

He took his hand away and gave her another look that sent shivers through her body. She realised that she was trembling and looked up into his eyes.

'You are very beautiful,' he repeated, 'and we are man and wife now. Do you understand that?'

She nodded, finding that his consideration brought a lump to her throat. He did not have to do that, she was his by law and by right he could do whatever he wanted with her and she would have no recourse for complaint. The very fact that he was taking pains to ensure she was agreeable to the fact made her grow a little fonder of him.

'I understand,' she said. 'I know what needs to be done.'

He looked away. 'Needs to,' he muttered and his voice was tinged with bitterness. Shame made Aurelia's cheeks redden even further than the thought of Jonathan kissing her had.

'I told you when I consented to be your wife that I would fulfil every part of a wife's duty,' she said. 'I meant it and I did not mean to imply I would find that duty unpleasant. If I did, I apologise.'

Jonathan reached for her hand and lead her slowly to the bed, whereupon he sat on the edge and waited until she did the same. She lowered herself and let her feet dangle, toes brushing the wool rug. They sat facing each other and once again Aurelia was struck by the thought that her husband didn't really want to be doing this. She was uncertain whether his hesitation was because he did not find her attractive enough or if he still did not believe she was willing.

She could think of no other way to assure him that she did not mind beyond touching him, so placed her hand on his knee. He jumped and then grinned at her shyly. She wondered if he, too, was a virgin and had as little idea how to proceed as she had. Now that she had begun, however, he seemed more willing to speed matters up. He put his hand on Aurelia's knee. The pressure and heat from his palm felt good and, when she did not flinch, he slowly ran his hand up the side of her thigh to rest on her hip, bundling the fabric of her nightgown beneath his fingers in the process and exposing her leg to the evening air.

As the previously untouched flesh began to ripple awake with the chill, Jonathan leaned closer and hesitantly kissed Aurelia's lips. However hesitant he might be at intercourse, he was good at that and she responded with eagerness so that when his lips grew firmer and began to move in unison it felt perfectly natural. Her head began to spin and Jonathan seemed equally affected because when he unexpectedly drew away his eyes brimmed with lust.

He moved his left hand to beside Aurelia's head and gently kept her chin tilting up. He brought his other arm around her back and rested his hand between her shoulder blades with his fingers spread wide. Aurelia put her arms around her husband's shoulders and without quite realising how it happened they were lying down, legs up on the bed, and were beside each other. Jonathan was still wearing his dressing gown so he paused briefly and undid the cord at the waist. Aurelia wondered if she should assist him, but he shrugged it off with ease, broad shoulders rolling back, first one, then the other. Aurelia watched in fascination as he shimmied it down his arms and let it fall to the floor, wondering if he was aware how the movement displayed the firmness of his well-shaped chest muscles through his cotton nightshirt. He rolled back over towards her and she felt something hard pressing against her thigh that she had not noticed before. Their eyes met and she saw in Jonathan's unconcealed excitement.

The light of the candle made his sandy hair glow with flecks of gold and carved his cheekbones into sharp planes. She was not sure what her own face would show, but was consumed by a sudden sense of coyness. She rolled away to extinguish the candle beside the bed, plunging them into darkness save for the splinter of light that crept between the heavy window curtains. She turned around back into Jonathan's waiting arms. He stroked his hand along from her wrist up her arm, then let his fingers trail over her collarbone and down until his hand came to rest on her breast. He squeezed it gently and a slight gasp escaped Aurelia's lips as the pressure sent a thrill of pleasure racing through her body that finished and intensified at the cleft at the top of her legs. How two such distant parts of her body were connected, she wasn't sure and didn't care.

She put her hand to Jonathan's chest, wondering whether the male anatomy was similarly joined. His nightshirt was fastened with a lace at the neck and a deep V-shaped opening down to just above his heart. There was room in the loose-fitting garment for her to slip her hand inside the gap and the muscles she touched were firm and covered with a light sprinkling of hairs. In her mind they were the same light brown as his hair. She stroked her fingers across them, slipping her other hand inside the neck of his nightshirt at the nape of his neck. He gave a sigh that had echoed her own and buried his head against Aurelia's neck, kissing the exposed skin with hot quick breaths against her ear.

He rolled her onto her back and eased one leg between her two. The length of her nightgown made his task difficult. He slid his hand to where it had bunched just above her knee and drew the fabric up so that Aurelia was exposed from the waist downwards. The cold air contrasted with the heat of his firm leg pressing against hers and once again the strange cramping, clenching spark between her legs coursed.

She wasn't sure what to do now, but fortunately Jonathan seemed willing and eager to take the lead because he drew his own nightshirt up until he, too, was half-naked. What a sight they must make, Aurelia thought, lying there in such a state. At least she now knew the answer to the question of whether she would need to be naked. Jonathan's fingers trailed across her belly with a light touch and the delicious sensation began to grow stronger within her, like the ripple spreading out from a stone thrown into the river.

'Are you…?' he murmured against her ear.

Until now they had both been silent so the question came as a surprise.

Am I what? Aurelia thought. *Scared? Excited? Ready?*

She wasn't sure what he was asking, but she realised that the three descriptions that had come to mind were all accurate so she turned her lips close to his.

'Yes,' she said. 'Yes, I am.'

She felt his hand wander down through her thatch of hair to settle at the parting between her legs. Jonathan slipped a finger inside her and the sensation of such an intimate breach caused her to gasp as her body admitted the digit with ease. He drew his finger away and lowered his body on top of her. Aurelia felt the hardness of his manhood pressing against her opening where his finger had been. She drew a sharp breath as her body spasmed.

'I will not hurt you,' he whispered. 'I will make it as quick as I can.'

She nodded and put her hands around his back, settling each one on a shoulder blade, and braced herself for discomfort.

That was not exactly the sensation she experienced. There was a slightly sharp lurch as he entered her that was not unpleasant. She tried to concentrate on the feeling of him moving in and out, upon how that action must be related to the increasing ripples of pleasure at the edge of her senses. It felt like trying to catch a dandelion seed that floated through the air almost within her fingers' grasp, but when she tried to clutch it, it darted out of her reach.

She became aware that Jonathan's breath had become audible moans that coincided with the increasing strains of his thrusts and the swollen hardness inside her. It was over quickly as he had promised, but far from feeling relieved, Aurelia was left with a sense that something had ended before it was resolved. Jonathan sagged onto her, his strength apparently gone. With one hand he brushed Aurelia's hair back from her cheeks where it had stuck, dampened by perspiration. He kissed her cheek, then drew himself out of her body and lay beside her on his back. Now she had grown accustomed to the light from the window she could make out the shape of his chest moving up and down in time with his breath. He felt for her hand and gave it a gentle squeeze.

'I hope that was not too uncomfortable,' he said.

Aurelia squeezed his hand back and smiled in the darkness. It hadn't been uncomfortable and, if that was the duty of a wife, she could endure it for as long as it was necessary for her to fulfil her part of their marriage contract.

'No, it wasn't,' she answered. 'But thank you for your consideration.'

Jonathan sat up and dropped his feet to the floor. Aurelia was momentarily confused until she remembered he had promised that once the deed was done she would have her privacy. He put on his dressing gown and tied the cord as she sat up and looked at him. She was almost sorry he was leaving because lying beside him hand in hand had been pleasant, but she had to remind herself that for him this was just a business exchange. She should no more expect him to stay with her than to keep the company of a customer once the transaction was complete.

He stood and turned to face her. 'Goodnight, Mrs Harcourt. I hope you will sleep well. I hope you will join me for breakfast at nine. I usually eat earlier in order to be at the mill at that time, but I thought tomorrow we might eat together. I need to pay a visit to your father to sign some papers and, if you wish to visit your family, we could ride together.'

'Thank you. I will. Goodnight, Mr Harcourt,' Aurelia replied.

Jonathan walked to the door and gave her one last look before he left, closing it quietly. As soon as he was gone Aurelia scrambled from the bed and drew back the curtains. By moonlight she washed herself with the jug of water Annie had left. The water was cold and she decided she would ask for warm water to be provided nightly. She brushed her hair loose and climbed into the bed. When she and Jonathan had lain together they had not even bothered to draw back the counterpane so the sheets were smooth and clean, though warmed a little from the heat of bodies lying on top of them.

Aurelia lay back and tried to recapture the sensations of what had taken place. Even though she had rinsed her skin, she could still catch the scent of Jonathan about her person. It was not unpleasant and, in the absence of her husband, it would have to be her only company.

Arthur's face rose in her mind and she tried not to imagine what their wedding night would have been like if circumstances had been different. Arthur had been a passionate suitor, continually trying to coax kisses from her, and he must have loved her dearly to risk ruining her in order to claim her as his wife. There could never have been a wedding, of course. She knew that.

She was glad that Jonathan had shown enough sensitivity to leave her in private because it meant there was no one to see her weep over the man who had deceived her so basely. Far better to be married to a man who did not expect or need her heart than cause scandal with one who had broken it.

Chapter Nine

Jonathan sat opposite his bride at the small dining table while she poured his morning coffee. One week on from the wedding, they had fallen into this ritual naturally and satisfactorily. If this was to be any indication of how their future lives would be, he could dare to believe marriage to Aurelia might not be too bad after all.

Every morning she would pour the coffee, then pass it to Annie, who would carry it to Jonathan at the other end of the table. She always waited until Jonathan had put his cream in before pouring her own cup and adding a single lump of sugar which she stirred slowly until the coffee was almost cold. Black and sweet. White and bitter. They were perfect opposites in their taste for that.

'Thank you, Annie. You may leave us,' Aurelia told the maid.

The girl bobbed a curtsey and left the married

couple together. She seemed content with taking both the roles of parlour maid and Mrs Harcourt's personal maid in exchange for her duties as the maid to all four of the Upford women. Presumably she was not party to the intimate knowledge that the marriage was a sham and believed her young mistress and new master to be rapturously in love and wishing to spend all their time together.

Jonathan felt a trickle of heat creep stealthily across the back of his collar. The marriage was not a sham. For the past seven nights Aurelia had admitted him to her bedroom when he had quietly knocked on the door and allowed him into her bed with the same quiet compliance and an expectant look upon her face. She consented to his touches and lovemaking without complaints. More than consented, he thought, now he considered it. She appeared to derive pleasure from the time they spent in her bed, though Jonathan was careful to ensure that when he felt his final strokes coming upon him he did not hold back in order to prolong his own enjoyment. Instead he submitted to the first warning of his body and let the climax flood out of him so he did not subject her to the act any longer than necessary.

They never spoke of what passed between them once the candle had been snuffed out, but he believed she was happy. He hoped she was.

He sipped his coffee and stared at her over the

rim of the cup. Aurelia lifted her eyes from the piece of toast she was buttering and glanced in his direction. When she realised he was watching her, she lowered her knife and gave him a shy smile. He held her gaze as his stomach did a somersault.

By God, she was beautiful. He was in danger of becoming besotted with her in a way that went far beyond the transactional nature of what they had agreed. It was just as well their unions took place in the dark because if he saw her expression and discovered it to be one of simple forbearance he swore he would break. Then again, if her face showed any fraction of the ecstasy that he himself felt, he would not be able to limit himself to just one attempt each night and would take longer and longer over each visit, which would not be a part of the agreement. After the first time he had laid her on her bed he had not kissed her lips. It was too intimate, too dizzyingly sensual, and if he allowed himself to indulge that need he knew he would lose himself too deeply in the whirlpool of emotions that he could feel himself edging closer to.

Her hair was swept back into a knot and she was dressed in a blue blouse which billowed out in layers of tiny ruffles over the breasts he knew by touch were full and soft. Each night she was waiting for him in the white nightgown with delicate lace, her hair in a loose plait. He imagined her clad in nothing but the finest, diaphanous silk his factory could produce as he stroked it over her belly, thighs and breasts.

'What are you thinking about?' she asked.

Jonathan's breath caught. It was an odd question and she could not have asked it at a worst possible time, given the images that were going through his mind.

'Silk,' he said. He placed his coffee cup down and rested his arms on the table. 'I'm thinking of what I have to do today.'

She looked at him with slight interest. 'I wondered if perhaps one day you might show me around the mill. I'm fascinated by how simple threads turn into such beautiful cloth—it seems impossible.'

Jonathan wrinkled his brow. He never tired of watching the fine spools of silk come together to create intricate patterns. She might be interested in the process, but his wife didn't even like to spend time in a room with too many guests. She would hate the clatter of machinery and relentless loud chatter of the workers.

'We've been married for a week and I haven't even seen beyond the gates,' she continued.

'It isn't a place for a lady,' he said. 'The noise and the dust can be overwhelming.'

His throat tightened, thinking of Edward and

the fibres that were suffocating his life day by day. He would not want Aurelia to be exposed to those, even though sense told him that an hour would not be enough to do much damage.

'But you have women working in your factory,' Aurelia pointed out. 'And children. Isn't it overwhelming for them?'

Jonathan looked at her, open-mouthed. It was the first time she had ever argued with him. The skin beneath his collar began to prickle at such flagrant confrontation.

'Women. Not ladies,' he said firmly. 'They need to work there, you do not have to. The factory is no place for you.'

Aurelia's eyes hardened. She turned the handle of her coffee cup ninety degrees, then pushed her chair back.

'As you say. In that case I shall bid you a good morning and occupy myself in other ways. Goodbye, Jonathan.'

She walked out, leaving Jonathan burning with fury at being dismissed so abruptly.

It was only when he was halfway to the mill that it occurred to him that Aurelia had called him by his name for the very first time. It had been anger, not passion, that had broken through her decorum. His temper rose and he could very clearly understand why his father and mother had been at odds and so often. And it was not something he wished to emulate in his own marriage.

A day in the mill only strengthened Jonathan's belief that he was right to forbid Aurelia to enter it. He was greeted with the news from Edward that the wooden rails on one of the mill's four skein winders had split. The spider-web-thin warp threads of silk that had been so painstakingly wound had slipped and the entire process would have to begin again. If this was not enough, he found the foreman on the second floor of the building stepping into what look like a brawl between two of the girls who each apparently held the other one responsible for the spilling of a basketful of bobbins.

He arrived just in time to witness the older girl leaping towards the smaller and seizing her by the hair. He had to rush to his foreman's aid to help separate them, each grabbing one around the waist. Both girls were eventually pacified and stood sullenly listening to their employer.

'It doesn't matter who caused the error,' Jonathan said as patiently as he could muster. 'But while we are standing here the work is not being done and the mistake is not being rectified.'

Both girls glared at each other, though the younger of the two, who was no more than ten in Jonathan's estimation, looked as if she was about to start weeping. Jonathan sensed that she had not been the one at fault. He held his hand up, stepping in between them.

'If there was anyone else capable of completing the task quickly, I wouldn't hesitate to show both of you to the gates myself, but you're both good workers and I'd hate to let your skills go to waste.'

He nodded briefly to the foreman. 'Give them a five-minute break for a cup of tea, then get them both back to work.'

He turned to the girls. 'By rights there is nothing to stop me throwing you out, but I'm placing my trust in you. Don't make me regret that.'

Both girls thanked him effusively and sloped off to the table at the end of the floor where tea was perpetually stewing in a pot. The younger one turned back and gave him a shy curtsey, then hurried to get her mug before the time was up.

Jonathan decided to leave his paperwork and instead spend the day walking the different floors, observing his workers.

By one in the afternoon he was irritable, with ringing ears and hair that felt stiff and greasy with the scent of human grime and silk threads. If Aurelia could see this, she would understand why he did not want her to be exposed to such a situation. He would try explaining that he had not commanded her without good reason.

* * *

Towards the end of the day he strolled down to the river. Work had already begun on clearing the ground in order to dig a trench to divert the supply of water. He stood and gazed over the slow-flowing river at the fields. Aurelia had been the means to get the land and he owed it to her to be a kind husband. He thought back to the ease with which they had conversed when they had accidentally met and a feeling of melancholy washed over him they were not on such easy terms now. He resolved to try to rectify the situation when he returned home that evening.

It turned out not to be so simple. If Jonathan returned home feeling tired and irritable, Aurelia's mood seemed equally dark. His attempt at reconciliation was met with a brick wall higher than that surrounding the mill grounds.

'You have no need to apologise, Mr Harcourt,' she said stiffly, not meeting his eyes, but looking slightly past him so that Jonathan had a sense she was inspecting his left ear. 'I forgot myself and presumed to intrude into your affairs. It won't happen again. I shall confine myself to the running of your home.'

Something in that last comment set a warning bell chiming for Jonathan.

'Are you finding that a trial?'

Her whole body stiffened. The expressive eyes flickered, then settled back on his ear.

'Mrs Harcourt, will you look at me!' Jonathan ordered.

She blinked and her eyes whipped to his face, growing wide at his unaccustomed tone. He cringed inside at the thought he had been impolite or, worse, aggressive.

'Are you finding your life unpleasant?' Jonathan asked softly. 'Tell me what I can do to help you.'

She glanced away again, tilting her head to look down. Her eyes closed briefly in what looked like distress and Jonathan shivered. He wanted to put his hand on her shoulder and console her, but she crossed over to the fireplace and brushed some imaginary dust off the mantelpiece. She looked into the mirror that hung over it and met the eyes of Jonathan's reflection. It was disconcerting to be looked at and yet not, at the same time. More so because Jonathan could swear there were tears beginning to brim in Aurelia's eyes that made them gleam so alluringly.

'There is nothing unpleasant that I can complain about. I am merely adjusting to the role of a wife and mistress of my own establishment. It is nothing that I won't become familiar with in time.'

Jonathan nodded. Even though she was capable of organising matters for her mother, running a house herself must be daunting. She turned back to face Jonathan, giving him a view of both the front and back curve of her shapely neck.

'Shall we go eat?'

They ate dinner in silence and Jonathan decided to curtail the evening by feigning a headache and informing Aurelia that he would not be visiting her room that night. He tried to ignore the flash of relief that briefly crossed her face.

'You may, of course, remain down here as long as you wish,' he said before leaving the room. He opened the front door and stood in the street, leaning against the railing at the bottom of the path and staring into the dark square as he smoked his nightly cigarette. The weather was dismal and a thick fog hung in the air, soon soaking through Jonathan's clothes until he felt a chill coming upon him. He pinched off the end of his cigarette and went into the parlour, intending to have a drink. He took off his damp waistcoat and looked at the garment in wonder. Before his marriage he would never have worn it at home and it seemed preposterous he was dressing formally in his own house. He loosened his collar and sat in his favourite high-backed chair in front of the fire, but found it hard to settle.

The room was beneath Aurelia's dressing room and he could hear her footsteps overhead as he sat with his untouched brandy in his hand. She seemed to be pacing back and forth and he tracked the footsteps from window to door to dressing table until finally she crossed to the door to her bedroom. He expected the footsteps to stop, but she returned and continued pacing around restlessly.

He thought back to what she had said and how difficult it must be to transform from a daughter to a wife. Their marriage had not been unpleasant for him, but she had left her home and family and the attempt she had made to share her husband's life had been firmly rebuffed. She must be lonely. He'd been a blind, unthinking, insensitive fool. Exactly the sort of husband he dreaded becoming.

Knowing she was up there, brooding and pacing and awake, was excruciating. When Jonathan could bear it no longer he left his brandy and made his way upstairs, determined to put an end to the awkwardness.

He didn't change into his nightclothes, but went straight to Aurelia's room. He knocked quietly on the door to her dressing room and waited. His heart began to stampede in his chest. He'd always been admitted by the bedroom door. She opened it halfway and peered out at him suspiciously.

'May I come in?' he asked.

'I'm not…ready,' she said. Her eyes moved over him and he wished he had remained fully dressed or changed completely. This half-state of shirt alone felt wrong. At the same time he felt a ripple of excitement at the thought of Aurelia removing his clothes herself. He really did want her. Perhaps this was the way to heal the breach between them.

'It doesn't matter if you aren't completely ready for bed,' he said. 'We're husband and wife. We should be able to see each other no matter what the circumstances.

She wrinkled her brow and bit her lip. 'Mr Harcourt... I...' Again she tailed off. 'Of course you are my husband and this is your house. I can't refuse to admit you, but...'

Her cheeks were growing red. He'd upset her a lot more than he had suspected.

'Mrs Harcourt, I can understand why you're still angry at me,' Jonathan said. He put his hand on her arm, hoping to emphasise that he was no longer angry himself. She jumped and drew herself up straight. Jonathan's heart twisted and he whipped his hand away.

'I'll leave you,' he said stiffly before turning his back and walking to the end of the landing.

'Stop. Jonathan! Come back!'

Jonathan looked round. Aurelia had opened the doorway fully. Her face was expressionless.

He gave her a wry smile. 'That's only the second time you've called me by my name and neither time has it been in affection.'

'Which is exactly how you wanted our marriage to be.'

He gave a mirthless laugh. 'As you say. What I wanted and what we both agreed upon. However, I had not expected my name to be reserved for moments of anger.'

She blinked and frowned in confusion.

'I'm not angry with you. As I told you before, I intruded where I shouldn't have. The fault was mine. That isn't why you can't come in, Mr Harcourt. I am not wilfully denying you your rights from spite—in fact, I would welcome a thawing of the atmosphere between us. However, I cannot permit you to visit my room tonight.'

Jonathan stared at her, nonplussed. She stood in the doorway barefoot, he noticed now, and looking no different to every other night, saving that now her hair was free from its night-time plait. Her hair was loose and tumbled about her shoulders in loose waves where chestnut and gold vied with tawny and coffee for supremacy as candle-light glowed behind her. She drew the neck of her nightdress tight, clutching it with one hand as if she feared Jonathan might rip it from her body. Her cheeks were growing pinker with every passing moment.

'Mrs Harcourt, you are talking in riddles,' he said. She dropped her head and made a small circle with her bare foot. It peeked from beneath the hem of her nightgown, narrow and shapely. Jonathan's imagination couldn't help but follow the limb that would be equally naked. He swallowed, wishing he'd drunk the brandy as his throat and mouth became sand. Whenever they had made love they had remained clothed and now he was struck by an overwhelming desire to see what his wife looked like beneath her clothes.

Jonathan walked back to her and took her face in his hands, the heat scorching his palms. She made a small noise in her throat and the pulse in her neck throbbed beneath his fingertips. He wanted to cover the spot with his lips and feel the rhythm grow quicker beneath his kiss. Whatever her reasons for refusing his company, not knowing was torture to him.

'Please be as frank with me now about your reasons as you have been on every other occasion we have spoken.'

She put her hands over his. Usually they were cool, but now they were hot to touch. Jonathan's heart leapt in alarm at the thought she might be sickening.

'Tell me,' he said, 'are you ill?'

'No, I'm not sick.' Her eyes flickered away and then back to his. 'I'm sorry, Mr Harcourt,' she said quietly. 'There is no baby yet.'

Jonathan had not expected there to be so soon, but her certainty confused him.

'Why are you so sure?'

Aurelia's cheeks flamed again, growing hot beneath Jonathan's palm. She sighed.

'If you are really determined to make me explain, then I will. I know there is no baby because my monthly courses have arrived. That is why you may not lie with me tonight.'

Her eyes bored into him with an air of open defiance. Berated him. *See what you made me admit*, they seemed to say.

Jonathan lowered his hands and stepped away from Aurelia. She wrapped her arms around herself, bunching the lacy folds of her nightgown over her breasts defensively. Jonathan cringed at having made her so plainly explain the situation. It should have occurred to him. His mother and their servant had used to bemoan their *monthly visitor* as they referred to it. Jonathan had not understood what they referred to for years, but he vaguely remembered coppers full of cloths soaking in hot water in the scullery. The maid had seemed to find her courses a reason for taking an afternoon off each month to lie in bed and groan.

'If there is anything I can do to help you,' Jonathan said, 'please tell me. A hot brick? Whisky and water? I am at your disposal.'

Aurelia smiled at him, but looked surprised. 'Thank you, that's very kind of you, but now I have everything I need. It is merely a question of waiting for the time to pass.'

'Then I shall leave you to wait,' Jonathan said. He held out a hand as if to shake it, then decided that was the wrong gesture and leaned in to brush his lips over his wife's cheek. He felt her shiver, or perhaps it was his own body that trembled at being close to her. He put his hand to the back of her head and had to stop himself from tangling his fingers deep into her thick tresses and letting them slide, glinting, through his fingers.

'Goodnight, Mrs Harcourt,' he murmured. He drew away and walked back to his own room.

Marriage is more of a trial than I anticipated.

Those were the words he wrote in his journal.

He had not achieved the release he craved, but he felt he had gone some way to mending the rip in their marriage before it grew too large. The knowledge, however, did nothing to alleviate the clinging sense of loneliness that he could not shake as he lay in his bed, missing the arms of his wife.

Chapter Ten

Perhaps she should get a dog. Aurelia tugged on the leash to bring Caesar to heel. The weather had turned cold and damp but she could not bear to stay inside Siddon Hall. After a half-hour in the company of her mother, fielding indelicate questions regarding her marriage, she had volunteered to walk the dog.

As she walked briskly down towards the river she reminded herself that, however odd and lonely her marriage might be, it was better than living under her mother's roof.

'At least now I am respectable,' she told the spaniel. She let him off his leash and he bounded away, barking loudly at his freedom. A dog would be nice, although a human companion would be better. She was pleased Annie had joined her, but the maid's conversation was limited.

As Aurelia neared the river she heard voices

raised in anger and the unmistakable joyful bark of Caesar. She lifted the hem of her skirts and broke into a run. By the time she arrived at the river the dog was in the process of causing havoc. A group of men were digging what looked like a ditch. The dog had crossed the river and was attempting to wrestle a spade from one of them.

'Caesar, heel!' Aurelia shouted.

The men turned to look at her and one of them laughed. A couple of the others nudged each other in the ribs. Aurelia adjusted her skirt and walked over to them. These were Jonathan's workers, of course, and would be engaged with diverting the river to widen it. One of the men nudged his nearest colleague, then muttered something and grinned. She doubted what he had said was complimentary or suitable for her ears. Suddenly Jonathan's refusal to let her visit his factory seemed fairer and more understandable.

Aurelia flushed.

'I'm sorry,' she said to the man. 'He just wants to play.'

'Don't we all, miss,' said the man who had grinned.

Aurelia gave him a cold look at such impertinence. 'Please could you catch him and bring him back.'

The man strolled over to Caesar, clicked his fingers and waved them in a circle. The spaniel began to chase his own tail in delight. He was utterly shameful.

'From the circus, is he?' the man asked. 'Why don't you come over here and join the fun?'

Aurelia folded her arms indignantly. A couple of the other men were starting to look uncomfortable at their workmate's behaviour. She hoped one of them would intervene because she had no intention of getting any closer to the river, but it seemed unlikely that they would do anything beyond mumbling it was time to get back to work.

'Will you please send him back?' she asked.

'What's going on? Why is there a delay?'

Jonathan's deep voice cut through the men's laughter.

Aurelia glanced in the direction it had come from to see her husband striding towards them. She had never been more relieved to see him. It was as well she knew his voice because she would not necessarily have recognised him otherwise.

He had left home wearing his usual dark suit with stiff collar and tie, woollen overcoat and hat. Now he was standing in shirt sleeves and braces, wearing a pair of dark brown trousers and heavy boots like the rest of the labourers. His top button was undone and his skin was flushed. His face glowed with exertion and his hair was disarranged and flopped across his forehead.

Aurelia shivered with excitement. How could seeing him dressed so informally make her quiver with excitement?

He stopped in his tracks and stared at her over the river.

'Mrs Harcourt,' he said, raising his brows in surprise. 'What are you doing here?'

She gestured towards the dog who had obviously recognised his previous playmate because he had abandoned his game with the ditch-digger and was now capering around Jonathan's sturdy boots. He bent and seized Caesar by the scruff of the neck and held him tightly.

'I was visiting my sisters and took a stroll in the gardens, but Caesar ran off.'

The men who had previously been unhelpful began to return to their work. The one who had taunted Aurelia picked up the shovel and turned away, but Jonathan stuck an arm out and barred his way.

He narrowed his eyes and squared his shoulders. Aurelia had never seen her husband angry before, but it was clear from the way he held himself and the slight flush beginning to appear behind his ears that he was furious with what he had discovered.

'If you would be so kind as to return the dog to my wife,' he said, leaving the rest of the sentence unfinished. His voice was cool, but each word was fired with the precision of a bullet from a shotgun. The man looked at the gulf of water that separated him from Aurelia. The men had been working quickly and the river was wider than when Jonathan had leapt across to join Aurelia what felt like ages ago. He would have to wade through. He looked back at his employer and clearly decided that a soaking was the lesser of two evils. He turned to the bank and whistled to the dog.

'Not like that,' Jonathan said. 'He's unruly and might run again.' He bent and picked up Caesar, holding him out to the man. Reluctantly the man took the soggy dog in his arms and waded across to Aurelia. He held Caesar by the scruff of the neck while Aurelia attached the leash.

'I'm sorry, Mrs Harcourt,' he mumbled, keeping his eyes averted from her face. 'I did not realise who you were or I would not have been so free with my jests.'

He gingerly crossed back and climbed on to the bank. The water was thigh deep and his heavy moleskin trousers were now sodden and clung to his legs uncomfortably. Jonathan had watched the entire process stone-faced. Now he folded his arms.

'You can pick up the morning's pay at the office, then leave,' he said shortly. 'I don't employ people who speak to a woman as you did.'

The man looked as if he was about to protest, then slunk away. His ex-workmates all studiously concentrated on digging the trench. Jonathan looked at Aurelia. She held his gaze, unable to tell whether he was angry or not.

'Mrs Harcourt, if you care to walk a little further along the bank to the bridge, I shall accompany you back to Siddon Hall.'

He did not look in the mood to be argued with so Aurelia obeyed. Jonathan donned a jacket over his shirt and spoke briefly to the remaining men. They walked parallel along their respective banks of the river until they reached the small bridge where Jonathan crossed over. He bent to greet Caesar, fondling him behind the ears with firm strokes, then stood and faced Aurelia.

'I thought I had made it clear I wanted you to stay away from the mill,' he said, fixing Aurelia with a stern look.

'And I have done as you told me. I have not crossed on to your land, but have remained on my father's side.' She lifted her chin and gave him what she hoped was an equally unyielding look in return, but then she remembered the flooding sense of relief when he had appeared and put an end to the encounter. 'I would not have ventured down to the riverside if I had known that your men were there.'

He looked mollified and his own face became

less forbidding. He had looked so angry when he appeared that it had startled her. She was glad to see his gentle expression returning.

'You didn't have to dismiss that man,' she said. 'He was rude, but he did nothing to harm me and now he has lost his livelihood. It seems vindictive.'

'Vindictive?'

Jonathan raised his eyebrows. He ran his hand over his hair, pushing it out of the way. It flopped forward immediately again and Aurelia wanted to twist her fingers into the locks and see if she could make them behave.

'You didn't have to make him wade across the river.'

'His behaviour was boorish and uncouth,' Jonathan said. 'Now I hope he'll think twice before repeating it. As for dismissing him, I do not want men like that working for me when there are plenty of others who deserve employment. Now do you understand why I told you to stay away from the mill?'

Aurelia nodded. 'It's my fault he lost his job,' she said quietly.

Jonathan put his hands on her shoulders and turned her to face him.

'Mrs Harcourt, don't think for a moment that you are to blame,' Jonathan said earnestly. 'I don't hold you responsible. It was his fault. He chose how to speak to you and he paid the consequences.'

His hands were heavy on her shoulders; warm and reassuring. She felt instantly comforted by his mere presence. Her saviour. Her husband. She reached up and covered his hand with hers, not wanting him to stop touching her. He stepped a little closer. Aurelia thought for one startling moment that he was going to kiss her, because he leaned in with his head slightly on one side, staring intently into her eyes. Her whole body tingled with excitement. She realised how much she had missed his company at night. Missed what they did together.

Missed him.

Three nights had passed since he had knocked on her door and she had had to send him away. He had made no further reference to her condition, nor did he attempt to visit her bedroom. Aurelia assumed delicacy towards her feelings had prevented him from asking when he might begin again and she wondered how long he would assume she was unavailable. Three nights since the excruciating admission of why she was refusing to fulfil her part of their bargain. Even though they had both agreed that intimacy was to be kept to the bedroom, she tilted her head back and waited for his kiss.

It never came.

Aurelia bit down the disappointment that she unaccountably felt. 'I still feel responsible. He has lost his job because he was unfortunate enough to be rude to your wife.'

'It isn't because you are my wife,' Jonathan said. He lowered his hands and stepped back. 'It was because of his behaviour. I would have done the same if he had spoken like that to any of my female workers, or any lady of my acquaintance.'

Aurelia blinked, not sure whether she was being insulted by his comparison of her to any of his workers. While she was pondering it Jonathan held out his arm for her to take. 'Let me take you back to your father, where I know you will be safe until I return to get you later.'

Aurelia was about to protest that she could make her own way to Siddon Hall and to her own home, but then changed her mind. Some company would be nice and Jonathan always talked sense.

She took his arm and was taken aback when he did not hold it at a right angle for her to rest hers on, but linked it right through and drew her closer to him than usual. He was warm and smelled faintly of mud and perspiration. It was unfamiliar but far from unpleasant and Aurelia wondered if he had been digging, too. She eased her body against his side, imagining the supple muscles of his arms and chest tightening as he toiled.

'Was your visit with your family difficult?' Jonathan asked. 'It seems an hour should be tolerable without you having to escape with this disobedient boy.'

Aurelia grinned.

'My mother was as she always is, with the added concern that now she has a married daughter and her mind is turning to her future role. She was trying in her subtlest ways to find out if I was already with child,' she said.

She blushed furiously. She had neither confirmed nor denied it, claiming the excuse of Jonathan's wish for discretion. She placed her hand over her belly briefly. Jonathan's eyes followed, settling on her.

'Our poor child, when you do conceive it, will bear such a weight of expectations,' he remarked.

'What if I am barren?' Aurelia said. 'What if you married me for no reason?'

Jonathan took her hand. She stiffened, startled, but then eased and left her hand in his.

'It will happen,' he said. 'Don't fear. We have barely begun to try.'

Aurelia bunched her fingers around Caesar's leash.

'What would you call the boy when he's born?' Jonathan asked.

'Don't you want to call him Jonathan?' she asked. All fathers wanted sons to bear their names, didn't they? She remembered the two boys born to Lady Upford. Poor pale scraps, neither of whom had lived past their first year and who both resided under small stones bearing the name Robert after their father. She wasn't particularly superstitious, but Robert was definitely not to be suggested.

'I'm not so vain,' Jonathan said.

'What about your father's name?' Aurelia asked.

Jonathan's arm tightened.

'No. It is enough that the child will bear our surname. What of the classical world?' he asked, brightening slightly. 'Your father clearly has a passion for all things ancient to have named you and your sisters and his dogs in tribute to Rome or Greece. Would you not want to continue that yourself? I'm sure he would offer you some suggestions'

Aurelia smiled to herself. She had no need to ask her father. She could produce a whole list of Greek heroes without help if Jonathan so wished and in the original alphabet.

'I think my father's love of all things classical is not as intellectual as you assume.'

She thought back to the plates and illustrations of vases in Sir Robert's books. Aurelia and Cassandra had once crept into his study and examined the volumes curiously and what Aurelia had seen remained branded on her mind. To think of men and women lying or standing in such postures and doing such things to each other! Some of them seemed physically impossible. Others morally so. She glanced surreptitiously at Jonathan and as his eyes flickered to hers Aurelia realised he was trying not to grin. He knew what she was referring to and for a brief moment they shared their amusement. Her throat grew hot at the thought of them conducting themselves in such a manner and the heat spread over and inside her like a pot of ink spilled across a desk.

There was no reason for him to shun her bed any longer. She wanted those arms about her again. She wanted that chest pressing against her breasts. She wanted all of him. The spark of hunger and snatched taste of that indefinable *something* that had eluded her was shuddering awake. She might have sighed, because he stopped walking and peered into her face, brow furrowed in concern.

'You aren't too distressed by what happened anymore, are you?' he asked.

She felt like a child caught guiltily with a hand in the cake tin. She couldn't explain what she had been thinking of, not to him. She shook her head.

'No, though I'm glad you appeared when you did. I don't know what would have happened otherwise, or how I would have got Caesar back.'

Jonathan grunted. Aurelia glanced up at him. The muscles in his neck were tight and his expression was as severe as it had been when he had confronted his worker. She realised his anger wasn't directed at her, but at the memory of what had happened. He untangled his arm from hers and slipped it around her waist. He'd never done that before. Always they had walked arm in arm or side by side. It did nothing to satisfy that longing for his touch.

'I almost didn't visit the site today,' he said. 'I have a stack of ledgers to inspect, but when Edward decided to leave with the excuse of supervising his cook for this evening I decided the bookkeeping could go hang!'

They smiled at each other. The incident had broken the ice between them and Aurelia found she was enjoying Jonathan's company. They began walking again and Jonathan once again put his arm around Aurelia's waist.

'Have you remembered we are dining with Edward tonight?' Jonathan asked. 'He's very much looking forward to beginning your campaign of socialising me.'

Aurelia smiled gently. 'I'm afraid he will find me sadly behind if that is the case. I have no intention of interfering in your life.'

'Of course not,' Jonathan said. The humour in his eyes vanished as quickly as it had previously returned. Aurelia bit her tongue. She had meant it as a joke, but it had been her wish to know more about his life that caused their argument.

'Tell me about Mr Langdon,' she asked quickly. 'I've only met him briefly.'

'You will meet him properly tonight,' Jonathan said, 'and one thing I know about Edward is that he will happily tell you anything you wish to know, probably a great deal more than you might wish if you aren't careful.'

This was the first time since he had refused her request to visit the mill that she had shown interest in speaking to him about more than purely household matters and she expected him to stop there, but instead he stared over the river at the mill grounds.

'Edward has been the greatest friend a man could hope for. He saw promise in me from a young age and it is thanks to him that I am in the position I am now. He knew my mother at some point in her youth. He was five or six years older than she was.'

He stared off past Aurelia as he spoke. She waited for him to continue, sensing he had not finished, but was gathering his thoughts. He had told her one night of how he came to be living in Macclesfield. How his mother had been made destitute and cast out of their family home by a distant relative when his father had died intestate.

How they were forced to move halfway across England to take the charity offered by Edward Langdon. It was no wonder he was so attached to his partner.

'When I was younger I wondered if Edward and my mother had been fond of each other, but she married my father instead. I thought his previous affection might have been the reason he offered us help, but I never liked to ask.'

He looked back at Aurelia with a solemn face. Her heart fluttered for poor Edward, lovelorn for a woman he could never have. 'If that had been the case, don't you think they may have reunited once your mother was widowed?' she asked. 'They were older, but if you had a second chance at happiness, wouldn't you take it?'

Jonathan looked away once more and once again his throat tightened. Aurelia wondered if he was aware of the visible sign that appeared whenever something troubled him. She certainly had no intention of telling him, useful as it was in discerning his moods.

'I don't know,' he said. 'There could have been other barriers. Perhaps love only comes once and when it is missed it is too late to chase after it. People change, feelings lessen.'

'I imagine he did his best to help them on their way,' Aurelia said quietly. 'Don't you think it would be better to do that than live yearning for something you could never hope to have?'

Sorrow placed its hands on her shoulders like an unwanted caress. She had not noticed its absence until it returned at the thought of lost love pining after something it was denied. After discovering Arthur's dreadful betrayal, she had believed her destiny was to remain unwed. She had been so easily tricked into loving him, when he had known from the start there was an insurmountable barrier between them. Even though her marriage was only a business arrangement, Jonathan was a pleasant diversion and time in his company had caused that ache to lessen. Life with Jonathan would never have the all-consuming ecstasy of the love she had felt for Arthur and that was safer. It was a tolerable substitute for spinsterhood under her father's roof and she knew she had made the right decision.

The roof in question came into view. They had walked slowly, but had reached the gates.

'You can leave me here if you wish,' Aurelia said.

'I'll take you all the way,' Jonathan said. He walked her as far as the gravel pathway in front of the main entrance before releasing her from his arms. 'You look presentable enough to return to your mother.'

He reached his hand out and brushed her cheek

with his thumb, leaving a trail of heat that made her tremble with desire. He tilted his head to the left and smiled. 'Perhaps I was a little angrier with him because it was you,' he said.

He turned and strode away before Aurelia could think how to respond.

Chapter Eleven

The odd confrontation seemed to have brought a change in the relationship between Jonathan and his wife. Until they met at the riverside he had been worried that the mood between them would affect the atmosphere at dinner with Edward, but their encounter and the chance to walk together had allayed those fears. That they had been replaced by other fears was something he did not want to dwell on too deeply. What if he had not arrived? Aurelia might have been harmed. She was at liberty to do what she liked with her days and Jonathan would never dream of confining her to the house, but he would have no idea where she was, whether she was in danger or distressed. Now he felt protective of her and the responsibility caused him more anxiety than he had believed possible.

He had been sitting with a cup of tea by the fire, but when she entered, wearing a gown suitable for an evening dining engagement, he could not resist leaping to his feet to greet her. Her shoulders were bare and her hair was piled high tonight, a mass of brown curls that seemed suspended with no visible support aside from a wide mother-of-pearl comb that sat at the back. Jonathan's fingers twitched at the thought of plucking it from her hair and discovering if the whole edifice would come tumbling down. She was not dressed extravagantly or immodestly—Jonathan had seen plenty of women with more of their bosom on display at dinner—but the effect of the off-the-shoulder gown and swept-up hair was to reveal much more bare skin than usual. Other small details on her indigo-silk dress drew his attention to her figure. He couldn't help but imagine what lay beneath the frothy edging of lace above her breasts and the bows that darted down her spine to an impossibly small waist above the dome of her skirt.

His blood raced hot with desire and the stiff collar and necktie seemed to tighten, cutting off his ability to speak or breathe.

'You look beautiful,' he murmured, unable to keep the admiration from his voice.

She gave him a cautious smile as if she believed he was lying, but it was warmer than any she had bestowed upon him since he had refused her request. She adjusted her sleeves, then checked her earrings—a pair of large pearls set in clasps of silver that dangled playfully on to her neck—were firmly fixed in her ears.

She had perfect ears, Jonathan decided as he watched her fingers nimbly toy with the ornament. Usually she wore her hair over them, but now he could see the lobes were pulled down by the weight of the pearl drops he had the urge to kiss them. To run his tongue from the shadowed spot on her neck where wisps of downy hair drifted free of her knot. To drag his lip down the curve of her neck until it met her collarbone. To...

He coughed, conscious of the erotic thoughts he was enacting while she stood waiting by the hearth, completely unaware.

'Would you like some tea?' he asked.

'If we have time, thank you.'

Jonathan poured her a cup and took it to her. He held it out, but kept his arm crooked and close enough to himself that when she took the saucer, their hands were almost touching. He gazed into her eyes and she looked back, neither of them paying attention to the cup they both clasped. When they'd danced together on their wedding day, he'd felt less attraction than he did at this moment. What would she do if he took her in his arms and began to waltz her around the room?

He didn't, of course. She would think he had

lost his mind. He contented himself by watching her lips on the rim of the cup as she drank and tried his best not to imagine his lips in place of the fine china.

'Would you mind if we walked to Edward's house?' he asked. 'It's only a short walk and the evening is fine so I thought we could go on foot as I know you enjoy walking. Or are you tired from earlier?'

'Not at all,' she said, lifting her chin and giving him a determined look. 'I can walk for miles without tiring.'

'In that case, let's be off.'

Jonathan summoned his valet to bring his overcoat and Aurelia's cape. He passed it around her shoulders himself and as he fastened the silver pin at the neck his fingers brushed against her bare skin. That close, the scent of her perfume made his senses tingle. It reminded him of candied violets and he wanted to kiss her throat to see if it tasted the same.

His pulse quickened and their eyes met again. He saw a spark of interest in her eyes and became truly aware, perhaps for the first time, that his wife did not find him unpleasant. He resolved that tonight he would visit her room once more.

Dinner was excellent, as it always was when Edward entertained. He seemed in good spirits and insisted that no mention should be made of the mill or business of any kind. Instead they talked of art and music. Aurelia and Edward discovered a shared enjoyment of the poet Shelley and Jonathan—who personally preferred Keats— was content to watch them bicker over whether *Frankenstein* would have been written if the weather in Switzerland had been more temperate. Aurelia argued her case intelligently and Jonathan was transfixed by the way her expression grew serious.

'I would love to see Switzerland one day,' she said. 'Or Paris. I've never been further than Brighton.'

'I first met your mother in France,' Edward remarked.

Jonathan sat forward, fascinated. 'I never knew my mother had even left England.'

Edward nodded. 'I happened upon her and your father while they were newlyweds travelling in France. We were guests at the same pension in Lyon. When we discovered we were all hoping to see the Alps, naturally we fell in together as companions.'

'Both my parents?' Jonathan asked. He shifted in his seat and twisted the napkin in his hand. He didn't even know if the swine was alive or dead and didn't particularly care, but the thought that Edward had been intimately connected with him was unnerving. His parents travelling happily together was something he found impossible to imagine. Had there ever been a time they had been happy?

'Oh, yes. For six months we travelled about as a little group.' Edward refilled his wineglass. 'Anne would read or paint while Christopher and I would disappear up mountain paths or over ruins. I think she was glad to have someone take him off her hands for a time. We parted when they returned to England and I went on to Italy. I had a yearning for Venice, you see.'

Edward sighed and his face grew wistful for a moment. 'When you appeared at my door all those years ago it seemed as if my past was standing before me. I had to stop myself from offering you a partnership on the spot.'

Jonathan met Aurelia's eyes. Her lips twitched into a slight smile and she cocked her head towards Edward, who was lost in his reminiscences. The movement made her earring drop against her neck, settling in the hollow between her jaw and ear, and Jonathan felt his heart speed up.

'Do you know Lyon is a centre for silk manufacturing, just as Macclesfield is?' he asked.

Aurelia shook her head. 'No, I didn't. How fascinating.'

Edward gave her a wide smile, returning from whichever memory had claimed him.

'You should persuade Jonathan to take you there. It is an excellent city to fall in love in and even he could not make the excuse that it was not good for business with those connections.'

Jonathan decided this was quite enough. It was one thing having his wife and best friend plotting to widen his social circle, but talking of love and holidays was too far. But then Aurelia turned her eyes on him. Vibrant and questioning.

'Perhaps we could,' he said. 'Though that will have to wait a year or two as Edward and I intend to present our merchandise at the Great Exhibition in spring.'

When Edward's servants began to clear away the dessert plates, Jonathan patted his waistcoat pocket and caught Aurelia's attention.

'Will you excuse me while I slip outside? Edward hates the scent of cigarette smoke.'

'Stench, not scent, Jonathan,' Edward chided gently. 'I keep telling you that.'

'And I keep suggesting you should try it, Edward,' Jonathan retorted. 'It is well known that smoking improves the lungs and it might do you some good.'

Edward eyes flickered briefly towards Aurelia and Jonathan felt chastened. He closed his mouth. Edward's condition had gone beyond the reach of any aid from any source. He mouthed an apology to Edward who gave him a brittle smile, then took Aurelia's hand.

'Mrs Harcourt, would you mind if I joined you in the drawing room while Jonathan partakes of his vice? I'm afraid it is rather unconventional, but I don't believe any of us here are particularly burdened by conventionality.'

Aurelia looked startled at his words, perhaps thinking as Jonathan had of their irregular marriage, then she laughed. 'Of course I don't mind. Usually I sit alone and wait for Jonathan to return. I must confess I rather hate the smell myself.'

'You've never told me that.' Jonathan raised his brows.

'You never asked,' she replied, giving him a long stare that made Jonathan almost resolve on the spot to tear each cigarette into shreds.

He stepped outside, opened his cigarette case, but paused before removing the cigarette. It worried him a little that Aurelia had said nothing about her dislike and he wondered what else she endured uncomplainingly. He closed the case again and stared into the night sky, enjoying the peace and wondering if it was that moment of contemplation which did him more good than the tobacco itself.

When he returned indoors he discovered Aurelia and Edward had left the dining room and were sitting side by side at the piano in the drawing room, playing a lively duet; a polka, he thought. They were both giggling as they stumbled a little over the tricky rhythms. Jonathan had never heard Aurelia giggling and the sound made his spirits rise. He could not see her face, but he could imagine the radiant smile that he had only seen on occasions. He had intended to go straight back in to join them, but he could not bear to interrupt such a perfect example of domestic happiness. He often felt as though such happiness was not for him, but now he gladly stood in the shadow of the open doorway to watch his friend and wife enjoying themselves and taking his pleasure from theirs.

Aurelia's fingers tangled across the piano keys while Mr Langdon thumped out the baritone harmony at the low end. When the piece ended they both burst into laughter and applauded each other.

'I bow to your skill,' Mr Langdon said. 'You would make an excellent teacher.'

'One of the first occasions Mr Harcourt and I spent time in each other's company he asked me to teach him,' Aurelia said, rearranging her skirts.

'Was he successful?' Mr Harcourt asked.

Aurelia laughed. 'Not particularly, but we did not have very long together.'

She smiled to herself. She hadn't thought of that quiet moment of mutual enjoyment for a long time. That evening that had been rather eclipsed by the unexpected proposal that had followed.

'I think he could play well if he puts his mind to it,' she said.

'You have all the time you need now you're married,' Mr Langdon pointed out.

'But he has not asked me again,' Aurelia said quietly. She looked at Mr Langdon.

'Then might I suggest you offer to resume teaching him,' Mr Langdon said. 'If you remember, I told you we should work on making him more sociable and that would be a good place to start, wouldn't you agree?'

'I'm not sure he would welcome that. He prefers his own company and interests,' Aurelia said uncertainly, toying with the sheets on the stand. It struck her she knew relatively little of what he did enjoy doing. When she had first tried to intrude into his working life they'd gone from lovers to strangers over the course of a single afternoon and the quarrel had lasted until that very afternoon. 'He's extremely devoted to his work as you know.'

'He thinks he knows best, but I believe he is not too old a dog to be taught new tricks,' Mr Langdon said.

'You care deeply for my husband, don't you?' Aurelia said.

'Anyone who knows him for a time would be fond of him. I have perhaps greater reason than many,' Mr Langdon said. 'I think of him sometimes as the son that I would never have.'

'And yet you persuaded Mr Harcourt to marry when he had no wish to do so!' Aurelia shifted on her stool and briskly smoothed her skirts. 'It seems to me that a simpler solution than forcing Jonathan to marry reluctantly would have been for you to provide your own heir.'

She bit off her words abruptly, hardly able to believe she had spoken so frankly to an older man in his own house. Jonathan would be appalled if he knew. To her surprise Edward laughed and held out his hand.

'I am a hypocrite of the highest order, I'm afraid. Please call me Edward, Mrs Harcourt. I would be honoured to be your friend.'

Aurelia took the proffered hand. 'Thank you, Edward.'

'Now,' he continued, 'I am a hypocrite, but a well-intentioned one. I knew from a young age I was destined to remain unmarried. I did love once, but that ended unhappily as I suspected it would from the start. I realised then that my life would be better spent as a bachelor, but at least I loved and was loved. Jonathan is different to me. He has a great capacity within him for love and his…shall I say *childish* refusal to countenance marriage as anything but unpleasant would cause more harm to him.'

Aurelia reached for her wine and sipped it, deep in thought. The picture Edward painted of a thwarted love and resignation to a life alone touched too close to her secret pain of Arthur's betrayal.

'Anne and Christopher did their child a great disservice with the disastrous impression of marriage they subjected him to and I took it upon myself to try rectify that. You must, as Jonathan has, forgive an old man for playing on your husband's good nature to force him into happiness despite his own reluctance.'

Happiness, not merely marriage. It was an odd word. Edward's description of Jonathan as a man too scared to try to find happiness touched Aurelia's heart. That was what she had intended to do after learning of Arthur's true nature. Marriage might be a chance for them both to achieve contentment.

'Do you think I could really make him happy?' Aurelia asked, uncertainly. She wasn't sure, but then again she didn't think she had tried too hard recently.

'I believe you could—if you made up your mind to do so,' Edward said. 'Jonathan has a heart that I believe would be easy to capture if only someone was determined enough.'

Aurelia said nothing. She ran her fingers over the piano keys, playing a tune absentmindedly that she realised was the slow movement of the *Moonlight Sonata*. The melancholy languor of the notes made her sad and she wished her mind had chosen a jolly air instead. Was that what came to her mind at the thought of making Jonathan happy? She stopped playing and took Edward's hand. She liked him immensely and had missed the intimacy of sharing thoughts and confidences with someone.

'I will do my best, Edward,' she vowed. 'And I would be honoured if you would address me as Aurelia.'

Edward smiled. 'I knew the first time we met that you would be the perfect wife for Jonathan. Now, where is he? If you do nothing beyond persuading him to cease smoking, that will be a marriage well spent.'

As if on cue there came the sound of the front door shutting loudly. Whistling tunelessly, Jonathan entered the drawing room with a smile on his face and his hands in his pockets.

'Are you satisfied now you have worshipped at the altar of your filthy habit?' Edward said.

'Perfectly,' Jonathan said with a smile.

'Then pour us all a glass of wine and come be civilised.'

Jonathan obeyed. He smiled at Aurelia as he

handed her the crystal glass. 'What have you two been talking about?'

She paused halfway through taking the glass from him, her fingers on the delicate stem, and her eyes flickered to Edward. She could never admit they had been discussing Jonathan. Any woman who had spent time in company would guess she would be the object of gossip when mutual parties were left together. It was inevitable. She hoped Jonathan was innocent of such cynical views on the world.

'I was playing the piano,' she said. 'We were playing together.'

'Your wife has let me into one of your secrets,' Edward interrupted. He accepted his own glass and ran his forefinger along the piano keys. Aurelia's expression relaxed.

'Aurelia admitted she has been teaching you this fine art. I would very much like to see how far her pupil has progressed.

Aurelia raised her hands and made a face of mock indignation. 'I said nothing of the sort,' she protested with a laugh. 'Mr Harcourt, Edward teased the information out of me and I told him we had only had one short lesson.'

Jonathan's lip twitched. Was it the use of their names that upset him? Aurelia still addressed him formally, which felt foolish now.

'Well, now it's time for another lesson,' he said.

'Move yourself, Edward, dear friend, and let me reclaim my wife before she falls head over heels in love with you and decides to leave me.'

Aurelia had started rearranging sheets of music, but at Jonathan's unexpected announcement she fumbled them and they floated to the floor, drifting wide beneath the piano. She exclaimed in annoyance and knelt to retrieve them in a flurry of spreading skirts. Jonathan dropped to his knees beside her and helped her to gather them. They reached for the same sheet of foolscap at the same time and their hands closed over each other's. A thrill of exhilaration ran the length of Aurelia's arm. They both laughed in embarrassment and looked at each other. Instead of looking away Jonathan let his gaze linger on her. Aurelia smiled at him shyly and felt excitement starting within her.

'Find me something easy,' Jonathan murmured, slipping the sheets into her hand, 'and I will do as you command me.'

He was looking at her with an intensity she hadn't seen since their wedding night. Aurelia's heart galloped in her chest.

'If that is your wish,' she murmured back, 'I shall do as *you* command *me*.'

Aurelia walked home in light spirits with the tune she and Jonathan had played running through her mind. At one point she must have hummed it aloud because Jonathan smiled down at her and finished the tune himself, taking the baritone harmony. It was such an odd thing to bring them closer but Aurelia felt warmth spreading throughout her. They passed a night watchman who gave them a suspicious look and they both had to stifle giggles until they had passed him. It must have been the excessive wine they had drunk which made them so reckless, but they clung on to each other's arm and it felt like they were dancing.

'Did you enjoy yourself tonight?' Jonathan asked.

Aurelia nodded. 'Very much. I like Edward. You have good taste in your choice of friends.'

'I have good taste in my choice of wife,' he answered.

Aurelia put her hand to her mouth to hide her smile at the unexpected compliment. Compliments had tripped off Arthur's tongue and all had proved to be built on quicksand, but this one sounded spontaneous and genuine. As they came to the crossroads he put an arm around her waist as he had done earlier in the day. Once again she allowed it.

'I think I shall purchase a piano,' he said. 'You might teach me a little and I shall perform for Edward.'

'You would willingly be taught by a woman?' she asked, impressed. Many men wouldn't, which was a continual thorn in Aurelia's side. How would women ever be allowed to learn if they weren't able to educate?

'I don't see any reason why women can't teach skills in the female sphere,' Jonathan replied.

Aurelia gave him a close-lipped smile. It was better than refusing to contemplate a female instructress completely.

'It is such a pity Edward and your mother never found happiness together,' Aurelia said.

The muscles in Jonathan's arm tightened, hard enough for Aurelia to be conscious of them through his coat.

'Indeed. I don't wish to discuss that any further,' he said.

He remained silent and distracted for the rest of the walk home and by the time they reached the front door he had not spoken two words to her since. She had intended to ask if he would like to visit her that night, but now she became convinced he would decline.

Jonathan helped Aurelia remove her cloak as they stood in the hallway and once again his fingers brushed against her collarbone. Her throat tightened and her stomach did a somersault as blood coursed through her body and desire made her quiver. Tonight might be a chance to begin again without the awkwardness of their first handful of encounters or the coldness of their disagreement.

She lifted her head and met his eyes. 'Would you... I wonder if you would care to visit my bedroom this evening?'

Jonathan paused in what he had been doing, unbuckling the clasp of her cloak. He had bent close to better see the clasp in the dim light from the oil lamp and she could feel the heat rising from his palm. His eyes bored into her.

'Yes. Yes, I would. Very much.'

He spoke in a low whisper that sent thrills running through her. She put her hand over his and finished undoing the cloak herself.

'I shall go wake Annie and ask her to help me prepare,' she said in a low, confidential voice. 'I shall send her to tell you I am ready.'

She walked up the stairs, lifting the front hem of her skirt out of the way with one hand, while the fingers of her other trailed up the banister.

'Mrs Harcourt,' Jonathan called.

She turned halfway round and looked back at him questioningly.

'Would you leave your hair as it is tonight?' Jonathan asked. He stood at the bottom of the stairs, hands clasped in front of him, eyes bright.

Aurelia lifted her fingers to the thick roll on

the top of her head, taken aback at the request. She nodded mutely, fearful that to speak would betray the anticipation she felt. The small touches, the brush of their hands and the feel of their bodies moving and touching as they walked had all served to stoke a fire inside her. Tonight, she knew on a level deeper than she had before that they would both discover what fulfilled them.

Chapter Twelve

~~~~~~~~~

As soon as Aurelia had turned at the top of the stairs Jonathan followed two at a time and entered his own room. He was about to undress fully and change into his nightshirt as usual when he thought again. He removed his tie and waistcoat, but slung his dressing gown over the top of his shirt and trousers. If this was a new chapter in his marriage, he intended to rewrite the rules. He was determined that tonight he would do more than simply lie atop his wife and do his duty. If Aurelia was leaving him her hair to take down, he would give her something to do in return.

It felt like the night was almost over when the soft knock came at Jonathan's door and he opened it to find Annie's cheerful face beaming at him.

'My lady is waiting for you, sir,' she said, with what looked like a far-too-knowing expression.

'Thank you, Annie,' Jonathan said. 'You may retire for the night. You won't be required again.'

Once the maid had bobbed her curtsy and vanished up to the attic where her room was, Jonathan walked to his wife's dressing room and knocked gently.

'Come in,' she said.

Jonathan heard an unmistakable tremor in her voice. Was it timidity or desire that caused the quivering? He burned to find out. He entered and closed the door behind him.

Aurelia was standing as she always did, in the centre of the carpet in her bedroom. She was dressed in the flowing white peignoir under which he could see the folds of her nightgown. He was pleased to notice her hair was still piled on top of her head as he had requested.

'Good evening, Mrs Harcourt.'

She returned his greeting and, although her voice trembled still, her cheeks were as pink as her lips and her eyes were bright. Her brow furrowed.

'You're still dressed,' she said in surprise.

Jonathan stepped a little closer to her. 'Yes, I am,' he said quietly. 'I hoped tonight you might assist me in preparing for bed.'

'You want me to undress you?' she asked in astonishment. Her eyes grew wider. Jonathan did not consider the request so outlandish, but perhaps it was.

'Do you object?' he asked, conscious that he

might be committing an awful faux pas. Perhaps this was something men did not ask of their wives.

'No… Only I'm not sure where to begin.'

Jonathan walked up to her and took her hand. 'Well…perhaps you could start with my shirt,' he murmured placing her hands on his chest, either side of the row of buttons. His heart thumped and he wondered if she could feel the steady rhythm in her palms.

She gave him a shy smile and bit the corner of her lip, then slowly slid her hands to his collar. Jonathan held his breath as every nerve in his body stood to attention. Silently Aurelia began to undo the buttons, starting at the top and working her way down. Her head was bent forward and the pearl-tipped comb glinted in the candlelight, catching Jonathan's eye. Now that he was closer to her, Jonathan could see that it was not alone in restraining her hair. Deftly, he reached out and plucked one of the many small ivory pins from the number that held Aurelia's hair in place. A lock of hair sagged to one side.

Aurelia paused, clearly startled by what Jonathan had done. She looked up at him, pausing in her task, and Jonathan could barely contain the lust that hammered through him when her gaze fell on him. Such innocence shone in her eyes. He held the pin up and grinned boldly.

'What should I do?' she asked.

'Keep going,' Jonathan urged. He was finding it hard to concentrate on speaking. 'There are still some buttons to undo.'

She resumed her task, but this time, she kept her eyes fixed upon Jonathan, her gaze never leaving his. Every time she undid a button, he plucked out another hairpin. When she reached the lowest button that she could see, she stopped. Her fingers brushed against the waistband of his trousers. Jonathan put his hand over hers to stop her. If she touched him any lower than that, he would not be able to hold back any longer. Already he felt close to erupting and they hadn't even touched properly.

In fact, what was he waiting for? Aurelia had already proven that she was willing and showing more interest in him tonight than he had seen before.

'What happens now?' she asked, looking down at their hands.

'Now this happens,' Jonathan breathed.

And kissed her.

Their previous kisses paled into insignificance. Greys and browns compared to this palette of colours. He kissed her and she was kissing him back eagerly, lips crushing against his with a passion he had never encountered in her before. A passion he had not realised he was capable of. He should never have left it so long.

He took her face between his hands, holding

her close. His fingers slipped into her hair and he tugged the comb free. The edifice that Annie had so painstakingly created came tumbling down around Aurelia's shoulders. Jonathan reached deeper into the mass of waves, twining his fingers to bring her closer.

'I want you,' he panted, taking her around the waist and tugging her peignoir. He felt her fingers slip beneath his shirt as she began to slide it down his arms. Releasing her briefly, he shrugged it off, tearing it from his waistband and let it drop to the floor beside her peignoir. Aurelia slipped her arms around his shoulders and he lifted her into his arms, carrying her to the bed.

He tugged back the coverlet and laid Aurelia down. She stared up at him. Her face was flushed and her lips reddened from their kiss. He stripped off his remaining clothes and Aurelia's eyes widened. It struck Jonathan that this was the first time he had been completely naked in front of her.

'I want to see you, too,' he whispered. 'All of you.'

She nodded. He climbed on to the bed and knelt at her feet, then began to slide his hands up her calves, gathering the folds of cotton and raising them inch by inch, moving up between her legs as he did. He stretched out alongside her and pressed the length of his body against the length of hers, savouring the warmth of her body, the muscles of her thighs and the softness of her breasts.

He kissed her again, trailing his fingers slowly down between her breasts and over her taut belly until his hand came to rest against the jutting curve of her hip bone. He was ready for her. He would hazard a guess that, from the tone of her complexion and the way she lolled back, legs splayed and eyes heavy, she was ready to receive him.

'I will make it as quick as I can,' he whispered. The same thing he always said in an attempt to make her duty less gruelling, but this time, instead of nodding as she always did, she put her hand to his chest.

'You don't have to.' She spread her fingers wide, causing Jonathan's limbs to become molten iron. She drew herself up and put her lips close to Jonathan's ear. 'I don't want it to be quick.'

'Are you sure?' he asked.

She slid her hand down between them, fingertips skimming across his belly and back up again.

'Very sure. I want you to take as long as you want.'

She lay back and looked up at him with eyes full of passion. Jonathan hesitated, before deciding that he would use every ounce of control he possessed to take her at her word.

* * *

Afterwards, they lay together covered in Aurelia's counterpane. Aurelia's head fitted into the crook of Jonathan's arm, a soothing heaviness that was causing him to drift in and out of sleep. Jonathan should have returned to his own room as soon as the weakening throes of climax had subsided. He always did that as he had promised, but somehow he could not bring himself to do it just yet and guilt of outstaying his welcome had begun to gnaw at him.

Aurelia was sleeping, making soft noises in the back of her throat. Jonathan wondered if she always did.

He closed his eyes and began to drift off, a wide smile on his face that seemed to spread throughout his body, warming him at the memory. He craned his head to look down at Aurelia. Her face was serene now and it would be all too satisfying to just lie here a little longer. He wanted to stay, but he'd promised she would not have to share a bed with him. Whatever enjoyment they had both taken from their encounter, he owed it to her to keep his word. Reluctantly he eased his arm out from beneath her head. She opened her eyes.

'Where are you going?' she asked sleepily.

'Back to my room.' Jonathan climbed out of the bed and tucked the counterpane around her. He laid her nightgown on the top. For the briefest of moments he contemplated kissing her. 'I was trying not to wake you.'

'You didn't wake me, I wasn't asleep.'

Jonathan thought about contradicting her, but what would be the reason?

'Please will you blow the candle out in my dressing room as you go?' she asked, stretching and stifling a yawn.

It was a clear dismissal. A bitter taste filled Jonathan's throat. Of course she wanted him to leave. Even after such rare intimacy. Why had he imagined even for a moment that she wouldn't?

'Of course.'

Aurelia pulled the nightgown to her and disappeared under the covers, only to emerge a moment later modestly clothed. She sat up and stared at Jonathan as he gathered his clothes, hands folded in her lap. Seeing her demurely dressed after the way she had shown such abandonment when naked was a clear signal that the two parts of their life were distinct. He felt a prickle down his back, conscious of her eyes on him, and dressed with his back to her.

'Is something wrong?' Aurelia asked.

Nothing was wrong. It had been the most satisfyingly, exhilaratingly, exhausting night of Jonathan's life. What they had done and the ways and places they had touched each other had been wild, almost animalistic. He grew short of breath as he remembered the breathy, high-pitched gasps that Aurelia had made while he sank himself into her, deeper and slower than ever before. Her face had contorted and he'd feared she was in pain, but when he slowed and tried to pull out she had wrapped her legs and arms tightly about him and refused to release him and he'd yielded willingly to the ecstasy.

He was ashamed now to think of it.

'I'm sorry,' he said, straightening and turning to face her. 'What I asked of you before was… Well, it was different to what I've asked before. I treated you like…'

He stopped before he insulted her and shook his head.

'I liked it,' Aurelia said. She climbed out of bed and stood before him. 'It was different, but I liked what we did. What you did. How it made me feel.'

'Really?'

'Yes. Do you think I shouldn't have?' She wrinkled her brow.

'I think you should,' Jonathan said. He couldn't measure the relief that filled him. 'I think we both should.'

'That's good.' She looked relieved.

'Goodnight, Mrs Harcourt, sleep well,' he answered, taking her hand. She held on to it and when he looked at her questioningly she gave him a nervous smile.

'I think after what we've just done it would be proper if you called me Aurelia,' she murmured.

Jonathan filled with elation. It was such a small gesture, yet meant so much. 'Then I am Jonathan from now on. Yes?'

'Yes, Jonathan,' she said.

He walked to the door and looked behind him. Aurelia was already lying back down, nestling back beneath the counterpane. He let himself out and closed the door softly. He held on to the handle and leaned his head against the panel of the door.

'Goodnight, Aurelia,' he whispered before making his way back to his room and his cold, solitary bed.

'The weather looks set to stay dry today. I was wondering if you would care to join me for a walk around the mill site this morning?'

Jonathan put his hand on Aurelia's shoulder and looked down at her. Aurelia tried to hide her astonishment at his words. The intimate touch was less of a surprise as they had grown increasingly physical with each other in the two weeks since the night they had dined with Edward. The night that Jonathan had decided, seemingly on a whim, to make changes to their lovemaking. The night he had knocked on her door and asked her to undress him.

Welcomed changes, of course. There was a passion in their lovemaking now that had not existed up until that night. He had seemed reluctant to touch her and she had ascribed that to his indifference to marriage, but he was being quick out of consideration for her, wishing to spare her the indignity of intercourse. It showed a sweetness in his nature that was endearing. But how fortunate he had accidentally revealed it and how fortunate she felt daring enough to correct his misapprehension.

Now that they both acknowledged the attraction they felt for each other, their nights together were much more adventurous and fulfilling. Jonathan regularly knocked at her door in various states of dress and Aurelia waited for him likewise. Last night, for example, she had removed her dress and shift, but kept on her corset and underclothes. Jonathan had barely closed the door behind him before he was upon her, desperately attempting to unlace it. His fingers had been fumbling, unused to the tiny hooks and laces, and the frustration that built because of the delay had only increased their longing and the satisfaction when they finally coupled.

She took a sip of coffee from the cup that had been halfway to her mouth when he had spoken, then placed it carefully in the saucer.

'Unless you have other plans for today,' Jonathan continued.

He was watching expectantly, eyes alert. Aurelia tried to comprehend what might have brought about this new change in him. The intimacy had stayed firmly in the realm of lovemaking, however, so, whatever his reasons for inviting her today, she welcomed the indication that he wanted to share a little more of his life with her.

As Edward had indicated, there was a capacity for affection within her husband, she believed, and if she had the opportunity to install herself into another part of his life she would not pass it up.

'I would like that very much,' she said. 'My sisters are coming here for afternoon tea, so the morning would be most convenient if that suits you. I have to spend an hour with Mrs Barnes to plan menus for the week and I need to give Sarah another lesson in dusting every part of the room.'

Jonathan grinned, causing the corners of his eyes to wrinkle appealingly. 'Shall I expect you to meet me at the factory gates with your bucket and dusters?'

Aurelia laughed at the reference to their first meeting. 'Do you think all married couples share such strange memories?'

'I don't know what most marriages are like,' Jonathan said. 'My experience of them is very limited.' The merriment in his eyes faded and Aurelia felt a rush of anger towards the father who had left his son with such a terrible view of life.

'In any case, I don't expect you to clean my house, Aurelia,' he said.

'I know that,' she reassured him. 'But now it is my house, too, and I still want to take everything in hand. There is a lot of work to be done.'

'Speaking of which,' Jonathan said, 'I should be going.'

He drained his coffee cup and walked to the door. As he passed Aurelia he paused beside her and touched her shoulder once again, letting his hand linger as he looked down into her eyes.

'I hope you slept well last night.'

She smiled up at him, feeling a blush stirring at the back of her neck. They never referred directly to the nights and the acts they committed together outside the confines of Aurelia's bedroom and Jonathan never stayed once it was over. As soon as he had recovered his strength and composure he rolled out of Aurelia's arms, dressed in whatever clothing he had discarded and returned to his own room.

As they had both agreed before they wedded, their marriage was strictly split into two halves and the intercourse was for one purpose alone: to get Aurelia with child. It was a happy accident that it turned out to be so pleasurable. Jonathan's eyes might tell the story of the passion that passed between them, but still he left her to sleep alone each night.

Aurelia knew she shouldn't mind. After all, the condition had been one that she had put in place and which he had readily agreed to, but more than once she had fallen asleep with a memory of him in her arms and his scent upon her skin, then dreamed that he had stayed with her until morning. Those mornings in particular felt empty. Aurelia never felt the day truly began until she and Jonathan met at breakfast and sat together, drinking coffee. It was a small indication of how used to marriage she was and how she had come to value Jonathan's presence in her life.

'Come to the gate for ten,' he said. 'I will wait there for you.'

Aurelia drank her coffee and poured another cup, thinking of everything she had to do. She buttered another piece of toast, but ate without enthusiasm. Her appetite this morning was not as great as usual and she hoped she was not sickening for something. Her fears seemed to be justified because her discussion with Mrs Barnes about the week's menu and the preparations that must begin for Christmas fare left Aurelia feeling nauseous to the point that she had to sip a glass of mint tea and lie on her couch for a quarter-hour before she felt well enough to meet Jonathan.

Jonathan was waiting for her at the gate as he had promised. He was speaking to a tall man, but when he saw her he shook the man's hand, clasped him on the shoulder and came over to admit Aurelia. She walked through the gate and into the small yard set with large cobbles. A group of four boys, all dressed in identical grey shirts and breeches, were busily heaving crates on to a flat wagon.

'They are heading for the canal at Manchester,' Jonathan explained. 'From there to London. Let's go down to the riverside. I'll just fetch my coat. Are you warm enough?'

Aurelia pulled her fur-trimmed cape closer around herself and adjusted her hat. The rain had stayed away, but so had the sun and the frost had not yet melted off the railings and walls. She was a little chilly, though the crisp air had helped her to stop feeling nauseous.

Jonathan dashed inside one of the doors, presumably the office he shared with Edward. Aurelia gazed around her at the high walls of the mill which she had only seen from a distance. Even from outside the thick brick building she could hear the clattering and thrumming of machinery. Inside it must be deafening and she had no wish to go any closer.

'Don't you find it makes your head ache?' she asked Jonathan when he returned.

Jonathan shrugged. 'I'm so used to it that I barely remember it was ever different. Shall we go?'

Arm in arm they walked together to the furthest end of the factory and through a small gateway. Before long they came to the clearing where trees had once stood. It was only a fortnight ago that Aurelia had been standing on the other side of the river calling Caesar back and already she could see the progress that had been made. The flow had been diverted, cutting off the horseshoe of what had once been her father's land.

'This is where I'm going to build the apprentice house,' Jonathan said. He strode out, leaving Aurelia standing at the edge of the clearing, and waved his arms at the imaginary building.

'They'll have a schoolroom, a bedroom to share and a kitchen to eat in. I think a garden would be nice where they can grow their own food. Perhaps even some chickens.'

Aurelia smiled to see her husband's enthusiasm. 'It sounds wonderful,' she agreed, crossing the frozen ground to stand at his side.

His eyes took on a faraway look and Aurelia wondered if he was even aware that he had slipped his hand into hers.

'The boys will be happier and better cared for here than if they stayed in the workhouse. I want to take care of my workers, you see. I want to see them educated. I should have gone to a fine school, but that chance was taken from me when we moved to Macclesfield. I was fortunate that my mother and Edward encouraged me to study, but it was hard. My boys will have a rudimentary education and a better future than they would otherwise.'

'Just boys?' Aurelia asked. 'Do you not also intend to have girls?'

Jonathan looked at her quizzically.

'You mentioned it before we were married,' she reminded him. 'On the night we agreed our engagement. If the life of the boys would be improved, why not also the life of the girls?'

'Of course,' Jonathan said. He straightened his cuffs in what appeared to Aurelia as an offhand manner, as if he was dismissing the importance of the idea. 'I don't think it as necessary for girls of their class to be as literate as those of yours or mine. They'll learn useful skills that will make them good wives and mothers one day.'

Aurelia forced a smile, though her jaw felt tight. She could contradict him, but that would raise the question of why she felt so passionately about it. Her husband knew as little of her appetite for learning as her parents had. It was interesting that he revealed he thought of the two of them as different classes, too. What would it take for him to stop feeling as if he did not belong? Jonathan might not have a string of titled ancestors and a baronetcy, but he was easily the intellectual and moral superior of her father and many of the titled men she had known.

Especially one, whispered a sneaky voice in the back of her mind. She silenced the voice firmly.

'I'm sure whatever they learn here will be of great use to them,' she assured him.

'Of course you have bought yourself another task now,' Jonathan said. 'If I am to find a teacher for the boys, then you may care to help me find a teacher for the girls. Someone capable of needlework and cooking will suit them and set them up well.'

'Perhaps I shall take on some of that duty myself,' she told him, laughing.

'I don't expect you to work for your keep,' he said, joining in.

She hid a smile that had suddenly begun to feel a lot more genuine as an idea began to bud. She would find a teacher willing to give the girls at least the basics of reading and writing. While the boys could learn in public, the girls would have to learn in private.

'You do make me wonder if I should purchase a piano for the apprentice house, however,' Jonathan said. 'If you can teach me to play, I'm sure you can teach anyone.'

His eyes lingered on her and Aurelia's stomach squirmed.

'I think I shall confine myself to one pupil

there,' she said. 'You are more than enough for me, Jonathan.'

'Am I?' he asked, giving her an earnest look.

An impulse to be close suddenly came upon her. She smiled at him and took his hand.

'Oh, yes, Mr Harcourt. You most definitely are.'

She wondered what Jonathan would do if she wrapped her arms around his neck and kissed him as fervently now as she had done the previous night. She was so convinced he would consider such intimacy outrageous that she was unprepared for Jonathan to take her in his arms. When he drew her close and cupped her head in his hand she felt as if she had been shot, but the instant his lips found hers it felt like the most natural thing in the world to be standing on the riverbank kissing the man who only made love to her so she would provide him with an heir.

When they returned to the mill yard the clock set into the arch over the double doors had just finished chiming eleven. Aurelia was surprised to realise a whole hour had passed. Jonathan bade her farewell formally, with a bow. She returned it with a curtsey. No one watching would have suspected they had been behaving in a manner that would scandalise anyone who happened to be walking along the river.

The amicable peace was shattered by the foreman striding towards Jonathan with an anxious look on his face.

'Mr Harcourt, we're having problems with the spools again. Those damned careless girls! Pardon me, Mrs Harcourt, I didn't see you there.'

Jonathan gave Aurelia an apologetic look. 'I need to go.'

'Of course. Don't let me detain you.'

She watched him stride away at the foreman's side, head cocked as he listened to whatever the foreman was saying and nodding forcefully. Her lips curved into a smile as she watched them go. Jonathan walked so fast, arms swinging, the foreman could scarcely keep up. It was curious how seeing him being so purposeful made him all the more attractive. She couldn't fathom it, but she could not ignore it. He moved through life with such determination that she could not help but admire him. Knowing that he was equally serious with everyone and not just her made it easier to forgive his occasional solemnity.

Chapter Thirteen

Aurelia let Dora and Cassandra chatter on while her mind wandered back to the morning with Jonathan and daydreamed about kissing him on the riverbank.

Of course she was interested in what their old friends in Oxfordshire were doing now, but that life seemed so far behind her now. Who was flirting with whom and where people chose to wear feathers rather than flowers in their hats was not her concern. Puzzling over why Jonathan had kissed her was much more intriguing.

The only time her attention woke properly was when Cassandra mentioned an old rival with glee.

'And Dottie Cleve wrote to tell me that Miss Burbage wore the same dress to the Earnshaws' party as she did to the wedding of…' She stopped and put her hand to her mouth, cheeks colouring, and looked down at her plate of sandwiches. 'I forget whose wedding. It might have been a christening in any case.'

'I can guess whose wedding it was,' Aurelia said quietly, 'and it doesn't matter.'

She could tell herself that she had no feelings for Arthur Carver, but this news was a blow that struck deep. He had deceived her and betrayed her, and almost caused a scandal that would have ruined her for ever, but as she brought his face to mind her heart fluttered. How much of that was fury at the way she had been tricked into caring for him, she could not say.

All the time he had been courting Aurelia there had been a young lady waiting for him to complete his studies at Oxford and return to marry her. He had been engaged since the age of sixteen. 'Oh, Lia, I am so sorry,' Cassandra said, leaving her chair to embrace her sister. 'I wasn't thinking.'

'Of course they will be married by now,' Aurelia said. From the moment the existence of Arthur's fiancée had come to light Aurelia had told him she did not believe he would end the engagement to be with her. What else could she have done?

She had ended all communication and Arthur's marriage became inevitable from that point onwards. But knowing it must happen and hearing the confirmation that Arthur had finally surrendered himself to the marriage he had protested against for years did not make that knowledge any easier to bear.

She wiped briskly at her eyes with the end of her napkin. Tears prickled her eyes and the feeling of nausea she had shaken off that morning rolled over her again. She bit her lip to stop it trembling and so the pain would distract her from weeping openly.

'That they would marry was never in any doubt. I'm only surprised it took so long to arrange the date.'

Aurelia burned to ask for every detail of Arthur's wedding. Where the wedding breakfast took place, whether the bride and groom rode in Arthur's cabriolet or if Lord Helsby had lent his son the landau emblazoned with the arms of the Helsby barony. Had they taken a tour of Italy as Arthur had promised Aurelia they would for their own honeymoon? Quite why she wanted to torture herself in such a way mystified her. Did she want to picture herself in the bride's place, or compare it with her own wedding day to Jonathan? No good could come of it.

'Is being married to Mr Harcourt terrible?' Cassandra asked. Aurelia wrinkled her brow. 'Does he mistreat you, I mean? He seems so nice and his home is so pleasant.'

Aurelia gave her sister a faint smile. She wondered if Cassandra regretted not accepting the proposal herself now she had become more familiar with Jonathan. 'Not in the slightest. We tolerate each other adequately and Jonathan is a good man.'

'And you are able to bear sharing his bed?' Dora asked. She waited with her arms folded until Aurelia and Cassandra had finished exclaiming aloud at the unseemliness of her question. 'All I mean is that I could not imagine doing anything intimate with a man I did not love. My skin would crawl at the thought.'

Aurelia went to the table and busied herself pouring more tea. The details of her intimate life with Jonathan were private and even if she was inclined to share them with her sisters, she would not dream of telling unmarried girls of some of the things they had done to each other's bodies. Far from crawling in revulsion, her skin took on its own life when Jonathan touched it. How innocent she had been when she had assumed that the act simply involved bringing two body parts into contact! Even now, the memory of her husband's mouth teasing her most sensitive, delicate parts was enough to excite her. Did that mean she loved him? She had never considered that. All she knew was that she was starting to value his company outside her bedchamber as well as in it and she was happy for that state of affairs.

'Being married to Mr Harcourt is bearable,' she said.

'I'm glad, but I wish you had stayed unmarried so we could have lived together always,' Dora said. 'Now, let's talk of more cheerful matters. Have you decided what you're buying Mr Harcourt for a Christmas gift?'

Aurelia frowned. 'I haven't,' she admitted. It pained her to admit to her sisters how little she still understood of her husband's likes, at least outside the marriage bed. Anything she could give him to enjoy within the confines of her bedchamber certainly couldn't be wrapped and laid beneath a tree.

'I know what gift I could give him, but that doesn't seem to be within my power. If I could only tell him I was expecting a happy arrival.' She blushed and waited while Cassandra giggled and Dora leaned forward as if she was about to take notes.

'That would truly make Jonathan happy and it is what he wants more than anything.'

'You have two weeks to find something. Or to get with child,' Dora assured her with a giggle. 'Why not ask Father what he thinks a man might like?'

Aurelia laughed. 'I would hardly imagine Father and Jonathan share many interests.'

A notion of an idea was beginning to form,

though. Jonathan had wanted to continue his studies of the classics. A book of illustrations of Greek or Roman archaeological finds might please him. And if some of the subjects were of an indecent nature, Aurelia could plead innocence, while hinting privately that she might not be averse to trying to replicate them.

She sipped her tea and let Dora and Cassandra gossip on as pictures danced behind her eyes and made her want to blush.

Jonathan returned home just as Cassandra and Dora were leaving. He strolled into the house, overcoat open and silk scarf flapping in the wind that swirled around him. Aurelia was glad to see him return and not just because of the purely physical reaction that the sight of him invoked. Her mind and heart were still in turmoil after the news of Arthur's marriage and seeing her husband made her feet feel like there was solid ground beneath them again rather than quicksand. She looked forward to the coming evening where they might sit together and exchange news of their afternoons.

Jonathan gave Aurelia a formal peck on the cheek, then gave an exclamation of delight at seeing his sisters-in-law. A flicker of jealousy bucked and reared inside Aurelia at seeing him greeting Cassandra so warmly. It took her by surprise, causing the breath to catch in her throat. She had not given too much thought to the fact that Cassandra had been Jonathan's first choice of wife, but watching him smile and bend over Cassandra's hand to kiss brought the memory sharply back to her. She hoped that by now she had proven a satisfactory wife and he did not regret being offered her.

'I hope you will both join us on Christmas Day,' Cassandra said as Jonathan straightened and released her hand.

'We don't spend the entire day in church, if that is what makes you hesitate,' Dora said before he had time to answer her sister.

'It wouldn't be Christmas without Lia,' Cassandra added.

Jonathan looked taken aback at the barrage. He glanced at Aurelia and raised an eyebrow. Aurelia walked to her husband's side. She slid herself between him and Cassandra, feeling the need to lay claim to him in some small way.

'We haven't discussed our plans yet,' she told her sisters. 'Mr Harcourt may have his own traditions and preferences. We shall discuss it between us and let Mother and Father know of our decision. Now, you had better go, the coach will be waiting.'

She ushered them to the door amid a flurry of kisses.

'I'm sorry,' Aurelia said as soon as the girls had left. 'Cassandra was wrong to ask you so directly.'

'Don't apologise. It was kind of her to invite us and you aren't responsible for your sister's impulsiveness,' Jonathan said. 'In truth, it hadn't even occurred to me to consider that this year would be any different to any other. Since my mother died I usually attend the service at the Methodist chapel with Edward. Then we go for a long walk across the hills and share a meal before I return home to read by the fire.'

Confirming the picture of Jonathan as solitary, Aurelia thought to herself. She wasn't sure she liked his fulsome description of Cassandra as impulsive, either.

'In that case we should extend the invitation to Edward,' she said. 'I would not want him to be alone.'

Jonathan put his hands on her shoulders and kissed her forehead. 'I'm sure he would be delighted at such a warm-hearted offer. Now, there is something else I need to discuss with you. I was very pleased earlier today when you said you are interested in the girls' welfare and I have both a proposal and a favour. Wait here, if you please.'

He went back outside and returned a short while later with a small girl who looked no more than ten.

'Millie here is not suited to working in the

mill,' he explained. 'She finds it hard to follow instructions. For whatever reason of their own, a few of the older girls have taken it into their heads to blame her for any mistakes and my foreman tells me she is suffering as a result.'

'Has this poor child been standing outside all this time?' she asked.

Jonathan looked shamefaced. 'She's been sitting in the delivery cart. I would have asked you straight away, but obviously we were distracted. I know you are finding the task of being a mistress of your own house a little challenging, so I wondered if you would be prepared to take Millie under your wing and begin to teach her some of the rudiments of being a domestic servant? It would kill two birds with one stone as they say.'

Aurelia looked at the child. Millie gave a nervous smile that revealed a gap-toothed mouth. She wore a shapeless dress made out of the same drab grey wool that the workhouse boys wore and looked as if she had never had enough to eat in her life. No wonder Jonathan thought his apprentices would be better tended under his own care.'

'Of course I will,' she said. '*We* will, I mean. It's your house.'

'It is yours, too. But thank you.' Jonathan looked relieved. Had he doubted she would agree? Surely he knew Aurelia better than that!

He squatted down opposite the child, placed

both hands on her shoulders and looked into her eyes. 'Go with Mrs Harcourt and be sure to do as she bids you.'

Aurelia watched her tall husband squatting uncomfortably in front of the small child and speaking to her so gently. Edward was right to suggest there was a capacity for affection in him that only needed to be brought to the surface. When he had children of his own Aurelia was sure all the love he seemed capable of would be lavished upon them. He was a good man. Kind and thoughtful. Their children would grow up in a happier household than their father had. Even though the marriage was not a romantic attachment, she believed there was enough affection in it to ensure that, certainly more on her side than she would ever have expected possible. She thought back guiltily to her pangs of longing when Arthur's wedding had been brought up. Jonathan was better in every respect than Arthur was and she had been foolish to waste even a moment pining after someone she could not have when she had a good husband here.

Jonathan stood. 'I'm afraid I shall have to seclude myself away for the evening and not join you for dinner. I have too much work to be able to spare any time.'

'Is there a problem?' Aurelia asked, recalling the urgency with which the foreman had summoned him earlier.

'Nothing too serious, merely tedious.' Jonathan sighed. 'Orders that were not fulfilled by our suppliers mean our production has slowed. Coupled with repairs needed in the spinning room we're behind and risk not fulfilling our orders. I intend to examine all our future commitments and see how best the time can be used so we don't sit idle. I had hoped to begin work on a new design, but that will have to wait.'

'Won't that be tiring?' Aurelia asked.

Jonathan shrugged. 'I've spent many evenings since I began working with Edward working into the night. I'm expecting a delivery of files from the mill any time now, so if you will excuse me I shall begin immediately.'

He shrugged off his overcoat as he headed to his study and closed the door. Aurelia watched with regret. Her hopes for a companionable evening with Jonathan melted away, but at least she had something to fill it with. She held out her hand to the child.

'Come along, Millie.'

Millie said nothing as Aurelia led her to the kitchen. When there she scuffed her feet on the floor as Aurelia introduced her to Mrs Barnes, Annie and Sarah.

'How old are you?' Mrs Barnes asked. The girl looked down at her feet and didn't answer.

'How old are you?' Mrs Barnes repeated a little louder. 'Surely you must know.'

The child was starting to shake. Remembering what Jonathan had done, Aurelia bent and took the child's face in her hands.

'Your name is Millie, isn't it?'

This time the girl nodded.

'How old are you?' Aurelia asked slowly, making sure that Millie was watching her lips.

'Twelve, missus,' Millie answered. Aurelia raised her eyebrows. Millie was older than she looked—moreover, it appeared her hearing was faulty. Whether this was from the machines in the mill or a defect at birth, Aurelia didn't know, but Jonathan's tender-heartedness was not misplaced.

Aurelia dined alone. The dining room felt too large and silent without Jonathan's company. When the grandmother clock chimed ten it struck her that Jonathan had not eaten. She piled a plate with bread and slices of cold ham, and a pot of tea, instructing Millie to carry the tray. She knocked cautiously at his door, hoping he would not be angry at her interruption.

He admitted her in a curt voice. He was at his desk, but as Aurelia entered the study he pushed his chair back and faced her. The desk was a mess and both oil lamps were burning brightly. Papers were strewn everywhere and he had removed his coat and waistcoat, which he had tossed on to a leather armchair in front of the window.

'Is something the matter?' He pinched the bridge of his nose and closed his eyes. They were ringed with dark shadows.

'I thought you might be hungry,' Aurelia whispered. She came fully into the room. It was the first time she had seen inside Jonathan's sanctuary and she tried not to look around too obviously. The walls were lined with bookcases and smelled faintly of leather, beeswax polish and Jonathan's cologne. It was a very masculine domain.

'Hungry?' Jonathan's eyebrows rose in surprise, then he blinked as if something was only just occurring to him. 'Why, yes, I am. I hadn't realised until you mentioned it.'

Aurelia wondered how many nights he had sat alone in the study in his bachelor years, failing to eat. She resolved to put an end to that habit now he had someone to take care of his needs. She beckoned Millie inside with her tray. The girl walked unsteadily to the desk and was about to put the tray down on the table on top of a large piece of paper with hundreds of tiny squares shaded in different colours and orders.

'Not there!' Jonathan barked, lurching forward and slamming his hand on to the paper. Millie began shaking so much that the tray looked about to capsize. Aurelia took it from her.

'You can go, Millie,' she said kindly. 'Sarah will show you where to sleep.'

She gave Jonathan a reproachful look as the girl backed out, bobbing curtsies all the while. He had the grace to look abashed and shuffled the pages back into some semblance of order. He gathered some of the ledgers and deposited them on the floor beside his feet and cocked his head to the space where they had been.

'Put the tray down there if you will. Poor child,' he murmured as Aurelia obeyed. 'I should not have been so short with her. She will think she has a monster for a master.'

His voice was heavy with remorse.

'No, she won't,' Aurelia said. 'She will know that her master is a kind man who has worked long beyond the hour when he should have finished.'

She peered at the strange paper with the coloured squares. 'What is this?'

Jonathan spread his hand out. 'Each of the squares denotes a hole in the card. That determines which threads appear on the finished cloth. I can alter the design by altering the pattern here.' He paused and gave her a bashful look. 'I'm sorry, I must be boring you. I know I get carried away when I plan them.'

'Not at all,' Aurelia said. 'It's fascinating.'

She meant it. He'd recovered some of his vitality when he had started speaking of his designs. Clearly that was where his enthusiasm lay, not in poring over ledgers. 'Will you retire soon?'

'I hardly think so,' Jonathan said with a long sigh. 'Not until I have broken the back of this pile at least. It is a mess, isn't it! My bookkeeping leaves a lot to be desired, but Edward seems to thrive on disorder. I can't make head nor tail of his filing system.'

He leaned back in his chair and scraped his hands through his hair, fingers digging at his scalp. His necktie was undone and hung loose and the top two buttons of his shirt was open. His bookkeeping might not be desirable, but Aurelia could not take her eyes from his throat and the triangle of chest that she could see just peeking over the neck of his undershirt.

'Can I do anything to help you?' Aurelia asked.

'No. Thank you,' he said. He pushed himself from his chair and strode around the room, raising his arms and rolling them above his head. Aurelia sympathised, knowing how the knots in her shoulders ached after she spent too long sewing with her head bowed. It must be the same for Jonathan. When he joined her in bed she might offer to knead away some of the aches for him.

In the meantime she poured him a cup of tea

and added a slice of lemon. He took it from her, then took her free hand, closing his palm around it and pressing it tightly. Aurelia squeezed his fingers in response as his touch awakened the craving which never seemed to be far below the surface. She looked up at him, her lips curving into a smile, but he was solemn.

'Go to bed, Aurelia,' Jonathan said. 'You can sleep without any disturbance tonight as I am afraid I will be too fatigued to join you.'

Aurelia withdrew her hand from his. Disappointment lurched in her belly. It was a gentle dismissal, but a dismissal none the less. She could see the weariness in his eyes and voice were not feigned and buried her disappointment. She felt remorseful that she had interrupted him and delayed his finishing even by the ten minutes just now.

'I shall bid you goodnight in that case and let you finish your task without any more interruptions.'

As she slipped quietly to the door Jonathan called out.

'Aurelia!'

She paused and looked at him questioningly. He was still standing where she had left him. He straightened his collar and ran his hand through his hair once again. The light from the oil lamps over his desk made his hair glow golden and caused shadows to turn his cheekbones into sharp planes. He smiled.

'The interruption was far from unwelcome.'

Aurelia glanced at the tray.

'I wasn't talking about the supper,' Jonathan said. 'I meant your company.'

He held her gaze intently until Aurelia felt a fluttering starting in her belly. She felt as if she was glowing inside. How silly to be so pleased at a small sign of appreciation, but to have been welcomed meant a lot more than she expected.

She should go before she started to demand he ended his task and came to her room after all.

'Drink your tea before it grows cold,' she said with a smile. She slipped out, leaving her husband to return to his books.

Chapter Fourteen

Naturally they spent Christmas Day at Siddon Hall. Jonathan had known from the moment Cassandra had pounced upon him that he would not deny his wife the chance to spend Christmas with her family. After the early morning church service the family walked back along the lane to the hall. Edward would be joining them to dine at noon and for the rest of the day.

Walking arm in arm with Aurelia along the frozen path, Jonathan realised he was happy. He hoped she felt the same, but asking her directly felt too intrusive. She seemed at ease in his company, but did ease equate to happiness?

'The last time we walked this way was our wedding day,' he remarked. 'I can barely remember making the journey.'

Aurelia tilted her head up to smile at him. 'I was thinking just the same thing,' she replied.

'Do you remember how the children stood and threw rose petals? I wonder if Millie was among them.'

'Possibly,' Jonathan said. 'I'm afraid I would not have known her then.'

They both glanced back to the line of servants that had accompanied their employers to the church service. Jonathan couldn't quite believe he had almost lost his head enough to try to kiss Aurelia in front of them all. He turned his attention to Millie. In the three weeks since she had entered Jonathan's house he had seen her grow both in confidence and stature. Good food and patience had turned the tearful, fumbling child into a happy girl. Now she was being petted by both Cassandra and Theodora, and Jonathan suspected that, if Aurelia was in agreement, employment could be found for her at Siddon Hall.

Aurelia broke his reverie, asking what he was thinking, and he repeated his thoughts to her.

'You're not taking her just yet,' she said with a laugh. 'She is invaluable to Mrs Barnes and you would risk her ire if you left us without her help.'

'Very well,' Jonathan agreed. 'It seems I must get used to being outnumbered by your sex at home.'

Aurelia's fingers tightened on his arms and he glanced down at her in concern. 'Did I say something to upset you?'

'Not at all,' she said. 'I have just never heard you use the word home before. It was good to hear.'

'It feels like a home now,' Jonathan said quietly. 'I didn't realise before how much it had just been a house.'

Since Aurelia had moved in it had become more than the four walls Jonathan inhabited. It was her presence that had made it so. He stopped and looked at her. He couldn't kiss her now in front of her family although he very much wanted to. 'I'm very glad I married you, Mrs Harcourt,' he said.

She fluttered her eyelashes and looked a little shy. Jonathan feared the news was unpleasant to her.

However, after a moment she looked into his eyes and replied, 'And I am glad I married you Mr Harcourt.'

'We made the right decision, I think,' Jonathan said.

'I think so, too.' Aurelia tucked her arm under his and looked into his eyes and Jonathan realised the answer to his question was right there. She bit her lip and looked at him sidelong through half-closed eyes. 'I was so nervous about being alone with you that night.'

They had slowed as they walked and were now lagging behind the rest of the party. He inclined his head and realised he was preparing to kiss her, but she had already turned to gaze at the hills. The sky was tinged with orange and clouds were beginning to gather heavily. 'The air smells of snow,' she murmured.

Jonathan inhaled. She was right. 'I wouldn't be surprised if we will get some before nightfall.'

Aurelia breathed in, closing her eyes and tilting her head towards the hills. 'Then we had better not stay too late before returning home.'

Home. Was it deliberate that she said that? He suspected from the look on her face that it was.

'Are you warm enough?' he asked, hoping she would answer no and give him the opportunity to put his arm around her.

'Very,' she answered. 'This keeps me perfectly snug.' She ran her fingers over the trim of fur that edged her new cloak and tucked it a little tighter around her shoulders. 'I couldn't have asked for a nicer gift. Thank you. The colour is exactly the one I would have chosen.'

Jonathan tipped his hat, pleased that the hours he had spent agonising over the colour had been worthwhile, while simultaneously regretting he had bought her such a warm garment.

'Now I come to think of it,' Aurelia said, 'I might be a little chilly after all and my back is aching a little.' She gave Jonathan a warm smile. 'If you would be kind enough to give me your arm again, I am sure I would be much warmer.'

Jonathan eagerly pulled her close by his side so that anyone watching would not realise that his arm was beneath the cloak and around his wife's waist. His mind went to the other gift which he had not given her yet, but which he intended to give her before they retired for the night: an altogether flimsier garment that he had acquired especially for her. It was a nightgown made of a silk lighter and finer than even his best produce. It had been worth the expense of sending abroad to Lyon in order to obtain the dark green silk and he did not begrudge a penny.

The afternoon was spent in riotous fun, playing games, singing and laughter. To Jonathan, having grown up as a solitary child, it was an experience unlike any other. Even when his mother had escaped the forbidding mantle of her marriage they spent the day quietly. Here everyone talked over each other, competing to say the wittiest things. He felt quite inadequate in comparison and slipped away to a sofa after a particularly competitive game of Snapdragon, assuming his absence would go unnoticed for a while.

He was wrong because less than five minutes had passed before Aurelia sashayed over and threw herself back on to the sofa besides Jonathan.

'You look quite exhausted,' she exclaimed. She still had three feathers sticking out of her hair from an earlier game. Despite his need for solitude Jonathan grinned.

'I've never seen you so fearsome,' he said. 'I'm not sure I know you today.'

Aurelia laughed. 'I have had years competing with my sisters. One time we became so competitive Cassandra's left ringlet caught fire and burned clean away!'

Jonathan sucked his fingers where he had not quite been quick enough to snatch the flaming raisins out of the bowl, quite able to see how that could happen. Aurelia took his hand and brought it close to her face to examine it.

'Is it sore?'

'Not too much,' Jonathan said. 'The flames were just a few small licks.'

Aurelia brought his finger to her lips and ran her tongue rapidly along the edge of the burn, causing fires to flare in Jonathan's loins. She smiled wickedly. 'There, another small lick to heal it.'

Jonathan glanced round to see if her daring action had been seen, but the rest of the party were busily throwing paper arrows at a target in the middle of the floor.

'By next year you will be more proficient,' Aurelia assured him.

Next year.

It struck Jonathan then that this marriage was not a short-term affair, but year after year he and his wife would spend occasions together. He swallowed a lump in his throat and blinked as his eyes threatened to water. This was what belonging to a happy family must feel like. He didn't belong yet. There were old jokes and arguments that were obviously brought out annually like the glass Christmas baubles, references that flew over his head and which Aurelia promised to explain once they were home. It gave him an unsettling feeling of both exclusion and inclusion and he fervently hoped that once Aurelia had given him the child he needed they would not become distant acquaintances once more. He closed his fingers and laced them through Aurelia's.

'What's wrong?' Aurelia asked, leaning closer to him and looking anxious.

Once more Jonathan was struck by how well attuned she seemed to his changes in mood.

'I was just thinking how different your Christmases must have been as a child to mine.'

'Well, now you are part of this family and you shall spend them in this manner. Come with me now,' she commanded. 'My father intends to play lotto and Mother always worries that once he starts playing he will never end the game until he has lost everything or won everything. Usually the former.'

There was a note of anxiety in her voice. Gambling, of course. Jonathan stood and helped Aurelia to rise. Even on this happy day there was the sense of anxiety. Of happiness teetering on the edge of destruction. His own father's vice had been his abrupt and inexplicable coldness towards the woman he had chosen to marry, whereas Sir Robert had threatened to destroy his family by other means. But Sir Robert at least was a loving father and husband whose children and wife were fond of. Would it be possible for Jonathan to uphold the terms he had agreed with Aurelia and yet still succeed in creating a happy marriage? As he walked arm in arm with his wife to the card tables he fervently hoped so.

It was late afternoon when Cassandra drew Jonathan to one side.

'You have probably forgotten, but I promised you a portrait of Aurelia. You must forgive me for not giving it to you before. Come with me while Aurelia is occupied.'

Jonathan had indeed forgotten. Truth be told, he had not particularly found the offer interesting. Aurelia was singing a duet with Lady Upford who had a surprisingly good soprano voice. He would not be missed for the time being, so dutifully followed Cassandra into the empty parlour to receive his gift. The picture was not a watercolour as he had expected, but a pencil sketch that Cassandra had then inked over to create depth, shadow and movement. Jonathan held it up to the light.

'This is outstandingly good,' he murmured in admiration. 'You've captured her likeness perfectly.'

Aurelia practically burst off the page. The only colour was a slight hint of cream and roses in her cheeks added with a deft stroke of pastel. Her eyes flashed and Jonathan could almost hear her surprisingly deep laugh as he examined her likeness. She looked as if she had been caught and pinned to the paper in the middle of a conversation. Her vibrancy made Jonathan's throat tighten. He'd never seen her looking this alive or full of exuberance. He was consumed by an urge to seek out his wife and see if he could replicate that expression himself. It mattered to him enormously to see the enjoyment she was capable of and know that he had never made her laugh in such a manner. Even though the nights they spent together were a typhoon of ecstasy, the barrier between them was as great as ever. Despite all his intentions of remaining at a distance he had grown deeply fond of her. So fond that thinking about it made his heart feel like the inner of a lobster, laid out to be picked and eaten at will once his shell had been cracked. He had no idea how to begin communicating that to her or reaching a state where she might feel as fond of him in return.

He wondered belatedly to whom she had been listening when Cassandra had made her sketch and hoped it was not another man. He reminded himself that he had no business growing possessive over her previous life. That was too uncomfortably like his father's behaviour.

'Aurelia will love it,' he said.

Cassandra's brow furrowed. 'She may not. It was done when we lived in Oxfordshire and I imagine she will have forgotten I ever started it. Perhaps you should keep this for yourself. Or perhaps I shouldn't give it to you at all.'

She held her hand out and Jonathan instinctively pulled the picture towards himself, not wanting to risk her snatching it away. He could not imagine why his wife would be upset to receive such a flattering likeness of herself. It should be displayed where visitors could admire it. However, he rolled it back into the tube it had come in and slipped it inside his breast pocket. He would not mention it to Aurelia and it would look well in a frame on his dressing table. Aurelia never ventured into his bedroom so it would be perfectly safe to place it there where he could look at it in the absence of the woman herself.

When Jonathan returned to the drawing room he discovered that Aurelia was absent. She had gone to lie down in her old bedroom, Theodora explained, after she was suddenly taken ill with a bout of sickness.

'Take me to her, please,' Jonathan requested.

He followed Theodora up the stairs and into the room that had once been his wife's. It occurred to him that he had never seen this room before and had no idea what it would have looked like when Aurelia lived there. Now it was without any signs of ownership. There was nothing of her personality in evidence, unlike the rooms she occupied in their home. She had completely left this life behind her to become part of his.

Aurelia herself lay on a low reading couch in front of the fireplace. Someone had placed a coverlet over her and her stockinged feet peeked out at the end. Her face was pale and she was sipping from a cup of water. She looked so unlike her usual self that it was all Jonathan could do not to bundle her into his arms protectively.

'What happened?' he asked dropping to one knee besides her and taking her hand. It was clammy and alarmingly warm.

'It's nothing,' Aurelia protested. 'I merely overindulged and now I am paying the price of far too many candied plums and sugared almonds.'

Theodora stood in the doorway, her arms folded. 'You told me you were cramping,' she said accusingly.

Aurelia glared at her sister and a little of her

vitality returned. 'I know you would love nothing more than to make a patient of me, Dora, but I'm afraid to disappoint you now. My nausea has passed and I feel well enough to go home. Mr Harcourt, are you happy to leave now?'

'Of course,' Jonathan said. 'I'll ask your father to bring the coach around. I'm sure he won't mind us using it if you are unwell.'

'There is no need,' Aurelia said. She pushed herself upright and swung her legs to the floor. 'I can walk home. I would like to clear my head and the cold air will help.'

Jonathan eyed her doubtfully, but she put her hand to his cheek and gazed into his eyes.

'Please,' she entreated, 'walk home with me.'

When she looked at him in such a manner Jonathan was incapable of denying her anything. 'Very well. I don't like it, but I will do it if it makes you happy.'

'Thank you,' Aurelia said. She brushed her fingers against his jaw, making Jonathan shudder with delight. 'Dora can help me dress. Will you go make our apologies to Mother and Father?'

As Jonathan left the room Theodora followed and caught him by the arm. 'You should have insisted that she ride in the carriage. You are her husband after all.'

'And I am not a tyrant,' Jonathan retorted, far

too angrily. 'If Aurelia wishes to do something, I will not forbid it.'

Dora's face lost some of its belligerence. 'I'm pleased to hear it, Mr Harcourt, but there is a fine line between tyranny and insistence that someone take care of herself.'

Jonathan pondered this as he went downstairs. His father had never conceded when his wishes were opposed. Had there been occasions when he was right to do so?

By the time they were halfway home he was regretting his decision because Aurelia walked slowly and uncertainly. She was obviously still in some discomfort, as she paused to press her hands against her belly and gave Jonathan an apologetic smile.

By the time they reached the front door she was barely capable of standing. She took off her cloak, but wobbled and looked as if she was about to fall. Jonathan did not hesitate. He swept her into his arms and off her feet.

'What are you doing?' she asked.

'I'm taking you to your room,' he said.

'I can walk,' she protested. 'You can put me down.'

'Not this time,' Jonathan said sternly and began to climb the staircase with her in his arms. It was no effort. Most of the bulk in his arms was her copious gown and layers of petticoats. Aurelia herself was slight and light as a feather. Jonathan nudged open the door with his foot and laid her on her bed. He lit the candle and both lamps, then sat back on the bed beside her.

'What do you need?' he asked, stroking the damp hair from her brow.

'Nothing,' she murmured, then grimaced. 'Water, please.'

She shuddered and clutched her abdomen, then groaned faintly, biting her lip. She was clearly trying to minimise her pain. It hurt Jonathan to see it. He walked to the door.

'I'll send Annie to help you undress and light a fire.'

'Thank you,' she whispered.

He returned to her side and squeezed her hand reassuringly. 'I won't be gone long.'

He filled a jug of water, then slipped into the dining room and poured a tumbler of whisky to steady his nerves before heading upstairs. He almost collided with Annie as she appeared at the bedroom door, white faced. In her hands was what Jonathan recognised as Aurelia's nightgown, bundled up but clearly bloodstained. His heart leapt to his throat and he pushed past the maid. Aurelia was on her bed, curled into a ball on her side with her hands clenching tightly to the rim of the bowl from her nightstand and looking sick. Her hair was loosely bound in a plait, but strands of hair were clinging to her cheeks and neck where she perspired.

'I started to bleed,' she moaned. 'More than I normally do and so suddenly.'

She screwed her eyes tightly and gave a loud sob. Jonathan did some rapid mathematics in his head, trying to remember when her last month's courses had been. Six weeks or maybe even longer, he realised, since the last time she had been unable to admit him to her room. She was clutching a bedsheet between her knees. With a shaking hand Jonathan poured her a glass of water and handed it to her.

'There is so much more blood than usual,' she groaned, squeezing his hand. 'It hurts, Jonathan, it hurts so much.'

Annie was loitering in the doorway. Mrs Barnes had joined her.

'Go back inside and wait with your mistress,' Jonathan commanded Annie. 'Mrs Barnes, please make a pot of tea for Mrs Harcourt. I am going to fetch a physician.'

'There is no need,' Aurelia protested.

Jonathan shook his head, staring in horror at the spreading crimson patch on the sheet.

'I'll be the judge of that. I'll be back as soon as I can.'

'No, Jonathan—' Aurelia said again, but he cut her off.

'You will do what you are told this time, Aurelia.'

He left the room and strode downstairs, grabbing his coat and stepping out into the bitter night.

Dr Tavistock was at home, although the manservant who answered the door told Jonathan he was dining with his family.

'It is Christmas night, sir,' he protested. 'The doctor won't come now.'

'I don't give a damn whether it is the day of Christ's second coming,' Jonathan growled. 'My wife is ill. Tell him Edward Langdon's partner is here and, if he wants another farthing from Mr Langdon, he will see me.'

As he had hoped, Edward's name and the threatened loss of custom did the trick and while Jonathan placed around the hallway Dr Tavistock gathered his bag and coat.

Before long the doctor was standing at Aurelia's bedside while Jonathan paced along the landing on the other side of the closed door, feeling like a bitch denied access to her pups. Aurelia could not be seriously ill. He was not sure if he would be able to endure that. When the door opened he rushed inside, demanding to know everything.

'It's possible she has lost a child very early in the pregnancy,' Dr Tavistock said quietly. 'I am unable to confirm it, but I have seen cases before.'

From the bed Aurelia groaned and gave a sob. Jonathan dropped to her side and took her hand. He stroked his thumb softly over the underside of her wrist.

'Did you know?'

She blinked furiously to clear her eyes of tears.

'I only started to suspect a few days ago. I was barely two weeks past my usual time,' she said. She covered her face with her hands and her next words were muffled. 'I didn't want to say anything until I was sure.'

Jonathan tightened his grip on her hand and closed his eyes.

'I'm sorry,' Aurelia wept. 'I am so sorry.'

'What for?' Jonathan asked, looking at her again. What on earth was she apologising for?

'Your child. Your heir. I keep failing. I hoped this month...'

It felt as if someone had plunged a hand into Jonathan's belly and ripped out his innards. She was in pain and weak, yet she thought it was the loss of an heir that he cared about.

'No! No, you haven't failed me.' He sat on the edge of the bed and took both her hands. He wanted to wrap his arms around her and hold her to him, but with the doctor present even this breach of restraint felt odd. 'There will be other chances. We don't even know if Dr Tavistock is right. You must not torture yourself.'

He found it impossible to grieve for something he had not known about until a moment before and that might not even have existed, but his heart broke for Aurelia's sake.

'Can you give her anything to help her?' he asked.

'I've prepared a draught of laudanum,' the doctor said. It will make her sleep and when she wakes there will be less pain.'

Less pain, but not less sorrow, Jonathan suspected. He took the glass that Dr Tavistock had prepared and gave it to Aurelia, holding the rim to her lips with his own two hands, then escorted the doctor to the front door.

'A sitz bath and wet-sheet treatment daily will help draw any congestions and the pain will ease over the coming days,' Dr Tavistock assured him. 'I'll send you my bill shortly. Goodnight and Happy Christmas to you.'

Happy Christmas? Jonathan smiled through a clenched jaw at the man's insensitivity. It was barely comprehensible that the nicest Christmas Day he had experienced should end in such a way. He sagged against the door frame, then returned to Aurelia's room with a heavy heart. She was still awake, though her eyes were growing heavy.

'Will you read to me until I sleep?'

Jonathan reached for the book on her bedside table, expecting something frivolous. It turned out to be an old copy of Malory's *Death of Arthur* translated into English. It was something he had never read, but from the look of the well-thumbed volume Aurelia had frequently returned to it.

Aurelia lay back. Already her eyes were starting to droop and she was struggling to remain upright. Jonathan pulled a footstool to the side of the bed and began to read. When Aurelia's eyes closed for the third time in succession, Jonathan put the book down quietly. Almost asleep, Aurelia's face was smooth and untroubled. He bent and kissed her forehead.

'Goodnight, my dearest,' he whispered. He wouldn't dare call her that under normal circumstances, but she stirred a little and smiled.

'Goodnight, Arthur.'

Jonathan grinned. The laudanum was confusing her and she must be imagining herself in the book. She would make a fine Guinevere. He left her alone, extinguishing the candle and lamps, and finally went to his own room. The green-silk nightgown he had planned to give her remained unopened in its gaily beribboned package.

Jonathan had spent the past five years alone on Christmas night, but none had seemed as long or lonely as the one where his wife lay in a drugged slumber a few steps away. She must recover. He'd do anything to know she would be safe. Anything to keep her safe in the future. He'd been given a glimpse of a happy family life that afternoon; something he'd never dared to consider could be his. To have Aurelia snatched away from him would be worse than cruel. It would destroy him.

Chapter Fifteen

After a week of convalescing Aurelia was convinced that any longer in bed would see her screaming like an inmate of the Bedlam Hospital. She felt better within three days, but had stayed in bed for a full week, only leaving her room to take the unpleasant cold sitz baths Dr Tavistock had prescribed. There she shivered in the hip-deep water of the tub, counting each day until she might stop taking them. The only thing that made it bearable was Jonathan's company. Being wrapped from neck to feet in damp sheets, she was perfectly modestly dressed, so he sat beside her and continued to read the tales of Arthur and his knights out loud to her. He read well, changing his voice and expression and clearly enjoying himself. He had started reading where her bookmark had been and continued each day. Aurelia hoped he never opened the book at the front and discovered the inscription there.

From your own devoted Arthur

She should have burned the book with all the other love tokens Arthur had sent her. His gifts had generally been what Aurelia considered safe and slightly impersonal, such as flowers or chocolates, and she could not bring herself to destroy the beautiful volume that had been uncharacteristically thoughtful. After a week she felt stronger, but her mood continued to be low and she grieved for the loss of the baby that might have been. She suspected that however many children she might eventually give birth to, she would always hold a special place in her heart for the first lost child.

Lying in her room did nothing to lift her spirits and she insisted upon leaving her room to mark the passing of the old year. Jonathan made a half-hearted attempt to protest, but submitted and they spent New Year's Eve sitting together in the drawing room. Edward called early but left at eleven, pleading a cold. As the clock chimed midnight and 1850 turned into 1851, Jonathan took her hand.

'Happy New Year, Aurelia, I hope this one will be good to both of us.'

He looked grave. He swore he did not hold her failure to give him a child against her, but she could not believe he did not regret that he had chosen a wife who was incapable of doing the one thing he had married her to do.

Aurelia leaned over and kissed his cheek and felt him stiffen. Since Christmas night when he had carried her in his arms and held her close he had seemed wary of touching her. Perhaps he was fearful of injuring her. She was feeling much better physically and now her body sang to her that it wanted to be touched again. Each month when her courses had prevented them making love, Jonathan had waited for her invitation to resume. This might be a similar situation and she would have to make the overture.

'It's late, but you don't have to go to the factory tomorrow,' she murmured. 'Would you like to come to my room?'

His eyes widened and he sat forward. 'Are you sure you are well enough?'

He had not been able to disguise the eagerness in his voice. She was right that he wanted to and she wanted to sing with joy.

'I think so,' she replied cautiously.

'Then, yes. Yes, I would,' he said. His face lit up, reminding Aurelia how handsome her husband was, but what gave her greater joy was seeing how eagerly he responded to her invitation.

'There's something I need to collect first.'

He went into his own room and returned carrying a flat box wrapped in red paper and a green ribbon.

'I was going to give you this on Christmas night,' he said, 'but, well...'

He didn't need to finish the sentence. Their eyes met and Aurelia saw a reflection of the grief that she felt. The powerful need to be close rose up again inside her. She unwrapped the box and lifted out a nightgown of such beauty that she gasped aloud.

'I thought you might enjoy wearing this,' Jonathan said.

'Very much so,' Aurelia murmured, tracing her finger over the pleats of lace at the neckline. 'Will you wait while I change?'

She quickly went into the next room and put on the nightgown. The silk was so fine it slid down her body. Tiny pleats gathered the scooped neck fully over her breasts while the wide sleeves gathered in ruffles at her wrists. She tiptoed back into the room, stomach tensing with anticipation. Jonathan had removed his waistcoat and tie and undone the top three buttons of his shirt. He lay on the bed, propped up on one elbow, but when he saw Aurelia he swung his legs over the edge of the bed and stood to face her. His eyes widened and he let out a long, low breath.

'I was right to choose that colour. You look absolutely beautiful.'

Aurelia put her arms out wide and turned a slow circle, enjoying the thrill that came with displaying herself. Though it was loose, the silk clung to her legs and breasts with a sensuousness that made her pulse race. She stepped into Jonathan's waiting arms, sliding her hands slowly up to his chest and resting her fingers on the first still-fastened button. He took her hand and kissed her wrist, then guided it back to his shirt. His own hands began to move slowly over her shoulders and down her back, fingers tracing her spine through the silk. She stopped undoing his buttons and moved closer to him, pressing her breasts against his chest and undulating.

'Silk feels so nice,' she murmured.

Jonathan scooped her up and carried her to the bed. She wrapped her arms around his neck to pull him down, but halfway he stiffened and pulled away. She felt his shoulders tense and tightened her grip, but he loosened her arms and stepped out of her embrace.

'This feels wrong,' he said. His face was solemn and he held himself awkwardly.

'Wrong?' Aurelia tugged at his shirt, but he resisted.

'I could hurt you,' he said.

'No, you won't,' she said. 'I feel much better now. Come lie with me. Nothing bad is going to happen.'

He walked to the door. Aurelia climbed from the bed and ran to him, unable to believe he really meant to leave.

'I'll leave you to sleep. Another night, perhaps.'

'Stop!'

'No. I can't do this.' He took her face in his hands and looked into her eyes. His expression was drawn. 'I can't let it happen again.'

'Let what happen?' Aurelia asked. But she knew the answer already and didn't need him to confirm it. Another pregnancy resulting in a loss.

'I can't risk it. The thought that… The blood…' He shuddered and pulled his hands away, clenching them into fists.

He left without another word and walked to his own room with his head bowed and without looking back.

St Valentine's Day was a fortnight away. Usually a date that Aurelia laid no significance on, but now she was married and she wanted to mark the day. She had agonised over what to sew onto a card for Jonathan. Any reference to love would feel wrong. Even though she was finding that words slid into her mind at odd moments, she had to remind herself that Jonathan did not return the sentiment. He still did not come to her bed. She had opened her heart before and had no intention of letting another man hold that power over her. She settled in the end for sewing a card from scraps of silk that Edward gave her. Jonathan would receive his own product worked into a touching scene of two hands side by side on piano keys. The message would require more thought.

As soon as Jonathan had left the dining room, Aurelia took her coffee and moved to the window seat. She had discovered that it was the most pleasant place to do her needlework in the morning as the light was brightest there. The door opened once more and she hid her workbasket under the table. Jonathan had returned and held out a letter to Aurelia. He furrowed his brow as if he realised he had caught her in a covert act and she felt a flush of guilt, even though her secrecy was innocent.

'This was just delivered to the door.'

She took it from his outstretched hand and recognised the handwriting.

'It's from Dora. How curious. I wonder why she's writing to me when I will see her today? She could have brought it herself.'

Dora and Cassandra were coming for afternoon tea as they now did twice weekly. Another ritual that had developed at Jonathan's suggestion and one Aurelia looked forward to.

She turned the envelope over. It was quite thick, suggesting multiple sheets were enclosed. She laid it to one side and smiled at Jonathan.

'Aren't you going to read it?' Jonathan asked.

'It can wait until I have finished my cup of coffee,' Aurelia said. 'I can't imagine it is anything particularly urgent.'

It was probably yet another pamphlet that Dora had found arguing women should be allowed to train in the medical profession alongside men. Good luck to her if that was the case as Dora would have to convince their father to let her attend a university. That would be a harder task than persuading all the dons at Oxford.

Jonathan leaned over and kissed her cheek, then left. His cologne lingered in the air and Aurelia inhaled it, her insides fluttering.

When she had finished the morning's work, she gathered all her scraps of silk and put them in her workbag, slipping the letter in with them. She had nothing to complain about. A husband who paid her attention, sisters who loved her and a full life. She should be grateful for what she had and not grumble about a lack of intimacy. Jonathan would come around eventually. If he wanted an heir, he would have to.

It was only when Aurelia had changed into her afternoon dress that she remembered the letter from Dora. She rummaged among her needles and thread and opened it. It was not a pamphlet at all, but sheets of paper which been ripped into four or five pieces, some of which were scorched around the edge. Dora had written a note in her sprawling careless script.

This came for you two days ago. Father tried to destroy it, but I thought you had a right to know of its existence.

Aurelia picked up the top piece. Her heart almost stopped beating and the heat drained from her body. Slowly she placed the fragments down and withdrew a trembling hand. It was little wonder Sir Robert had been determined to destroy this. And Dora had been right to try to save it for her.

Only half of the letterhead was there, but she would have recognised the family crest and handwriting of Arthur Carver, presumptive Seventh Baron Helsby, anywhere.

Aurelia's first instinct was to finish what Sir Robert had started and destroy the letter without even reading it. There was nothing Arthur could say that would make up for what he had put her through. If she did that, however, she knew she would spend the rest of her days wondering what it had said and was not strong enough to live with that torture.

She knelt and spread the scraps of paper out on sofa, piecing together what she could. Dora had obviously not managed to salvage the whole thing as the start of the letter was almost intact, but segments were missing. Even so, it told her all she might want to know.

Aurelia read it three times, each time becoming more distressed.

My dearest Aurelia...

...no right to call you that, nor to address you in any terms at all, yet I find I cannot stop thinking of you as such. You are the dearest being...

...ine is dead. The illness which tormented her for so long finally...

...ffering is mercifully at an end. I am free, my dearest one...

...be yours. If there was any hope at all that you...is then a single word would make me the...

And that was where the letter ended. Aurelia clutched the pieces in her hand, screwing them tight.

'How dare he?' she exclaimed aloud.

Even without the entire letter, the meaning was clear. The woman Arthur had been secretly engaged to throughout his courtship of Aurelia had, according to him, been frail since childhood. Now Emmeline Carver had died a few short months after their marriage and Arthur thought Aurelia might be willing to overlook the grave deception he had carried out.

The monstrousness of such an arrogant, unfeeling presumption made her want to retch. Tears welled in her eyes and she felt a rush of anger and revulsion, but underneath was a feeling that was even more unwelcome. Affection for Arthur.

She had loved him so deeply. She had fought with that love and had spent the time since her discovery of his deception working hard to make sure all her emotions towards Arthur were placed firmly inside a locked box where they could not hurt her. Now even the sight of his handwriting threatened to split the box open and let all emotions burst out uncontrollably. She felt giddy with sickness that she thought had abated. She stumbled through to her bedroom where she threw herself on to the bed, still clutching the pieces of Arthur's letter to her chest. It was only then, as she lay on her bed, that something occurred to her.

Arthur had written to her at her father's home. He did not know she was married. Aurelia buried her face in her pillows and moaned. Whether or not she could forgive Arthur, whether or not she could bring herself to believe the words he had sworn to her, whether or not she loved him, none of that mattered. She was married now and beyond his reach. Her last reserves of strength gave out and she lay there sobbing until Annie knocked at the door and announced Cassandra and Dora had arrived and were waiting in the parlour.

Aurelia quickly washed her face and checked her appearance. Her eyes were red and her face was puffy, but she decided it didn't matter. Her sisters would understand why. She gathered the pieces of Arthur's letter that had been salvaged and locked them in her writing desk along with her Greek dictionaries, then made her way downstairs.

'You read the letter, didn't you?' Dora said upon taking one look at Aurelia.

Annie was still lingering at the bottom of the staircase. Aurelia shot a warning look in her direction. The maid must have been aware of the scandal that had almost enveloped her mistress, but Aurelia did not want her reminded of it now she was living in a house with other servants who knew nothing of it.

'I didn't know you had a piano,' Cassandra said quickly.

Aurelia nodded, grateful for the change of subject. 'Jonathan bought it for me as a Christmas gift.'

She had been presented with it when she had emerged from her convalescence, still grieving for the child she might have lost. Jonathan asked her to begin teaching him and night after night since her illness they sat side by side while Aurelia instructed her pupil and Jonathan painstakingly learned to play. It had been such a considerate gift and one of the ways they had grown closer.

'I did read Arthur's letter, but I wish I hadn't,' Aurelia admitted when the three women were settled in the parlour and alone.

'Might you reply to him?' Cassandra asked.

'Do you think I would demean myself in such a way?' Aurelia said sharply. The fact that she had considered it, if only for a moment, made the question even more intolerable. She was ashamed of herself.

'But you and Arthur loved each other so deeply,' Cassandra said. 'You would have married him if he had been free and he loved you deeply enough to lie.'

Aurelia poured the tea out. Her hand shook terribly.

'Let me do that,' Dora said. Aurelia smiled gratefully. Dora was always sensible.

'If Arthur had been honest about his circumstances from the start, I might have forgiven him,' Aurelia said. 'If he had told me when we met that he had been promised to Emmeline, but did not love his fiancée, I could have borne it. I would have pitied him. But instead he lied to me and did her a grave injustice. Why would I ever trust a man who could behave in such a way and how could I humiliate myself by allowing myself to love him once more?'

'So you allow that you might love him?' Cassandra said, a hint of victory in her voice. 'Doesn't love conquer all faults?'

Aurelia turned away. Only in stories. In real life it was better not to dwell on past happiness, but instead concentrate on the present.

'I told Arthur I wanted nothing else to do with him and I meant it. Besides,' Aurelia said, sitting back in her chair, 'I am married now.'

Married to someone who doesn't love you, her inner self whispered. *Someone who can't bring himself to touch you.*

'But what if you weren't married?' Cassandra asked. 'You aren't with child, are you? You could procure a divorce.'

Aurelia stared at her sister in horror. She didn't know about the possible miscarriage on Christmas Day, so her insensitivity was excusable, but the morality was not.

'You don't love Mr Harcourt and you only married him because Father wanted you to,' Cassandra continued. Aurelia looked at the cup in her hands. She couldn't honestly agree with Cassandra's verdict. Not the part about love.

'What sort of woman do you think I am that I would consider breaking off my marriage under such a pretext?' she said coldly. 'I would be as bad as Arthur. Worse even, because he was not actually married when he began to court me.'

'You could claim you were coerced,' Dora supplied.

'What is wrong with you both?' Aurelia exclaimed. 'Has something happened to make you lose all your scruples? I made vows to Mr Harcourt. My husband is a good man. He's kind and generous. He works hard to make his business prosper and cares for his workers. What has he done to deserve such base treatment when he has been only good to me?'

Dora looked chastened. 'Are you fond of him after all?' she asked.

Aurelia took her time before answering. The frustrating state of affairs regarding the lack of lovemaking had continued, but while the intimacy Aurelia had enjoyed and desperately craved had vanished, it had been replaced by a different sort of intimacy and one that was equally enjoyable. As well as the piano lessons, the habit of reading aloud had continued and they sat together in front of the fire taking turns to read. The dark nights of January had passed in a rush and Aurelia's mind had been kept too busy to dwell on her loss. She found herself waiting for Jonathan's return home each evening with more and more eagerness, genuinely enjoying his company. Far from being the businesslike transaction she had agreed to, her marriage had become a friendship. And though it pained her to admit it, her own feelings had grown into something deeper.

Aurelia looked down at her hands. 'I am fonder of him than I expected to be.'

She loved Jonathan. In admitting it to her sisters she finally admitted the depths of her feelings to herself. But what use was knowing that if Jonathan saw their marriage as a business arrangement? It was obvious that he enjoyed her company, even if his feelings stopped short of love, but since the horrible night when he had given her the beautiful silk nightdress, then run from her, he had not come to her bed. He would not—or could not—bring himself to make love to her. He had said he didn't want to hurt her again. The fear of a repetition of the nightmare of Christmas was stopping him, but what if there was also a sense of revulsion brought on by what her body had done and what he had witnessed? He had talked about the blood with such horror.

What if Jonathan might prefer to take another wife who could give him what he needed? What if he regretted not pressing harder for Cassandra's hand, for instance?

Chapter Sixteen

When Jonathan returned home that evening Aurelia's eyes were brighter than they had been for a while. Clearly an afternoon in the company of her sisters had done her some good. It made a change from seeing her placidly sitting and sewing or reading, as she walked around the room purposefully as they waited to eat. A warm glow settled on Jonathan's chest until he realised there was a mania behind her movements and her smile was fixed and brittle.

She was too happy. Too lively. It worried him, in fact.

'How are you this evening?' he asked.

'Very well,' she answered. Her smile widened further as she brought Jonathan a tumbler of whisky, but her hand was unsteady. Jonathan took the drink, but held on to her wrist. Her pulse was rapid and sent his skin fluttering.

'Did anything happen to excite you today?' he asked cautiously. 'You seem a little agitated.'

'No,' she answered, tossing her head. 'Nothing out of the ordinary. Cassandra spoke of gossip. Dora intends to join the Young Ladies' Subscription Library women in an effort to provide clothing for destitute mothers and their children. I think perhaps I may join her. It will give me something to do.'

She began rearranging flowers in a vase so viciously that she broke off one of the heads and gave an exasperated sigh. Jonathan set down his whisky and walked to her side. He put his hands on her shoulders and turned her to face him. It pained him that she resisted a little at first.

'You seem unhappy today,' he said gently. 'What can I do to help you?'

She glanced at him and then quickly looked away. In that flash Jonathan had seen an expression he had so often relished. The hunger and desire that burned also in him. He knew what she wanted because it was the same thing that he did. He wanted to make love to her so much it hurt. Even the feel of her arms tensing under the palms of his hands was enough to cause blood to rush and begin strengthening him. But how could he bring himself to possibly inflict a pregnancy on her again after seeing the harm it had done before? Every time he thought of approaching her, the image of Aurelia's face twisted in pain caused him such fear of losing her.

Until the memory faded of her lying weak and in pain while he stood by helplessly, he could not bring himself to make love to her. He wondered if that was why his father had found his mother so repellent that they only had one child together. What had caused his parents to become distant to the point of hatred?

He took the broken rose from Aurelia's hand and tucked it into the curl of hair above her left ear.

'There. It won't go to waste now.'

She gave him a slight smile, but the longing was still there.

'Will you play something for me?' Jonathan asked. 'Something cheering.'

'Don't you want to practise?' she asked.

'I'd rather watch you,' he replied, taking her gently by the elbow and escorting her to the stool.

He sat beside Aurelia at the piano, watching her hands move swiftly over the keys, but his mind was not on the music. He leaned in towards her until his arm touched hers. She stopped playing and flashed a sideways smile at him.

'Are you tired?'

'Yes, but not too much to listen to you play.'

She resumed playing and Jonathan let his mind wander again.

How could he make his wife as happy as she

made him? The depth of his affection for her ran so much deeper than he had suspected was possible. He had to do something that could lift her spirits and it had been her mention of Theodora's plan to join a charitable group which gave him the idea. He could not imagine Aurelia sewing trousers and shirts, however he had a ready stock of children among his workers who still needed a teacher. Why not Aurelia? He had seen the way Millie had bloomed under her care. Construction of the apprentice house was well underway and by spring it would be ready to house the first occupants. His mind began to work as he weighed up the advantages and disadvantages of his plan and he only half-listened to the music. By the time it was bedtime he had decided.

Since he had been unable to make love to Aurelia, the evening ended at the top of the stairs in a ritual that had become a habit. Aurelia gave him a pensive look as if she was trying to decide whether this night would be the one he made love to her again. He wanted to so much that it made him hot and weak at the mere idea. He knew Aurelia desired him as much as he desired her, but did she really want to risk such a painful and heartbreaking outcome? It mystified Jonathan. Somehow he could never find the words to ask her and inevitably she would give an almost imperceptible shake of her head as resignation filled her eyes. Jonathan took Aurelia's hands and kissed her cheek.

'Goodnight, Aurelia, sleep well,' he murmured as he always did. Ordinarily he turned resolutely to his own room where he spent his nights fighting the longing for her and the temptation to go to her that racked his body and soul. Tonight he added something extra to his farewell.

'Will you visit me at the mill tomorrow?'

She looked surprised, but pleased. 'Of course. Why?'

He lifted her hand to his lips and grinned over the top of it. Her eyes danced beneath the thick frame of lashes and Jonathan had to work doubly hard not to just pull her to him and begin seducing her.

'That's for me to know and you to discover tomorrow.'

He walked away as usual, but with a lighter spring in his step.

As he lay in bed that night he gazed by candlelight at the portrait that Cassandra had given him. He ran his finger over the painted Aurelia's cheeks, wishing it was the real woman he was caressing. He had only married her for an heir, but now that was the least of his concerns. Keeping her safe and making her happy was all he cared about. What heir mattered in comparison to losing Aurelia? She was the family he had been searching for and he'd rather spend the next forty years enduring the frustration of not making love if it meant Aurelia was alive to share them with him. They would never become enemies like his parents, but until Aurelia was content he could never be satisfied.

The following morning they walked the short distance to the mill together. The temperature had turned, taking the frost with it, and the cycle of dull, fog-shrouded days was upon them. Umbrellas were useless. It didn't as much rain as surround them with a wet shroud that slowly soaked every article of clothing. When Jonathan had taken Aurelia to the site of the new buildings before they had walked on frozen earth. Now slabs had been laid and surrounded with gravel. He couldn't help remembering that the last time they had kissed passionately and indiscreetly with hands roaming to places they shouldn't have. He was glad now that there were men working on the site so he had an excuse not to do it again and give in to his temptation.

'This is where the apprentices will live,' he announced, gesturing to the two-storey house that stood alongside the river. He took Aurelia's hand and led her closer, keen to show her everything. 'I thought a kitchen garden could go at the front and a privy and washhouse in the yard at the rear. The house isn't finished inside, but the floors and staircases are in place. The bedrooms will fit twelve younger boys and eight girls. The boys will move to a third room once they reach the age of fourteen.'

He carried on, describing the kitchen and schoolroom, the private room set aside for a wardress to live in and supervise the children, then realised he had been talking non-stop and giving Aurelia no opportunity to speak. He stopped and grinned.

'What do you think?'

'It looks wonderful,' Aurelia said enthusiastically, squeezing his arm. 'They're lucky to be working for you. I'm so pleased you brought me to see it.'

'There is another reason I brought you,' Jonathan admitted. 'I have failed to find a teacher I believe could perform the role adequately and with due care for their welfare. I will be too busy between now and May preparing for the Great Exhibition to spend any further time on the matter.'

He reached for her hand as if he was proposing to her. Any excuse to touch her, feel her warmth. 'I wondered if you would like to start teaching the children?'

'Me?' Aurelia was clearly taken aback and

made no attempt to hide it. He'd expected her to show more enthusiasm.

She wrinkled her brow. 'I don't know if I could.'

It was uncertainty of her ability rather than a lack of interest, Jonathan realised. 'Only the younger boys at first,' he explained. 'The rudiments of counting, reading and writing their letters. Some Bible verses and enough words that you deem necessary for them to prosper.'

'And the girls? What of them?' Aurelia asked.

She'd spoken before of her wish for the girls to be educated, too. Jonathan wondered briefly whether she would feel more confident teaching the girls. He had no objection to them learning the rudiments of literacy eventually, but to start with the boys needed to take precedence.

'I've seen the care you have taken over Millie and believe you would be ideal to encourage them with household matters.'

Aurelia stared up at the building.

'Will you take the role?' he asked.

'If you think I'd be capable.'

'Of course I do,' he answered. 'I think you are capable of anything you set your mind to.' He kissed her cheek. The brim of her bonnet was so big it almost enveloped his head, too. Who cared what the men might think?

When they returned to the office, Edward had left and they were greeted by Jonathan's clerk,

Matthews. He was an efficient young man who had a habit of peering through his spectacles and gave Jonathan the impression he was far more organised than even Jonathan could contemplate.

'Mr Langdon has returned home, Mr Harcourt, sir,' Matthews said. 'He would like you to call at his house at your earliest convenience. He seemed a little ill, if you will permit me to express an opinion.'

Jonathan and Aurelia exchanged a worried glance.

'Ill?' Aurelia asked.

'His cheeks whitened and he gave a gasp in his throat,' interrupted the mill boy who was busy piling coals into the scuttle by the fireplace. 'Sort of like this, Mr Harcourt.'

They were treated to the sound of wheezing and gurgling from the lad who clearly imagined himself on the stage. It would have been comical if it hadn't suggested Edward's lungs were troubling him.

'Do you mind returning home alone? I really should go to Edward,' Jonathan asked.

'Not at all,' she replied. 'Is there anything I can do to help?'

Jonathan held her hand and squeezed it tightly. 'I'm sure everything will be fine,' he said, but anxiety twisted his guts. Aurelia still didn't know the whole extent of Edward's illness. She wrapped her arms around Jonathan's waist and pressed herself tightly against him, with her cheek against his chest. He put his arms around her and they stood, husband and wife together, comforting and receiving comfort. Jonathan caught a trace of the violet perfume she wore and it had the intoxicating effect of a glass of finest brandy. But for the presence of Matthews, Jonathan would have buried his face against the enticing spot behind her ear that so demanded to be nibbled. As it was he merely patted her on the back and bade her farewell.

'I shall be home shortly.'

They parted at the gates. At the end of the road Jonathan turned back to watch her as she crossed at the furthest end of the road. His heart felt lighter than it should be considering Edward's possible condition, all thanks to a simple embrace that had lasted a moment longer than was proper. He was infatuated with her, searching for any signs that she might return his growing affection. He believed his feelings to be one sided, but the embrace she had just given him might be a hint that her regard for him ran a little deeper, too. If he was to lose Edward, then knowing Aurelia cared a little for him would sustain him through his grief. Alternately it might have been a comforting gesture from a kind woman towards a man she could see was troubled and he would be as alone as he always feared he might be.

* * *

Edward was lying on the sofa in his drawing room when Jonathan arrived. He was wearing a green-striped-satin smoking jacket with a yellow and blue tartan blanket pulled up to his waist and had a copy of *Punch* open face down on his chest. His cheeks were a good colour and it was clear to Jonathan's relief that his condition had not deteriorated since last they had spoken. Upon expressing his relief Edward waved a hand.

'Dr Tavistock worries over everything,' he said. 'I merely felt the chill and damp this morning and a fit of coughing made my head reel a little. I am not ready to leave this existence yet.'

Jonathan pulled up a stool and sat beside him. 'Is there anything I can do for you?' he asked.

'As I am ordered to rest I shall spend the rest of the day planning some new patterns to take to the Great Exhibition. Florals or tartans, do you think? I have some fashion plates I would like to look through,' Edward said. 'Will you go to the desk in my study and bring me the pile in the top shelf? It's the one with the red ribbon tied around it.'

Jonathan made his way through to Edward's study. It was a complete contrast to his own, well-ordered room, with stacks of newspapers and periodicals piled high among ledgers and books. It made Jonathan's brain itch just to cross the threshold. How could Edward locate anything! He spent a good five minutes trying to locate what Edward had sent him for and when he finally unearthed the correct pile of papers it sent a whole sheaf of letters and papers sliding to the floor. He let slip an expletive as he knelt to gather them. As he did, a familiar address leapt out from amid the pile.

Darbrough Court.

He'd read it almost before he had realised what it was and felt vomit rise in the back of his throat. He squatted back on his heels and stared stupidly at the date and greeting.

My dear Edward

A letter dated a month previously.

The handwriting was unfamiliar to him, but the signature at the bottom was a name he knew well.

What he did not understand—what he could not comprehend in the slightest—was why the father he had not seen for over half his lifetime would be writing to Edward and signing the letter *Affectionately, Christopher.*

He looked at the rest of the pile he had gathered and identified among the jumble the same paper with the same handwriting at least another five times. He knew he should not read them, but his curiosity was too great. He would read only the dates. The letters were all dated January and July. Thanks to Edward's haphazard organisation they were not in consecutive order, but often enough to suggest the correspondence was habitual. The oldest was from six years' previously and the most recent was from this year. It was clear his father and Edward wrote to each other twice yearly. Jonathan carefully folded the letters, trying his hardest not to read any of the contents. His hand trembled and he felt a spreading dampness across the back of his neck where his collar felt overbearingly tight and hot.

He pushed himself upright and returned to Edward's parlour, carrying the requested plates in one hand and the letters in the other. Edward was reading *Punch* when he entered the room, but looked over the top of the edition and chuckled.

'This is masterful. The caricature of...'

Jonathan stopped in front of him and held out the pile of letters, stone faced.

'I think you have some explaining to do,' he said.

Edward lowered the periodical and steepled his fingers. Even then, Jonathan hoped Edward would have a satisfactory explanation, but from the look of shock that crossed the older man's face, it seemed Jonathan was about to hear something that would wreck any friendship they had.

'Yes,' Edward said. 'I rather think I do.'

Chapter Seventeen

Aurelia looked at the grandmother clock for the fifth time. Only ten minutes had passed since her previous visit to it. The hands now pointed to twenty-three minutes past eight. She bit her fingernail and tried to suppress the dread that filled her stomach and bubbled up whenever she counted the passing minutes.

When Jonathan had not returned home at the end of the working day she had been a little surprised. He usually kept his hours so precisely. When an hour had passed her surprise had turned to anxiety at the thought that Edward's condition must have been more serious than she had suspected. When dinner was almost ready she sent the kitchen boy to Edward's house to ask after her husband and had received a reply that Mr Langdon had taken to his bed and Jonathan had left the house shortly after four.

She ate alone, but with little appetite, and had instructed Mrs Barnes to keep a plate of the mutton stew hot and ready for Jonathan's return. She tried to read, but did not want to go too much further in the story without Jonathan or he would lose his place. She went to her sitting room and began to translate a passage of Hesiod from Greek to English, but stared at the words as if she had never encountered them before and found the Greek as incomprehensible as Millie was finding the reading of English letters.

When the clock struck nine she would consider sending a message to her mother asking advice. It would pain her to do it, but she could think of no alternative. Many wives were used to their husbands staying out all the hours of the night, drinking or keeping company with their friends, or worse, but Jonathan's habits were usually so regular. He had never given the smallest hint that he ever visited one of the town's women of questionable morals, but what if he was no longer interested in spending his nights with her because he was finding satisfaction elsewhere? She bit her lip anxiously and resisted returning to the clock once more.

The chimes were only halfway through the count of nine when she heard the front door slam. Dropping her book and pen, she reached the top of the stairs in time to see Jonathan vanish into his study. Aurelia swept downstairs after him and followed him into the room.

Jonathan was standing with his back to her, both hands on the back of the chair in front of the desk. His head was bent over and he had not even removed his outer coat.

'Where have you been?' she asked nervously. 'How is Edward?'

His head snapped around, but he wasn't looking at her. His eyes were fixed on the oil painting of the mill that hung on the wall.

'How is Edward?' he muttered, shaking his head.

He left the room abruptly and went into the dining room. He stumbled slightly as he entered, knocking into the small three-legged table. Aurelia jumped in surprise. Her husband was usually so precise in his movements and so elegant that seeing him not fully in control of himself was unnerving. He looked at her and she saw with horror that his eyes were bloodshot and rimmed with red.

'What is wrong?' she asked. He appeared to notice her properly for the first time. He didn't answer, but turned away and poured himself a tumbler of whisky with a shaking hand, leaving the stopper out of the decanter. It rolled towards the edge of the table, but he simply stared at it.

Aurelia moved forward and grabbed it before it fell to the floor.

'Have you been drinking?' she asked.

He stared at the glass in his hand and grimaced.

'Mr Harcourt, tell me what is wrong,' she demanded.

He flinched and tipped back the whisky in one abrupt and violent motion, draining the glass. By now Aurelia could barely contain her anxiety. Her husband did not drink to excess. When he took spirits it was measured and enjoyed over time.

'Jonathan!' she exclaimed. His head snapped up and his eyes were glazed. Anger flared in them, dying away almost instantly like a match extinguished by the wind.

'Jonathan,' she said once more in a gentler tone. 'Tell me what has happened please.'

'My father is dying.'

He stared at the glass in his hands as if not sure what it was.

'My father is dying,' he repeated and it was as if these words punctured him because he sagged into his chair with his head in his hands.

'Your father?' Aurelia frowned in confusion. 'You mean Edward?' Grief made her reel. 'He seemed so vital only recently.'

'I mean my father,' Jonathan said, lifting his head. 'I mean Christopher Harcourt of Darbrough Court near Durham.'

'But he's been dead for years,' Aurelia blurted out. 'Your mother was a widow.'

Jonathan shook his head violently. 'No. He hasn't,' he said in what was almost a snarl. 'My mother was never widowed.'

Aurelia felt for the edge of the dining table and sat down. She opened her mouth, shut it again. He watched her through bloodshot eyes while she tried to comprehend what she was hearing.

'My father was a cold, controlling swine who made our lives miserable. My mother and I lived constantly in misery thanks to his coldness and bitterness. Rather than live under his roof after I was sent to school my mother left and took me with her.'

'But you told me…'

'Of course I did,' Jonathan snapped. 'As I told everyone who asked. Only Edward knew the truth and he was sworn to secrecy. Our whole lives here were based on that lie.'

His eyes flashed and he took her hands, fingers gripping tightly. 'As you are now.'

'Why are you telling me?' Aurelia asked.

'Because you deserve an explanation of why I'm not entirely in command of myself,' he said, pointing an unsteady finger at her. 'And because you are my wife. And a husband and wife should have no secrets from one another. I am done with secrets.'

Aurelia dropped her head, thinking of the letter

from Arthur that was still hidden in her writing slope and the secret of her romance that she had never shared with Jonathan. She should have told him. Jonathan walked unsteadily to the table and abandoned his whisky. He poured a large measure of brandy, tipped it down his throat and placed the tumbler carefully down again, nudging it until the glass was perfectly at the centre of the coaster and lined up with the whisky tumbler.

'You see, Mrs Harcourt, I've received a great blow today,' he said. 'Edward asked me to retrieve some papers from his desk in the office. As I've mentioned before, his filing system needs a complete overhaul and while I was looking I found a letter addressed to him from my father. One of a series.'

He curled his fist around the brandy glass tightly enough it could almost shatter. 'My father always knew where we were, but, thanks to Edward's intervention, he chose to let us live in peace. I don't know why. Presumably Edward used their previous friendship as a lever, though why he would be friends with that swine I don't know.'

Aurelia gently prised the glass free and put it softly on the table. She stood quietly, uncertain what to do while her husband raged.

'That's not the worst of it,' Jonathan continued. He took a deep breath and his face contorted in disgust. 'It appears my father had been attempting to support my mother ever since she left her marriage. He had been sending her money and she refused to spend it on herself. No wonder she died leaving such an inheritance.'

'That's good, isn't it?' Aurelia asked.

'No!' Jonathan's head whipped around. 'She left him. *I* supported her. I worked hours in the mill, working the machines amid the noise and dust. Spending my nights learning so I might prove capable enough to work as a clerk in the office. I need not have bothered. My path was already arranged. Edward always intended to offer me employment in some capacity. I bought my shares in the business with that devil's lucre.'

Aurelia added a large measure of soda from the siphon to the half-empty glass of whisky and held it out to him. He took it and gave her a bleak smile. She drew up the footstool and sat down beside him while he sipped the whisky and soda and gradually his trembling stopped.

'I confronted Edward with the letters and he admitted everything. He asked me if I would visit my father before he dies. He asked for my forgiveness, but I refused. I told him our friendship was over and I would begin proceedings to dissolve the partnership. We parted angrily and I returned to the mill. An hour later Edward's valet sent a boy to fetch me. Edward had taken to his bed, overcome with grief. I refused to go. I couldn't forgive him and I may be too late.'

Jonathan bit back a sob. 'My greatest friend and I turned my back on him. If his end comes quicker as a result of my words or actions I shall hold myself responsible.'

Aurelia put her hand on his. He stared at her bleakly.

'I'm sorry. You shouldn't see me like this. I hoped you would have gone to bed.'

'How could I go to sleep not knowing where you were? Now I'm even more glad I stayed up. I hate the thought that you might have been grieving alone.'

Jonathan shivered, then seemed to pull himself together, but his eyes grew bright with pain and the tears that he was holding back pooled on his lower lashes, turning his eyes a startling topaz blue. Aurelia tried not to notice, ashamed that at the time of his greatest grief she was thinking about something so trivial.

'Alone...'

Jonathan ran his hands through his hair which was in disarray in an attempt to straighten it, but only succeeded in disordering the waves further.

'Edward was everything to me,' he muttered. 'Mentor, friend, confidant. Sometimes he felt like a father to me and now that means nothing. I am alone.'

He drained his glass and sighed. Aurelia took the glass and refilled it. As an afterthought she poured one of her own, topping them both up with a good quantity of soda.

'You aren't alone,' she said quietly, holding the glass out. 'I'm here. If you want me.'

Did he understand what she was trying to say? She wanted to tell him she loved him outright, but fear of adding to his turmoil held her back.

'It was Edward's doing that I married you, you know. What next? I discover his lungs are perfectly healthy and he will live another twenty years and that was merely a pretence?'

He turned his face away. Aurelia's heart missed a beat. What small consolation it must be to lose his greatest friend and be left with the wife he had never wanted. How fortunate she hadn't shared her heart. She finished her drink and put the glass back beside the decanter. She had drunk it too quickly because her head was already starting to feel fuzzy and when she picked up her sewing basket her hand trembled. She walked to the door.

'You don't have to go.'

She hesitated and looked round. Jonathan held a hand out and gave her a crooked smile. It was nowhere near as warm as his usual ones but at least it seemed he was trying to gather himself together.

'I mean... I didn't mean that I regret marrying you. I don't. I'd appreciate your company. I'd like you to stay.'

She returned to her seat opposite him, but he had lapsed into his thoughts. She opened the basket and took out the blouse she was hemming. She hoped it had been the whisky that had made them both get Jonathan's meaning muddled and he hadn't accidentally spoken the truth in his heart. She irritably stabbed the needle through the cloth, missed a couple of stitches and then pricked her finger and gave a cry of irritation as a drop of blood welled.

Jonathan looked up, the sound seemed to have drawn him from his reverie. He furrowed his brow. 'Did you hurt yourself?'

'Not greatly,' she replied. She held out her finger for him to see and was surprised when he took it and brought it close to his eyes. He wiped away the bead of blood with his thumb and pressed it hard on her finger to stem the bleeding. He held it for a moment, released the pressure and examined her finger intently. Then, to Aurelia's surprise, he lifted it to his lips and kissed the spot. It was how she might treat a child's injury, but as the warm moistness of his lips closed around the soft flesh of her fingertip, the feelings that spread through her were anything but childlike. She looked up and discovered his eyes were on her. A drum began to beat in her head; a fast rhythm that drowned out any other sense. Her husband watched her closely. Keeping his eyes raised to hers, he put his mouth in the palm of her hand and kissed it once again. Her insides jolted and she took a deep breath. He hadn't touched her so intimately since New Year's Eve and now the slightest tenderness was overwhelming. She felt the familiar spinning sensation as desire coursed through her and she curved her fingers over the back of his hand.

Jonathan moved his lips further up until they were over the veins in her wrists. She wondered if he would be able to feel the excitement that raced along with her blood beneath the surface of her skin. He kissed her there fiercer now and more fervently. Aurelia bit back a gasp of pleasure. She ran her free hand over his other arm and slid her fingers beneath his shirtsleeve, scraping her nails over the inside of his wrist, mirroring the place where he kissed her. He growled in the back of his throat and pressed his lips harder against her wrist, then all at once pulled away and looked back into her eyes.

She had never seen such raw hunger. He held her gaze with a challenge, like an animal begging to be free. She was not sure how this creature had come to replace her husband, but his expression was more intoxicating than whisky. When his mouth closed over hers there was no hesitation whatsoever in her and she met his waiting lips with fierce passion.

Somehow they were standing, lips locked, arms tight, each trapping the other within an embrace. They pulled apart to stare at each other, both breathing heavily. Jonathan's face was flushed and Aurelia expected hers would be similarly reddened from the heat that blazed in her cheeks.

'I want you,' Jonathan growled.

'I need you,' Aurelia answered.

His lips came down on hers again, crushing, pulling. A frenzy that was unmatched. She revelled in it. He pulled her close, gripping her buttocks through the mass of skirts. She pushed herself towards him, wishing she was rid of the cumbersome obstacles. Jonathan picked her up and swept her into his arms. The rush as she was lifted off her feet and crushed against his chest was exhilarating.

'What are you doing?' she gasped.

'Taking you to bed before I have you here and now on the dining room floor,' Jonathan replied, his eyes burning into her fiercely.

Aurelia wrapped her arms around his neck. 'Then we had better go quickly.'

When he had carried her before she had been insensible with pain and had not appreciated the ease with which he lifted her, but now she grasped his strength.

At the top of the stairs Jonathan hesitated. Aurelia's stomach seized. He was going to stop as he had done on New Year's Eve. The thought of that rejection and disappointment was too much to bear. She could not risk those associations and memories ruining tonight.

'Take me to your room,' she said.

He didn't hesitate and for the first time in their marriage Aurelia found herself in her husband's domain. She had little time to appreciate it, however, because as soon as he settled her on her feet, his hands were at her clothing and his lips were on her neck. They undressed each other frantically and barely made it as far as the bed before the hands that had torn at clothes were teasing at their naked bodies, stroking and pulling and touching. Their hands collided as they scrabbled downwards. She took hold of his erection and he plunged his fingers up between her thighs.

There was no holding back now and any reservations Jonathan might have had were absent. He backed her towards the bed, clutching her to him tightly. Aurelia fell back, pulling him with her. She wrapped her legs around him and jutted her hips up so that his delicious hardness was pressing where she needed him to be. If he did have second thoughts, she would trap him there and not release him until the longing that had been pent up inside her was beaten into submission.

She needn't have worried. Jonathan showed no hesitation. He seemed to be pouring all his anger and pain into his lovemaking, surging against her until he was practically lifting her off the bed in his passion. When finally it was over, he dropped beside Aurelia and held her to him as if he never intended to let her go.

She lay sated and contented with her head resting on his shoulder. Usually afterwards Jonathan left her and returned to his own room. Now it was she who should leave, but he held her so tightly that she could not slip free. Nor did she want to. She closed her eyes, thinking that a few minutes more would be acceptable.

'You don't have to go,' Jonathan murmured, adjusting his arm so she could nestle more comfortably. 'I'd like you to stay.'

'I'd like to stay.'

Aurelia pulled the sheet over them both and stared around at the unfamiliar shadows on furniture and ornaments she hadn't even had time to notice. Soon she felt her limbs beginning to grow heavy and her eyes shutting of their own accord. She burrowed down closer to Jonathan.

'Thank you,' Jonathan murmured. He rolled on to his side and pulled her close, his top leg crooked over hers. The room was chilly, but Jonathan's body was warm and curiously it appeared that naked flesh was better at heating her up than a body clad in wool or linen. Aurelia rolled on to her side, lying with her spine pressed against Jonathan's chest and her feet tucked between his, drowsing. She wriggled to get a little more comfortable and her buttocks rubbed up against something hard that she would have sworn wasn't there a second before. She heard Jonathan give a long, drawn-out sigh.

'Aurelia, are you still awake?' he murmured softly. His lips were very close to her ears and tickled delightfully.

'Yes,' she whispered.

'Good,' Jonathan answered, 'because when you brush up against me like that it makes it extremely hard to settle to sleep.'

His hand slid softly down across her front and his fingers began to gently stroke across her skin. He traced the curve of her belly then began to caress her breasts while he kissed the back of her neck. She arched her back to encourage his mouth and fingers to reach further and she discovered with delight that Jonathan only needed to shift the smallest degree to enter her from behind. They made love for the second time, lying in that position. At first, Aurelia doubted that the same result could be achieved by almost no movement as by the frenzied acrobatics they had previously performed, but sure enough, with Jonathan moving in a leisurely rhythm and his lips and fingers providing a harmony to their tune, she felt the rising tide cresting within her.

Afterwards there was no talk of her leaving and they lay wrapped in each other's arms until the sun rose.

Chapter Eighteen

Jonathan awoke with a pounding headache and a numb arm. The headache was easily explained away by the amount of whisky he had drunk and it became apparent that the arm was caused by Aurelia's weight pinning it down.

The events of the previous night gradually formed in his mind. He'd returned home in a drunken state after frequenting the sort of establishments he had never entered before. He'd blurted out everything to Aurelia in a bitter tirade. Then, incredibly, they'd made love—although the animalistic coupling they had first done could hardly be termed that. It had been raw and frantic; a show of all the pent-up emotion and hunger Jonathan had kept so firmly under guard. At one point she had cried his name aloud and he had answered with hers, repeating it over and over as he kissed her face, hair, breasts.

He'd asked her to stay for the night because the

thought of being alone—of being without *her*—had been unbearable. He should never have made the request, having promised her she would always have her privacy to sleep, but astoundingly she had agreed. And she was still there now. She was the rock he had instinctively clung to. The one he had sought for consolation and he never wanted to sleep without her by his side again.

He craned his head to look down at her and discovered she was already awake.

'How long have you been awake?' Jonathan asked.

'Maybe a quarter of an hour,' she answered. 'I didn't want to wake you. You looked so deeply asleep.'

Jonathan's insides squirmed a little at the idea she had been watching him sleep. It made him feel both vulnerable and excited at the thought. Aurelia put her hand on his chest. Her fingers were icy cold. A shocking contrast to the warmth of their bodies. Jonathan blinked in surprise and shuddered.

'Good grief, Aurelia, you're an icicle!'

He took her hand and wrapped it in his, bringing it to his lips to warm it with his breath. Aurelia giggled, deep toned and infectious.

The room was beginning to warm up. The fire was crackling softly in the grate, which meant that some time earlier Sarah, the maid, had slipped into Jonathan's room and lit it. She did this every morning, usually without waking Jonathan, and presumably paid her employer no attention. He hoped she would not have noticed there were two bodies in the bed, especially as it now dawned on him that both he and Aurelia had slept naked. Then again, why on earth should his wife not spend the night in his bed? Why should they not spend every night together?

He rolled on to his front and embraced Aurelia. 'Thank you for last night,' he murmured. 'Please forgive what I said and did. I was not fully in possession of myself. It won't happen again.'

Aurelia put her hand to his cheek, fingers a little warmer now thanks to his efforts. Her fingers scratched in his stubble. He needed to shave and wash, but the teasing sensation of Aurelia's fingernails against the roughness felt too good. Far too good, because that simple touch had set his body alight. They had only ever made love at night before and he wondered how different the experience would be in the morning when they were both still sleepy and warm.

He decided to find out and began to kiss her. Immediately her lips began to crush his and she rolled closer. This passionate side of her always took him by surprise.

'Slowly,' he murmured. 'We have got all day.'

Aurelia frowned. 'Don't you need to go to the mill?'

'That can wait,' Jonathan said. 'I don't want to think about that now. I'd rather concentrate on you.'

She slid her fingers down his neck, tickling his collarbone and smiled at him, eyes dancing. 'Then, Jonathan, I would like it very much if you would kiss me again.'

So he did. And much more.

It was mid-morning when finally they both agreed they were sated. Breakfast would be cold or had been removed from the dining room. He wondered idly what his servants would be thinking and decided on balance it was worth the gossip to have spent half the morning making love to Aurelia.

Lying with one leg over his, she stretched and yawned.

'Should you be going to work now?' she asked once again.

Jonathan stared at the ceiling, an unfamiliar sight in daylight. The arguments of the day before weighed heavily on him. 'I suppose I should. It's still my factory for the time being and Edward will most likely not be there.'

'Then shouldn't you be going to see Edward instead?' Aurelia rolled on to her side and gave him a stern look.

Jonathan clenched his fist, gripping the coverlet between his fingers. 'No. There is nothing I want to say to him, or that he could say to me.'

'I think you're wrong,' Aurelia said, 'And I think you know it.'

She lay on her belly and lifted herself on to her elbows as she looked at him. Her hair fell forward over her breasts, but Jonathan could still see the outline of them.

'You remind me of a Sphinx, lying like that.'

She giggled, then grew serious. 'Don't think to distract me,' she cautioned. 'But if you like, here is a riddle for you: what creature has the magnificent member of a bull and the obstinacy of a donkey?'

Jonathan pouted. 'I assume the answer should be myself, so I don't know whether to thank you for your flattery or be incensed at your insult, Aurelia.'

'Both,' she said with a smirk. 'If you are going to be so pig-headed as to ignore a decade or more of friendship, then you are the biggest fool in the British Empire and beyond.'

'I don't want to talk about it,' Jonathan growled. Despite his genuine irritation he liked this new boldness. If that had grown from sharing his bed, he would have to ensure she did it more frequently.

'You don't have to talk about it,' Aurelia said.

'You just have to think about it and come to the decision that you know is fair and sensible.'

She leaned into him closer and stroked his cheek as if a soft touch could take the edge off her words. It worked, too, damn it all!

'I don't deny Edward was wrong to keep the knowledge a secret, but at least think of the years of friendship between you. They are worth more than this argument, surely?'

She looked past him and her hand grew stiff on his shoulder.

'Where did you get that?'

Jonathan leaned round, wondering what she was referring to, and saw the likeness that Cassandra had done. It had been caught in the thin sunlight that had made its way across the room.

'Your sister gave it to me on Christmas Day,' he answered. 'She had promised it to me on our wedding day.'

'I didn't realise you had spent time alone talking.' Aurelia's fingers tightened, her nails biting into Jonathan's shoulder. Her face was full of fury and he had no doubt she was unaware of causing him pain. He was bewildered at her reaction.

'Are you angry Cassandra and I spoke about it?' Jonathan asked.

Aurelia looked away. 'She had no right to give you that. It wasn't done for you!'

'Why does it matter?' Jonathan asked. 'It's a

very good likeness of you. You look beautiful in it.'

'It wasn't done for you,' Aurelia repeated quietly. She pressed her lips together until the pressure whitened them. Her eyes misted.

'Who was it done for?' Jonathan asked gently.

She shook her head and climbed over Jonathan, out of the bed, and began rummaging among the discarded clothes for her shift.

'Aurelia!' Jonathan said sharply. 'Talk to me, please.'

She pulled her shift over her head and gave him a weary look, shaking her head. Jonathan sat up and swung his legs over the bed, pulling the sheet across his lower half.

'Cassandra told me to keep it a secret from you. She said it would upset you, but I didn't really believe her.'

'And yet you have it on display on your dressing table,' Aurelia exclaimed, throwing her hand towards the picture.

'I never expected you to come in here,' Jonathan pointed out. He didn't want to admit how many nights he had lain looking at her image and wishing she was beside him.

She lowered her hand. 'I suppose not. It doesn't matter. It was something I wasn't expecting to see again and surprised me.'

It had done more than surprise her; she had

been distressed and angry in equal measure. Jonathan let the sheets fall away as he stood and put his hands on her shoulders, trying not to be conscious of his nakedness.

'I want to understand why it upset you. I know so little about you even after months of marriage and I'm beginning to regret that. Why did you even agree to marry me?'

Her lips twisted into a wry smile. 'We have been married five months and you've only just thought to ask me that.'

He felt abashed. 'I suppose it never occurred to me to ask you outright.'

Aurelia began picking up her clothes and laying them on the bed. Her movements were so determinedly casual he could tell immediately she was avoiding the subject. 'You know why. Because Father wouldn't sell you the land otherwise and I wanted you to have it.'

'That can't have been the only reason,' Jonathan said. He took her hand. 'I told you about my mother's marriage last night, things I've never revealed to anyone else. Will you tell me the truth about this now?'

She gave him a long look. 'Promise me you will go see Edward and I will tell you.'

Jonathan raised his eyes. 'A secret *and* a promise in return for an explanation! That isn't a fair exchange.'

'But it is my offer,' Aurelia answered.

'Very well, then,' Jonathan said. 'Tell me now and I will go directly to Edward's house afterwards. I swear it.'

Aurelia sat on the edge of the bed and stretched her legs out in front of her, curling her toes into the thick rug.

'We moved back here suddenly as you know. I never told you why we had to leave Oxfordshire and I assume the rumours haven't followed us.'

'Weren't your father's gambling debts the reason you had to move?' Jonathan asked.

'It was one of the reasons, but my father is not entirely at fault.' Aurelia gave him a faint smile. 'You know, the first time I saw you I thought you had been sent to try to settle his debts. You had such a purposeful air as you strode along the path.'

He hadn't realised she had been watching him then. 'Considering I mistook you for a housemaid, I can hardly complain about that.'

'I was cleaning to try to distract myself,' Aurelia said. 'When I moved here my heart was broken. I had been in love with somebody else—deeply in love—but I couldn't have him. I decided that as I couldn't imagine loving anyone else and you didn't require me to love you, I may as well marry you. It would help the family and I didn't care what happened to my heart.'

'Who was he?' Jonathan asked. His stomach contracted with an unwelcome burst of jealousy at the thought that Aurelia had already given her affections elsewhere.

'It doesn't matter. I couldn't have him. I was hurt. We no longer communicate.'

Her voice was as clipped as the statements. He couldn't bear the pain that was still evident in her voice.

'Please,' Jonathan urged. 'I'd like to know.'

Aurelia's eyes grew misty. She closed them and turned her head away.

'He was a student at the university, though he moved in my father's circle. There was some distant family connection that my father enjoyed parading. Whenever Arthur dined with our family we spoke frequently. I was young and silly and his attention turned my head, I suppose. We grew close and I had hoped he would ask me to marry him. But he couldn't.'

Arthur. Even hearing the informal use of his name on Aurelia's lips caused Jonathan more fits of jealousy. Something struck him. 'Couldn't, not wouldn't? Why not?'

'Because it transpired he was already engaged to another woman.' Aurelia turned to him and shook her head. Her complexion was pale apart from a flush of scarlet that blossomed on each cheek.

'He already had a fiancée who lived in the

town close to his estate, far away from Oxford. They had been engaged since they were both very young. It had been arranged by their parents. Naturally Arthur tried to tell me he was intending to break it off with her, but he had deceived me. When my father discovered the truth he grew furious and cut off all ties between us. He didn't need to. I would have gladly done it myself if he hadn't stepped in on my behalf.'

She looked so sad that Jonathan wanted to wrap her in his arms and offer her some comfort.

'Cassandra's portrait was meant for him,' she continued. 'I told her to destroy it. That was why it was such a shock to see it here.'

Jonathan writhed inwardly. He should have obeyed Cassandra's instructions and hidden it. He should never have accepted it in the first place.

'Do you still love him?' he asked quietly. Why did he care? Why torture himself with hearing the confirmation that his wife longed for another man?

Aurelia shook her head. 'Not any longer. I trained myself not to. I decided I was done with love and marriage, even though living at Siddon Hall for ever seemed inevitable. When you told me you didn't need or want me to love you it seemed the perfect solution and I'm so pleased you asked me.'

Her assessment of the circumstances pained Jonathan deeply. He had laid his indifference towards marriage out for her to see and she had grasped it eagerly. She had only married him as a way of building a protective wall around her heart.

He covered her hand with his and gave it a gentle squeeze. Aurelia stared at it for a moment.

'Excuse me. I really must go dress. I promised to accompany Dora on an errand. You will go see Edward as you promised, won't you?'

She pulled her hand free from his, gathered her clothes and left the bedroom swiftly with the pile trailing in her arms. Jonathan sank back on the bed as he pondered her words. Yes, he hadn't required her to love him, but he was finding it hard now to live with the knowledge that she didn't when he was growing so fond of her in return.

If he hadn't claimed her, she might in time have met someone she could have loved. More than that, if he'd waited and courted her properly, she might have grown fond enough of him to accept a true proposal.

If he'd known then how his feelings towards Aurelia would grow, would he have ever asked for her hand and risked subjecting himself to this anguish of unrequited love?

He was trapped in a net of his own weaving and it was an unpleasant place to be.

* * *

It was with a weary heart that Jonathan called on Edward. Again he was admitted to the drawing room where Edward lay on the same reading couch under the same blanket. Only the change of smoking jacket for a silk dressing gown showed Edward had moved from his place. His eyes were wary when Jonathan entered the room, but he sat up a little straighter.

'I hoped you would return,' Edward said, wheezing slightly. 'Please take a seat.'

Jonathan folded his arms and remained standing.

'I didn't intend to, but Aurelia made me promise to come.'

Edward gave a grunt of satisfaction. 'She's a sensible woman.'

Jonathan didn't reply. So sensible she could train herself to fall out of love? Was it possible she could ever train herself to fall in love, again with Jonathan? That was something to think about another time because now he wanted answers.

'You promised to protect my mother,' he said coldly. 'She came to you for help, thinking she was safe here, but you told my father where we were living.'

Edward rolled his eyes theatrically. 'Do you think a man such as your father would not have been able to find your mother with or without my help? People cannot just disappear. I gave your mother sanctuary and a home with independence. She never had to work to support herself. I kept her safe through my intervention. Christopher promised never to seek her out, but to support her financially. How many women in her situation could claim to be so lucky?'

Jonathan was silent. He'd seen poor women forced into the factories and workhouses and genteel ladies reduced to taking rooms in boarding houses because their men had abandoned them. It would have been so easy for his mother to end up in the same situation. Edward no doubt spoke sense and had acted with her best interests at heart. Still, it rankled to think that all the time he had believed his progress and achievements had been entirely his own doing. The man he loathed had been the source of his success after all.

'Why did my father agree to those terms? What influence did you have over him?'

'Are you sure that is a question you want answered?' Edward said.

After Aurelia's revelation Jonathan wasn't sure he could stand any more secrets being revealed. 'No,' he admitted. 'It isn't, but if I don't ask I will always wonder.'

'Good,' Edward said. He rang the small silver bell he kept for summoning his maid and called for tea.

'It is always better to regret something you

did rather than something you were never brave enough to do,' he continued once the girl had departed. 'But be warned—when I tell you this I fully expect you to turn your face from me and I want you to feel no remorse at doing so.'

'Was it blackmail?' Jonathan asked.

Edward regarded him coldly. 'I have many faults, but resorting to extortion is not one of them.'

Jonathan hung his head.

'You always believed I loved your mother, didn't you?' Edward asked.

Jonathan shrugged noncommittally. Edward gave him a piercing look.

'You were right, of course I did. Anyone who knew Anne would have loved and admired her.'

Edward reached for his teacup and took a small sip, then a larger one. His hand shook, causing the cup to rattle in the saucer as he replaced it. He put it down and looked Jonathan in the eye.

'I loved Anne, but I was in love with Christopher.'

Jonathan recoiled and saw the look of pain that flitted across Edward's face.

'I don't understand.'

'Oh, I think you do,' Edward said. 'You're a man of the world, Jonathan, not an innocent babe, and my predilections are hardly unique, as distasteful as they must be to you.'

Jonathan tried not to wrinkle his nose at the thought of what acts Edward referred to. He had long suspected Edward's tastes were contrary to what nature intended. It was not something that particularly troubled him, but if what Edward was admitting was true, then he was not sure what repelled him more: the confirmation of what at times he had suspected of Edward's nature, or that the father he loathed was the object of his friend's love.

'Why my father?' he asked.

Edward shrugged. 'No one chooses who they fall in love with, but the moment Christopher and I laid eyes on each other we both knew. I doubt you would understand, never having experienced that immediate connection to another. The physical reaction is so overwhelming it is almost pure agony, along with the all-consuming need to be in the presence of the object of your affection at all times.'

Jonathan paced around the room, straightening disordered ornaments and newspapers. He hadn't, had he? He'd glimpsed the edges of such emotions at times with Aurelia. Beyond the need to touch her there was a wild yearning to be more to her than he was and to have even a fraction of his affection returned. Was that love? He suspected it might be. It scared him.

Jonathan sank on to the chair at Edward's side. The whole tale was overwhelming.

'It was a tragedy for all three of us. Christopher realised he could never be happy with Anne once he had discovered what true love felt like. Once they returned from Europe he offered to end the marriage, but she declined.'

'Did she know why he asked?' Jonathan asked. His poor mother, trapped in a marriage to someone who did not love her. Who was not capable of doing so.

'No,' Edward replied firmly. 'Anne knew Christopher and I were close, of course, but I don't think she ever suspected such love between two men was possible. She knew he was unhappy with her, but not why, and it tortured her.'

'So my father was unfaithful to my mother, and with you,' Jonathan said furiously.

'No. At least not in the way you mean. Your father took his marriage vows seriously and remained faithful to Anne throughout their marriage. But every time we met the temptation and the longing was there.'

Edward rubbed his eyes. They were growing red. 'If she had, of course, she might have understood Christopher's callousness towards her. Oh, yes,' he said, holding up his hands, 'don't think I was such a besotted fool that I could ignore his faults. He became incapable of making her happy and was cold to her as a result. At times I hated him for it. It was the only thing we ever argued over.'

'If she never suspected, why did she leave him?' Jonathan asked.

He recalled the long journey to Macclesfield; the flight across the north of England, changing coaches and his mother's determination to put distance between herself and Christopher.

'She was stronger than Christopher was,' Edward said. 'She knew that once you had left to go to school, life would become unbearable for both of them. Imagine living out your days in a house with someone you had grown to resent. She did what Christopher did not have the courage to do. Of course she came to me and I promised to help. Your father guessed straight away where she had come. I told him he must stay away or risk losing my affection for ever. He kept his word, though it broke his heart to lose you.'

Edward folded his hands. He avoided Jonathan's eyes. Clearly his tale had come to an end. Jonathan raked his hands through his hair, feeling the bubbling of emotions growing inside him. If he stayed any longer, it would burst out. He pushed himself from the chair.

'I need to go.'

'Must you?' Edward asked. 'I hoped we might

speak more and come to some sort of reconciliation. I care for you deeply, you know.'

Jonathan's throat tightened. The admission was spoken with such sincerity and he had no doubt Edward meant it. Not enough sleep and too much to drink the previous night was taking its toll and it was too much to take in everything that he had learned.

'I have spent a day on my own interests when I should have been at the mill.' He could not resist adding, 'Even if my involvement in your business is a legacy that was contrived as an inheritance of some sort, I intend to fulfil my duties to the best of my abilities.'

Edward flinched as if he had been struck. He looked away. When he met Jonathan's gaze next he looked more wounded at his words than at any other time. Jonathan felt a surge of guilt.

'Don't take me for a fool, Jonathan,' Edward said drily. 'Whatever Christopher and I meant to each other I can assure you that if you had been anything other than capable I would never have proposed you became my partner. You got where you are thanks to your own efforts.'

The two men locked eyes. All Jonathan saw in Edward's was the same affection and sincerity there had always been. He wondered if Edward could see any of the confusion that consumed him.

He nodded, picked up his hat and left. There

was work to be done, but as he strolled to the mill his mind returned over and over to what he had learned.

One thing in particular tormented him: his father had been married to his mother while he loved another. Edward and Christopher had been denied the chance for love that was so close, yet so far out of reach. After what Aurelia had told Jonathan that morning about her own broken heart the similarities were disturbingly uncomfortable. He had to hope she had been telling the truth about not being in love any longer with the despicable Arthur. The thought that she was still pining for another man while Jonathan's heart was hers was too terrible for him to contemplate.

Chapter Nineteen

Aurelia was waiting by the fire when Jonathan returned home. She had feared he would be as late as the previous night and return in the same state of inebriation, but he strolled through the door whistling to himself. She let go the breath that she had been holding since hearing the door and sat at the piano. Softly she began to play an old folk song she had been trying to teach Jonathan. She heard the door open, but didn't turn to greet him. Instead she carried on playing and waited to see what he would do.

He stood at the edge of the rug; she could hear his footsteps stop. He began to whistle along with her playing, adding a harmony of his own invention. When the piece was ended she finally turned and greeted him. He strolled across the room and sat beside her. As always, she felt a flutter deep inside her as his leg brushed against her skirt and she caught a hint of the fragrance surrounding him.

'You seem happier this evening,' she ventured.

'I accomplished a lot this afternoon. The new dyes will be perfect for my designs for the damask. We'll have a fine selection to exhibit in London.'

'We? So you settled your differences with Edward?'

'No.' His face changed. 'Not yet, at least. I learned some things that I need to consider. About my past and my family.'

He took her by the hands and ran his fingers up over the inside of her wrists. The warm, firm digits on her sensitive flesh sent sparks of delight racing over her. 'I mean we. Us. I'd like you to come with me to London. If you wish, that is.'

'I'd like that. Very much,' Aurelia replied. They held each other's eyes. Jonathan was the first to break eye contact.

'I recognise that song you were playing,' he said.

Aurelia gave him a playfully severe look. 'You should. It's one I told you to practise. I don't believe you've been attending to your lessons.'

Jonathan scratched his chin ruefully. 'I know. I am a terrible pupil. I hope your boys will prove better than I am.'

Aurelia smiled, but her conscience wormed inside her belly. She was determined that the girls would be taught as well as the boys. Then she would reveal her work to Jonathan and he would have no hesitation in letting the girls learn openly. All afternoon she had talked with Dora about how to accomplish this. She disliked keeping secrets, but this one could do little harm, she reasoned.

'It always confounds me that you can look at the holes in a Jacquard card and know exactly how the threads will wind together when you have hundreds of squares to consider, yet the keys of this piano are beyond you,' she said.

Jonathan shrugged and laughed. 'I know. It's a mystery to me, too.'

Late that night as Jonathan struggled to undo the hooks and eyes of Aurelia's corset, her mind returned to that conversation.

'Your fingers would be nimbler if you practised your scales daily as I instructed,' she said with a grin.

He looked at her gravely as he undid the last remaining hooks, then scooped her over his shoulder, strode to her bed and placed her on top of the coverlet. He knelt beside her and began to run his fingers up and down her belly, humming the tune from earlier. She giggled and squirmed as his fingers tickled her.

'Jonathan! What on earth are you doing?'

'I am practising scales as you told me,' he said. He tapped out a rhythm as he moved his right hand from the hollow of her throat to her navel and his left from her navel to her groin. 'You should provide the melody and tell me which end of the keyboard I should play at.'

Aurelia bit her lip and stretched out. Jonathan in a playful mood was rare, but if it stopped him brooding over his fight with Edward she was more than willing to play.

'Which end is which?' she asked.

'Why don't you hum something and find out?' he said with a glint in his eye.

She hummed a low arpeggio and discovered the answer in a way that made her gasp out the final note. Jonathan looked pleased at the effect his 'playing' had. She raised her head and looked up at him through her eyelashes coyly.

'I wonder if my pupil has mastered playing with two hands simultaneously?' Aurelia murmured.

Jonathan lifted her hand. He brushed his lips over the knuckles while giving her a look that set her heart pounding.

'I'm not sure. I think I should practise very thoroughly this evening. My teacher can be quite demanding, you know.'

A thrill raced through Aurelia, sending her stomach pitching up and down. 'I think you should, too,' she said, stretching out and letting her legs flop apart.

Jonathan flexed his fingers and bent over her. Aurelia began to hum once more and managed to get quite a long way through her tune until Jonathan's fingers began tickling her in such a way that she was reduced to making tuneless gasps. Shortly after that they abandoned all practice.

Afterwards they lay in a lethargic tangle of limbs. The reluctance Jonathan had had and his reservations about getting her pregnant seemed to have disappeared completely. Jonathan had made no attempt to leave Aurelia's bed, but now he let his hand fall to the floor where his discarded nightshirt lay.

'You don't have to go, Aurelia murmured. She slid her hand across his bare chest and downwards to settle on the hard muscles of his abdomen. She loved that part of him—the fine hairs of his chest that became a single line like a map guiding her fingers to the thicker thatch below his belly. She walked her fingers down the line and was dismayed when Jonathan took hold of her hand and gently guided it back up to his chest.

'I will stay the night with you on condition that you let me sleep now, you insatiable creature. I must not neglect my work tomorrow and don't have the luxury of staying in bed all morning like today.'

Aurelia settled against him and closed her eyes. Sleeping in his arms was a new and exciting pleasure enough to satisfy her. She was on the cusp of sleep when Jonathan gave a great sigh, sounding as if the world was on his shoulders.

'What's wrong?' she whispered. 'Can't you sleep?'

'I'm just thinking of the past.,' he said quietly. 'My father loved another and my mother would not set him free. All our lives might have been so different if she had.'

'That is a tragedy for both of them,' Aurelia agreed. She waited to see if he would continue, but he lapsed into silence and she listened to his breathing grow slower as he fell asleep. She rolled over and lay on her side and after a moment Jonathan turned behind her, tucking his legs in the crook of hers and wrapping his arm around her shoulder as he nuzzled down behind her.

Aurelia slept uneasily. She didn't think Jonathan loved anyone else, unless he was regretting not marrying Cassandra. Even if that were the case, Aurelia was not sure she could bear a life of loving him when that love was not returned.

Relations between Edward and Jonathan were still cool in the weeks leading up to the Great

Exhibition. Edward had taken to working from his study at home, using a series of bobbin boys to relay messages to Jonathan who worked in the office on the mill site.

Sometimes Aurelia took the messages herself as an excuse to visit Edward. She was dismayed at the change in her friend who had lost most of his vitality since his argument with her husband.

'Won't you tell me what happened between you?' she begged on more than one occasion, but all her entreaties were met with a firm refusal.

'You know enough already,' Edward said. 'Anything Jonathan chooses to tell you is his choice and I won't risk incurring his ire further by going behind his back.'

'I hate to see you both at odds.' Aurelia sighed. She finished arranging the flowers in the vase. Now it was April the blossoms were in full force and her mother's gardens were full of hyacinth and marigolds. Edward insisted on keeping his fire lit even on the warmest day and the scent was almost too sweet for the stifling heat. It turned her stomach and made her long for the cool air of the small square her house looked on to.

'So do I,' Edward admitted, 'but I fear it was a natural consequence. I am very pleased Jonathan has you, Aurelia. My suspicions were correct that he needed a wife.'

'And an heir,' Aurelia pointed out. 'That's why you told him to marry me, after all.'

Edward patted her hand. 'Do you know, my dear, I believe that is the least of my considerations compared to the change I have seen in Jonathan since you and he married.'

Aurelia smiled inwardly. She resisted the urge to run her hand across her belly and thought to herself that her husband and friend were not the only people capable of keeping secrets. It was too soon to be certain, but she had missed the last two months' courses. If she had counted correctly, she had moved beyond the time when she had bled in agony at Christmas.

She had said nothing to Jonathan and, though it pained her to deny them both the pleasures they enjoyed, she had maintained the pretence that she was indisposed and he was unable to visit. She would wait until they returned from the Exhibition in London when she would be more certain and Jonathan would not be so distracted with his work. May was approaching and, though everything was prepared for the transportation of the examples of silk ribbons, brocade and even a ribbon loom to the Exhibition site in London, Jonathan spent a lot of time fretting and poring over letters and plans.

Despite that Aurelia realised she had never been happier—or busier. Jonathan shared his concerns and plans with her now that he seemed determined not to speak with Edward. They spent hours discussing ideas as if she was a partner in the business. She would never have expected marriage could be so involving. If Arthur crossed her mind at all, it was only to wonder how she had ever thought a life of idle compliments and chit-chat would ever have made her happy. Life with Jonathan had turned out to be so much more than she had dreamed it could be. He might not love her, but he valued her and that was almost a good enough substitute.

The end of April arrived, bringing warm sunshine and a sense of purpose. Aurelia and Jonathan walked home as usual along the river path on a fine evening. The newly formed routine had been settled since the apprentice house had been finished two weeks earlier.

Aurelia always arrived at the house for five o'clock to instruct the two girls whose turn it was on the rota how to prepare the evening meal. Millie accompanied her and Aurelia secretly hoped that in time she would take her place as a superintendent in the house and pass on some of the housekeeping skills she had learned under Mrs Barnes. Her confidence had grown and seeing her guiding the younger children made Aurelia happy.

At six o'clock the rest of the apprentices would

return home, the girls to finish preparing the meals and the boys to begin an hour of lessons with Aurelia. At seven Jonathan would arrive at the house, inspect the boys and listen in on some of the learning before escorting Aurelia back home while the children ate their supper.

What Jonathan didn't know was that while the girls were preparing the meal Aurelia was also teaching them reading, writing and some necessary arithmetic using the recipe books and household manuals she had brought with her. Each day a different pair of girls would receive her instruction and then pass that on to the others while Aurelia taught the boys. So far it was proving effective and Aurelia looked forward with anticipation to the day when she could reveal her results to Jonathan and prove girls had an equal claim to education.

She was absorbed with thinking of this and missed what Jonathan had been saying until she realised he had grown silent and was looking at her questioningly.

'I'm sorry, my mind was elsewhere,' she apologised.

'I said I have taken the liberty of booking us a suite with adjoining rooms,' Jonathan told her. 'I hope you don't mind. We don't have to use both rooms, of course…'

Aurelia squeezed his arm.

'I'm sure whatever you have decided will be perfect,' she assured him and she meant it, too. He was considerate and, dare she say it, loving and she could not imagine a time without him in her life. She was truly happy and the other secret she was nursing, which she was becoming more and more certain of, would seal that happiness for both of them.

She was so certain that there was nothing that could happen to end her happiness that it was doubly a blow when the moment came.

The house was in a state of disarray as Jonathan and Aurelia prepared to travel to London the following morning for the opening of the Great Exhibition. Annie was to accompany her mistress, while Jonathan's valet had already travelled ahead to prepare the hotel for their arrival.

Since Aurelia and Jonathan now spent every night sharing one of their beds, some of their possessions had found themselves moving between rooms and it was no surprise to Aurelia when Sarah bobbed a curtsy on the landing.

'I found your book, Mrs Harcourt.'

Sarah held out a thick book bound in brown leather.

'This isn't mine. What makes you think it is?' Aurelia asked.

'It has the odd writing you read,' Sarah said. 'The one that looks like shapes.

Aurelia opened the book at the first page, curious to see what the girl meant.

Η ταλαιπωρία της μητέρας μου έχει τελειώσει. Δεν έχω χάσει.

The Greek script was written in a confident hand.

"'My mother's suffering is ended. I am...'" She translated the words under her breath, struggling with the final verb.

The book wasn't hers. It was Jonathan's. This was a diary entry.

'Thank you. You may go now, Sarah,' she said absentmindedly.

She had not realised Jonathan kept a diary, or that he understood Greek and could write in a hand better than her own. Fascinated, she couldn't help herself and flicked through the volume as she walked back to her sitting room. The date on the first page had been from a few years previously. He didn't write in it every night. There were weeks with only one or two entries and three months were missing completely. Towards the middle of the book they became more frequent and one of the most recent entries caused her blood to run cold. Jonathan talked about marriage being a trial. He was unsure of his decision. Aurelia's eyes stung. She flicked back further. She knew that to intrude into Jonathan's thoughts was wrong, but couldn't help herself. There had to be something, even a sentence, that would suggest he might be happy with her. She found an account of their first quarrel and deciphered it.

My wife wishes to visit the mill. Why she would like to surround herself with noise and workmen is beyond me and I will not expose her to that.

Turning the pages further back, she let her eyes fall on a list, methodically set out. She read it and immediately wished she could pluck the words from her memory, but it was too late.

She closed the book and sank into her chair, clutching the book tightly to her chest. Jonathan had listed all the reasons he should marry Cassandra. Through blurred eyes Aurelia found the page and read it again. Some were practical, dealing with the need for the land, others—the ones that were harder to read—listed Cassandra's beauty, her wit and so on. There was no mistaking the meaning. Jonathan had even finished the entry by declaring on a fresh line his intention to marry Cassandra.

Aurelia bit her lip, feeling sick. Jonathan had

only asked for her hand because Cassandra had refused him. She'd known that from the day he had proposed and had thought herself immune to any pain caused by the knowledge. To see her sister's merits and advantages laid out so clearly with the incontestable conclusion that she was the right bride for Jonathan filled her with anguish. She stifled a sob.

Because the fact was, she had fallen in love with her husband. She hadn't meant to and was not even sure when it had happened, but little by little through the kindness he had shown, the dedication to ensuring her happiness, the gentle touches and passionate kisses, she had come to realise what a prize she had won. She closed the book and walked out of her room to return it to Jonathan's. She didn't want to see the hateful volume any longer and already felt guilty for having pried into his private thoughts.

'There you are, my dear. What are you doing?'

His voice made her jump like a child caught in the act of stealing lumps from the sugar bowl. Jonathan was walking up the stairs towards her, carrying a pile of newspapers. Aurelia's first impulse was to hide the book behind her back, but honesty wouldn't let her deceive him. She held it out to him.

'Sarah brought this to me, but I think it must be yours.'

Jonathan's eyes widened and Aurelia saw a flash of panic momentarily cross his face. Then the anxiety was gone, replaced with relief. Aurelia felt similar relief flood through her. He had assumed she could not read it. Why would he ever suspect she could read the Greek alphabet or whole words and sentences? How fortunate she had kept that side of her a secret.

Jonathan smiled and held his hand out.

'Thank you. It's a journal of mine. I never quite broke my childhood habit of jotting down my thoughts. It must have fallen from the table beside the bed. Are you almost ready to go? The train leaves in half an hour.'

'Nearly, I just want to gather a few more items,' Aurelia answered.

'Good. I must admit I am looking forward to the journey. Hours spent in a compartment with my wife will be a much more agreeable way of travelling than usual.' He kissed her on the cheek and went into his room.

Aurelia put her hand to the spot, capturing the memory of his soft lips on her skin. She wanted to cry, but that would serve no purpose. She had enough secrets already, so keeping one more from Jonathan was hardly a burden. Yet the secret that she loved her husband was the one that weighed on her heart the greatest.

Chapter Twenty

Aurelia seemed unusually withdrawn on the journey to London. They had the compartment to themselves and Jonathan considered the length of the journey ahead of them before they arrived at the next station where they would need to change trains. He wondered if he should sit beside Aurelia instead of opposite and put his arms around her. Once he would never have even considered it. A day earlier he would not have thought twice before touching her, but now he hesitated.

'I've never travelled by train before' was all she said in answer to Jonathan's query as to whether she was unwell. She ran her hands over the walnut frame of the window and peered through the glass at the countryside rushing by in a blur. They must have been doing all of forty miles an hour. 'It isn't at all what I was expecting.'

Maybe it was the jolting of the carriages that was making her feel off colour. She turned her head to look out of the window and her book in her lap remained unopened. Jonathan frowned to himself, seeing the slim volume in her hands. She had opened his journal to discover it was his book and a small germ of worry in his brain whispered to him that she had read what he had written there, and that was the cause of her unhappiness. He knew deep down this could not be the case because he had written in Greek, but all the same he could only connect her change in manner to the point at which they had left the house.

'Are you sure you made the right decision by coming with me?' Jonathan asked. 'It isn't too late for you to return to Macclesfield on tomorrow's train.'

He wanted her at his side. Exploring the Exhibition halls would not be half as much fun without Aurelia to share it with him, but if she preferred to return home he would not object. To his relief, she shook her head.

'No, I would like to see London and the Exhibition. I want to see the Great Shalimar, this "crystal palace" that everyone has been talking about with such excitement. I don't really believe it can contain as much glass as the reports claim. How will it not fall down if the wind gets too strong?'

Her voice filled with enthusiasm, but too soon her eyes dulled. 'Of course I would be happy to amuse myself if you would rather I left you to do your business without me. I'm sure I will be able to find plenty to occupy me.'

Jonathan clenched his jaw. How stupid he had been to ever tell Aurelia she was not welcome in that part of his life. How sooner they might have grown close if he had granted her request to see the mill the first day she had asked.

She turned on her seat to face him and held his gaze. 'I do wish you and Edward had reconciled before we came away.'

Was that the cause of her mood? The last time Jonathan had spoken to Edward for more than a few minutes had been three days before the planned trip to London. Edward had looked frail and had shown little interest in the arrangements. He had begun his journey two days earlier than Jonathan and Aurelia after saying he would prefer the chance to recuperate from his journey before the grand opening.

'Aurelia, you know how I feel about Edward and you know it hurts me to have quarrelled with him,' Jonathan said, but Aurelia interrupted.

'Do I really know how you feel about anything? I am not sure I do. What I do know is that Edward was your greatest friend and if you do not mend your disagreement before he dies you will regret it for ever. Living life with regrets is enough to make anyone's life miserable.' She sounded weary again and dropped her head. 'If you will excuse me, I think I shall close my eyes for a few moments.'

She leaned against the velvet headrest and pulled her veil over her eyes. Jonathan rested his head back and closed his eyes. He could not escape the nagging sense that Aurelia was correct and he should at least speak to Edward again. He'd as good as forgiven him in his heart. Far from hating Edward, he was filled by a deep sorrow for the old man's tale. Three lives had been blighted. Four, including Jonathan's own. His mother had married a man who could never love her. His father and Edward had loved against nature and the law. Jonathan's entire future had changed. None of them had achieved the happiness they had craved. But none of that was Edward's fault. Aurelia's other words haunted him more.

Living with regrets.

He had thought she was happy. She seemed happy and full of purpose, as passionate as ever in their bed, and willing to spend time with Jonathan. So why did she speak so bitterly of regrets?

The Great Exhibition of the Works of Industry of All Nations. How to describe it?

Jonathan wouldn't be able to resort to Greek to record the experience as surely they would not have had the words to describe what he saw.

The initial impression was of a great crush. A

mass of people dressed in their finest streaming towards the Exhibition. Men and women with skin and hair of every shade. A vibrant multi-coloured river of coats and capes winding to the entrance of the glass structure of the Exhibition hall that itself glinted in the sunlight like the crystals it was compared to. Children scuffed their feet, bored with the wait. Self-important-looking older and richer couples grumbled audibly about how they should have preferential treatment and be allowed to bypass the queues.

'This is one of the beauties of our Prince's endeavour,' Jonathan remarked to Aurelia. 'No one is treated better than anyone else. A viscount must queue just as a man such as I.'

'What do you mean, a man such as you?' Aurelia slipped her hand through his arm. 'There is nothing that makes you a less worthy person than the highest duke in the land and this baronet's daughter is happy to be standing in line with you.'

Her words warmed Jonathan's heart. He spread his fingers over her hand, enclosing it in his, and she smiled at him.

'What would you like to see first?' she asked. 'Personally I want to see the elephant and then the silks from the Orient. Would you like to see those, too?'

'Very much,' Jonathan agreed. 'It's strange to think something that starts half the world away in

China ends with us in Cheshire, isn't it? Perhaps one day you and I could travel there together and see the mulberry bushes in their original setting.'

Aurelia's face lit up and her eyes widened. 'To China? That's so far,' she breathed. 'I can't imagine it.'

Jonathan placed his hand over hers and gave it a gentle squeeze. Through her silk glove he could feel the shape of her wedding band on her finger. She appeared to be happier now than when they had journeyed down to London. A good night's sleep at the hotel seemed to have restored her spirits, even though she had claimed to be too weary to make love.

His stomach fluttered with a mixture of excitement and trepidation. He had presumptuously made plans Aurelia was not aware of, but which he hoped would please her and further cement their marriage. Rather than returning to Cheshire immediately after the Exhibition, they would be travelling to France and take the honeymoon they had never had. Together they would visit Paris and Lyon. Perhaps even reach the mountains Edward had talked of. It would be the perfect opportunity to spend time together and Jonathan dared to hope that through their shared experiences Aurelia might begin to return the feelings he bore towards her.

They inched slowly forward, but hours seemed

to pass before they were inside the glass palace and standing among the living trees that had been contained within it and surrounded by more delights than Jonathan could list. Someone jostled against them and he put his arms around Aurelia to protect her from the bustle. She glanced up at him, held securely in his arms.

'It's so busy here. Much worse than I expected it to be,' Jonathan muttered.

'You hate crowds, don't you?' Aurelia said. Her eyes scanned the great halls that stretched away left to right from the central atrium. She stiffened and her eyes widened, then narrowed.

'What's wrong?' Jonathan asked. She was still staring at a point in the distance and he wasn't sure she had heard him. He put his hand on her shoulder and looked at her anxiously. She appeared to recollect where she was.

'It's nothing. I just thought I saw someone I recognised from Oxfordshire, but it couldn't have been. Let's go find somewhere to take tea. I'm so thirsty I believe I could lap water from the fountain.'

Jonathan agreed that after standing for so long to gain admittance the elephant and silks could wait and their first priority was to visit the Western refreshment court.

'Is there someone who could relay a message for me?' Jonathan asked the impeccably dressed waiter who led them to a small table for two set in one quarter of a vast tearoom.

'I'll find a boy, sir,' he answered, as he drew Aurelia's seat out for her to descend on to, spreading her skirts as she sat. She had bought a new outfit for the occasion that Jonathan had not seen before, though as he looked at it now he recognised the brocade and grinned.

'I wondered when you would pay attention to my dress, Jonathan dear.' Aurelia giggled. Her eyes glinted with delight. 'I decided that as we were displaying the best of Great Britain's industrial produce, what better way to exhibit your wares than to parade them in public?'

Jonathan gazed at her dress in admiration, though at least half of that was for the woman rather than the spreading skirt and tight-fitting jacket in burgundy brocade shot through with copper. She met his eyes and he gave a low whistle of appreciation. Aurelia's smile deepened.

'I started planning it the day after you invited me to come. Edward arranged for me to obtain the cloth and I had my mother's dressmaker create it.'

'And you kept it secret so well,' Jonathan said. 'How devious you are, my dear. This will teach me to pay more attention to what is going on under my nose, I suppose.'

Her smile dropped a little. 'It was only a small secret. Surely you can forgive me that.'

'I don't think that secret is likely to change my world too drastically,' Jonathan said, giving another laugh. The arrival of their order distracted them and they set to work devouring disappointingly small sandwiches. Their refreshments were interrupted by the arrival of the same runabout boy who had taken the message to Jonathan's exhibit arriving back at their side.

'Please, sir, I was told to give you this, sir.' His eye strayed to the plate of bath buns.

Jonathan realised his card had been returned with a message written on the back.

Please call on receipt of this reply. We have visitors who might be to our advantage.

It was signed by Edward and Jonathan couldn't help but notice his handwriting was shakier than usual. Aurelia was still toying with her bun less than enthusiastically. Jonathan showed her the note and she raised her eyebrows with interest.

'Will you mind if I go now?' he asked. 'The Machinery in Motion gallery is practically next door. You can stay and finish eating and I'll come back as soon as I can.'

Aurelia shook her head, unable to answer for the mouthful of the stodgy dough she had just taken. She swallowed and licked a trace of butter from her lips. Even the sight of something so simple was enough to send Jonathan's imagination spiralling. He decided he would order a plate of cakes to be sent to their hotel room where he could enjoy licking the cream from Aurelia's lips himself.

'Go, of course. You don't know what opportunity this might be. The exhibits might set all of Europe marvelling, but the food will certainly not.' Aurelia arched her brows and pushed the remains of the cake away. 'I think I will drink my tea, then go exploring.'

'Don't go too far,' Jonathan cautioned. 'I could imagine never finding you in this crowd and having to wait until we were the last two remaining people in the building.'

'Would you really wait that long?' Aurelia asked.

She gave him a smile of such sweetness his insides melted. How did she not guess what she meant to him? He could live with her disapproval that he had broken the terms of their marriage, but could he live with knowing his love was not reciprocated? Perhaps he would be brave enough to tell her when they were abroad. Paris was the city of love, after all.

'I will find my way to the elephant and wait for you there.' Aurelia laughed. 'I never imagined saying such a thing, did you?'

'Not at all,' Jonathan answered. He stroked her hand, then walked away. He would not leave her long.

* * *

Aurelia waited until Jonathan had left the refreshment court before summoning a waitress.

'May I have another pot of tea?'

The waitress bobbed smartly and left, returning after a brief delay with no tea, but bearing a piece of paper.

'If you please, ma'am, there's a gentleman at the table by the window. He has asked me to give you this.'

The waitress's eyes sparkled with excitement as she held out the folded piece of paper. Aurelia looked past her, trying to see who might have sent it and wondering if Edward was there. She couldn't see clearly past a party of older couples blocking the view. She accepted the note with curiosity. It looked to have been written in haste on a page torn from a small notebook and folded in half. She recognised the writing immediately and her stomach plummeted.

Arthur.

He was here, watching her. The hairs on the back of Aurelia's neck stood on end. She had thought earlier that she had caught a glimpse of him, but had decided she must be mistaken. Now, having her suspicion confirmed made her stomach flip over. More disconcerting than the fact she had received the note at all was that it was addressed to Miss Upford. Arthur presumably still did not realise she was married even though he must have seen her and Jonathan taking tea together. But then, they were hardly intimate in public so why would he? She took a pencil from her bag and scribbled a reply.

I have no wish to speak to you, now or ever. If you have any of your former regard for me, you will respect that wish.

Aurelia looked up at the waitress who was lingering nearby and held the note out.

'Please return this to the gentleman and tell him my reply is enclosed within. And please do not bother bringing me tea, I am leaving.'

The girl looked disappointed. Presumably she had hoped to see an illicit affair taking place. 'Of course, madam.'

As soon as the waitress left Aurelia flung a handful of shillings on to the table. It was more than the bill would come to, but she didn't care. She wanted to have left by the time Arthur received her reply. She walked purposefully out of the refreshment court through a different door to the one Jonathan had taken, but made the mistake of hesitating before choosing which way to turn and heard Arthur's voice calling.

'Aurelia, please wait.'

He was following her as she strode past galleries of furs and shawls so quickly she barely noticed the hues and textures on display. She had suspected he might follow, but had hoped she would have been deep enough into the crowds for him not to spot her. She pulled her bonnet forward and carried on walking, choosing the nearest gallery on a whim and finding herself surrounded by medieval altars and candlesticks. She felt the unsettling experience of having walked straight into a church.

A hand took hold of her elbow and she spun around with a cry.

'Take your hand off me at once!'

Arthur withdrew his hand.

'I knew it was you,' he said. His face lit with delight. He had not changed. If anything he was even more handsome now he had a few lines on his face and had grown his hair into a longer style.

'Aurelia, I'm so pleased to see you. I thought we would never meet again. You must forgive me for ignoring your message.'

Aurelia glared at him. 'I do not forgive you and I did not intend that we ever should meet again. I have nothing to say to you.'

'But I have lots to say to you,' Arthur cajoled. 'Please walk with me. Didn't you get my letters? You didn't answer them.'

Letters plural, Aurelia noted.

'What do you want with me, Arthur?' She sighed.

'Only to see you and talk to you. I miss you. Is that so wrong after the way we parted?'

'And is it so wrong or surprising that I should decline!' Aurelia shot him a withering look. 'After the way you betrayed me—not to mention how you betrayed Emmeline—no woman with any scruples would let you anywhere near her!'

Arthur's handsome face dropped. 'You're right. I know that now. I'm grateful Emmeline died before she learned how duplicitous her husband is.'

Aurelia's eyes strayed to the black band on Arthur's upper arm, the outward sign of mourning. She doubted his grief went deeper than the sleeve of his jacket.

'I read one of your letters and chose not to respond,' she told him. 'As I choose now no longer to spend time in your company.'

She turned away, but was prevented from leaving by Arthur clutching at her sleeve again.

'What do you think you're doing, Mr Carver?' she exclaimed. 'Take your hand off me immediately!'

He dropped his hand, but did not step away. 'Is there no hope for us?' he asked.

His face had taken on a sullen aspect. Why had Aurelia never noticed how petulant he could be when she had first known him? He seemed like a sulky child in comparison to Jonathan.

Jonathan.

Where was he?

'There is no hope,' she answered. 'Even if I was so lacking in dignity that I would forgive you, I am a married woman now.'

She turned and walked through the galleries until she found herself in the Indian Court where she had arranged to meet Jonathan. Frustratingly Arthur followed.

'Was that your husband you were taking tea with? Where is he now?' Arthur said. 'He abandoned you to walk about the finest exhibit the world has ever seen on your own.'

'He had to attend to his business,' Aurelia said defensively.

'A businessman?' Arthur raised his eyebrows again and glanced down his nose. Why had Aurelia never noticed how infuriating the habit was? 'You married a tradesman. I'm sorry I drove you to this.'

'I married a good man,' Aurelia snapped. 'An excellent man. Better than you could ever know or attempt to mimic.'

'Mimic?' Arthur raised his brows in surprise.

'Yes, mimic. Because any outward signs of goodness that brought you within a mile of Jonathan's good character would be a sham!' Aurelia leaned against the wall, weary of the confrontation.

'You told me that I had broken your heart, yet you sound as if you love him.'

He reached a hand to touch her face, but withdrew it as she glared at him. He sounded genuinely contrite and looked at her with some of the love in his eyes that she had once treasured.

Aurelia smiled. 'You broke my heart, but Mr Harcourt has mended it and more. Go away, Arthur. My husband will be here soon and I would not wish him to encounter you. And I would not exchange him for one hundred baronets, earls or dukes.'

Arthur leaned towards her as if he was about to embrace her. Aurelia gave him a stern look and he stepped back. He fumbled in his pocket for the note she had given him and pressed it into her hand.

'Goodbye, Aurelia. I wish you well. Can you wish me the same?'

Aurelia gazed at the man she had once loved, wondering why she ever had. She did not doubt his love for her had been genuine, but it had been a selfish love. He had been willing to risk scandal and the disapproval of his family to win her hand. Such love was not enough to build a marriage on and never would have been.

'I do wish you well. I hope you find happiness, but it will never be with me. Now goodbye.'

She watched as he walked away with not a single regret in her heart.

Chapter Twenty-One

❧❧❧❧❧

The scale of the endeavour continued to amaze Jonathan as he made his way to what amounted to a whole weaving shed, with machinery contributed by a whole range of manufacturers. Pride raced through him at the sight of Langdon and Harcourt's display with fine brocades and silk hanging or half-completed on the loom. Edward was standing talking to a tall gentleman who had his back to Jonathan. Edward was leaning on the cane with the ivory-topped handle he had started to use since his recent bout of illness. Jonathan hated the cane. It was an ever-present reminder that Edward was growing weaker. He looked older, but his expression was as animated as ever. Jonathan was transported back to the first time he had stood opposite Edward outside the mill office so many years ago, never dreaming that he could become Edward's equal…or friend. Edward caught Jonathan's eye and gave him a small nod.

'My partner has arrived at last. Jonathan, allow me to present Viscount Turnott of Street Hatton, Worcestershire.'

The man bestowed an enthusiastic smile on Jonathan, who bowed. He hadn't been warned to expect the aristocracy and thought gratefully of Aurelia who had given him the confidence to move among higher circles.

'I was telling your partner how beautiful your fabric is,' Viscount Turnott said. 'I am wondering what your capacity would be if I were to place an order. How quickly could you manufacture what I needed? Are these machines powered by water?'

Jonathan explained with enthusiasm what the process was and how his new wheel would drive up production. After ten minutes of conversation, the young Viscount appeared just as enthusiastic about the new technology as Jonathan and Jonathan was on the verge of offering him a personal tour of the mill. They finally drew the conversation to an end.

'I have friends who I believe would be just as interested as I am,' Viscount Turnott said. 'I would like to introduce you to them. We intend to return to the Exhibition every day as there is far too much to see on one visit.'

'I would be delighted and I agree with your assessment,' Jonathan said with a laugh. 'In fact,

I have abandoned my wife to explore by herself. Would you deem it terribly rude if I went to find her?'

'Not at all.' Viscount Turnott handed Jonathan a card and they bade each other farewell. Jonathan turned the card over to look at it. The young man had seemed an unassuming type of gentleman and yet his card clearly suggested he was a member of the Queen's household. Jonathan held it out for Edward to inspect.

'If we are noticed, this will be our making!'

The two men smiled at each other in delight. Jonathan shook his old friend's hand, temporarily forgetting their quarrel. Edward stiffened and sniffed and Jonathan realised then how much he had missed the friendship.

Jonathan broke away first. Public affection unnerved him. 'I need to go find Aurelia. I've abandoned her for far too long. That's something I owe you thanks for,' he said, smiling. 'You were right about marriage being good for me.'

'You love her, don't you?' Edward said.

Jonathan felt heat spreading across his chest and neck. 'Yes, I do. It took me longer than it should have to realise how much she meant to me.'

'And does she know that?' Edward asked.

'I've never told her. It was not part of our arrangement. I'm not sure she would be pleased to hear it.'

Edward rolled his eyes. 'If I know Aurelia, I don't think that will be a concern to her. Tell her before too long.'

Jonathan made his way to meet Aurelia at the elephant. It was later in the afternoon and the great crowds had thinned a little so it was easy to spot her standing in one corner of the room that housed the immense pachyderm.

It was equally easy to spot that she was not alone. A broad-shouldered man with a shock of chestnut hair and a moustache that had clearly been modelled on Prince Albert's stood beside her. He was resplendent in an immaculately cut suit of grey silk with a black band around one arm.

What was equally clear to Jonathan as he approached was that the two were not strangers, but clearly knew each other. Jonathan paused and backed against the wall. He could not see Aurelia's face because she had her back to him, but her companion was speaking and looking grave. Aurelia shook her head and said something. The man leaned closer to listen and his face took on an expression that Jonathan could not fail to recognise.

It was a sentiment he knew well because it was one he felt on a daily basis. This man was in love with Aurelia.

Jonathan froze to the spot, unable to move as he watched the charming fellow flirting with Aurelia. If only he could see her face and understand whether the attention was welcome. Aurelia shook her head and the man leaned forward to press something in her hand and then walked swiftly in the opposite direction from Jonathan.

Jonathan waited until the man was out of the room before he joined Aurelia.

'I'm sorry I took so long. I hope you haven't been waiting too long for me.'

She shook her head and gave Jonathan a smile that looked forced.

'Not at all. I only arrived myself a few moments ago. Did your meeting go well? Was Edward there? You must tell me everything.'

Her face lit with a smile more like the one Jonathan had grown used to. He nodded, but couldn't bring himself to smile back, knowing that Aurelia was deliberately omitting to tell him what he had seen with his own two eyes.

Secrets, always secrets, he thought. Well, he was determined not to fall into the same trap as his parents had, even if what he discovered tore him to shreds. He felt the pulse in his neck begin to speed and took a breath to calm himself.

'When I arrived you were talking to somebody. Who was it?'

Aurelia's face fell, but she quickly blinked and her calm expression returned. Jonathan wondered if she was intending to brazen it out and deny everything, but she pressed her lips together and then looked at him.

'That was Arthur,' she whispered.

Jonathan's throat filled with acid. Of course it would have been Arthur. Who else was in love with Aurelia? Something occurred to him.

'He was wearing a band of mourning. Who for?'

'For his wife,' Aurelia answered. 'She passed away shortly after Christmas.'

Jonathan felt a wave of nausea. A cold trickle of perspiration down the back of his neck. Aurelia's former love was free now and they had sought each other out here. His body felt weak with the anticipation of impending sorrow.

'Did you know this before?' he asked.

Aurelia nodded. 'Arthur wrote to me shortly after the event. He asked me to forgive him for what he had done. Dora saved the letter from my father and sent it to me.'

Jonathan searched his memory. Something stirred: a letter from Theodora that he had handed to Aurelia himself one morning. He tried to recall if she had seemed different that evening, but she had seemed distracted or secretive on so many occasions. Even as they drank tea and he had teased her about her dress, she had seemed unsettled at the mention of secrets and now he suspected he had discovered why.

'And what do you intend to do with that information?' he asked. His voice sounded harsh in his ears and must have appeared equally forbidding to Aurelia, because she stepped back and her mouth dropped open.

'I intend to do nothing! I am your wife now.'

For better or worse, Jonathan thought grimly. This very afternoon, when they should have been exploring the exhibition together, he had left her and given them the opportunity to meet. No wonder she had turned to her first love when Jonathan had been so neglectful.

His path became clear, like fog lifting, only to reveal a deep chasm on either side. It would kill him to lose her, but if it meant she could be happy with the man she loved he would not stand in her way. He would not be another Anne Harcourt clinging on to somebody against their will.

He took a deep breath and turned his head away, rapidly blinking to rid his eyes of the sharp tears he knew were almost ready to brim, then turned back to Aurelia.

'Yes, you are my wife.' He drew a long, uneven breath. 'But perhaps that is something we need to discuss.'

Astonishment flashed across Aurelia's face, then her eyes grew cold.

'I see,' she said. She brought her chin up and pressed her lips together hard until they were bone white. 'As you wish. I would prefer to discuss matters later in a less public place, but let me say this—if you want to end our marriage, then be honest enough to say so and don't attempt to pretend it is out of a sense of betrayal.'

She gave a strangled sob, spun on her heel and walked swiftly away, pushing through the crowds that gathered around the elephant. Jonathan followed, trying to keep sight of the burgundy and gold gown through the crowds. Was she hoping to catch up with her Arthur? Jonathan wasn't sure, but he didn't think so. She had swept off in a different direction. She walked past the central fountain and into the tropical gardens. Jonathan saw her pause and look at the piece of paper in her hand that Arthur had given her. She screwed it up and hurled it into a flowerbed, then carried on walking. She turned back to the main atrium and was swallowed up by the crowds.

Jonathan sagged, feeling all the energy leaving him. She had not objected to his suggestion of ending their marriage, but had jumped to the conclusion that he wished to end it for reasons of his own. He stopped by the flowerbed and picked up the piece of paper that Aurelia had discarded. He spread it out, prepared to torture himself by reading whatever words of love Arthur's note contained. As he read it became clear to Jonathan that the meeting had been a matter of coincidence, not an intentional plan. He read Aurelia's reply. They were written in her firm, assured hand, but pressing so hard that it left an impression that went right through the paper. As he read her words Jonathan wanted to curl into a ball of remorse. It was clear that Aurelia had rejected Arthur in the strongest terms possible.

How could he have jumped to such unfounded conclusions?

She didn't want Arthur. Was it beyond the bounds that she could learn to love Jonathan as he hoped? He had to find her and tell her how greatly mistaken he was and, more importantly, untangle why she thought he would want to be rid of her.

Finding Aurelia, however, proved to be much harder than Jonathan anticipated. He made his way first to the Chinese silks and to every room he thought she might have been interested in. The galleries were still heaving with people and there were so many rooms that Jonathan soon came to the conclusion it would be impossible to locate her. She might be in the room directly above him, one gallery away or at the opposite end of the building and he would be none the wiser. She might have left altogether, although he hoped she would have had more sense than to go off into Hyde Park alone. Wherever she was, she would not be found by Jonathan running from one end to the other with no plan.

He returned to the Machines in Motion gallery. Edward would help him look or would keep watch for Aurelia. Then Jonathan would stay by the exit until he was the last person in the building if it was necessary.

Chapter Twenty-Two

Aurelia ran on through the galleries, not caring that she was attracting looks from other visitors. She found a staircase and ascended, hoping the upper floor would be quieter, but it was still teeming with visitors.

Jonathan was having doubts about their marriage. She had scarcely believed what she was hearing when the words came out of his mouth. It was so sudden and she found it hard to believe that merely seeing her in conversation with Arthur had been the catalyst for his decision. She recalled the diary entries she had read and her lip wobbled. Jonathan must have reached the decision of his own accord and this was the pretext he would use to rid himself of the wife who had proved a disappointment.

Her stomach heaved and she felt a swell of nausea. She stopped running, suddenly and painfully out of breath, and leaned against the railings of the balcony that overlooked the central hall. She gripped the railing tightly with one hand while the other pressed against her belly. She was sure now that she was with child. If that was the case, the matter was more complicated. Jonathan would not find it so easy to rid himself of her and she did not believe he would treat her so ill.

She looked over the edge and the drop made her head spin. From above the women on the ground floor were a mass of colourful flowers and feathers, nets and veils adorned their hats while the men were discs of plain felt and silk. She would never find Jonathan amid them.

'Miss, do you need help? Are you unwell?'

Aurelia looked round. A woman had stopped beside the railing, her black eyes full of kindly concern.

'Do you have friends we can find?' She spoke to the smartly dressed man beside her. 'Isiah, you go see if you can find someone to help this poor lady.'

'No! Thank you, but I won't trouble you,' Aurelia said, before Isiah could walk away. 'I know where my friend is. I'll go to him now.'

Edward would be kind to her. He would help direct her to someone who could find a hansom cab to take her back to the hotel where she could wait for Jonathan and decide what to do next. She thanked the couple and made her way to the gallery where Jonathan was exhibiting. The sound of cogwheels turning, shuttles clattering and other complicated-looking machines going about their business was overwhelming. Aurelia walked slowly through the rows of looms and spinning machines, imagining this must be what it was like daily in Jonathan's mill. She'd never experienced it and it was unlikely she ever would.

Edward was standing by a machine upon which finished silk was being wound around a great wooden frame. He smiled as he saw Aurelia approaching, then as she drew nearer his face fell.

'My dear Aurelia, what on earth is the matter? You look so pale,' he exclaimed, rushing as fast as he could to take her by the hand. 'Where is Jonathan?'

Aurelia shook her head wordlessly. If she spoke, she would spill out the whole tale and would not be able to stop from sobbing. She bowed her head and felt Edward pat her on the back.

'Never mind, here he is now,' Edward said, lifting her chin.

Aurelia turned around and saw her husband had entered the room. He froze mid-step as their eyes met, then he lifted his eyes to the ceiling and ran his hands through his hair. His hat was nowhere to be seen and his tie was askew.

'I thought I'd lost you,' he said, rushing towards her. He seemed so relieved that Aurelia found it hard to believe he wanted to leave her. They were friends, though. Whatever deeper feelings he lacked, they liked each other's company. It was her fault for allowing herself to grow too close.

'I was beside myself with worry when I couldn't follow you. I thought I'd have to stay here until I was the last man in the building.'

He stopped short of embracing her and they faced each other awkwardly.

'I must speak with you,' Jonathan said.

'Have you two quarrelled?' Edward asked, his expression pained.

'Not exactly,' Aurelia said.

She drew Jonathan to one side, out of Edward's hearing.

'I need to know. Are you still in love with Arthur?' Jonathan asked before she could speak. 'I know he is now free to marry. I don't want to dictate your actions or force you to remain in circumstances which are abhorrent to you.'

'Absolutely not!' Aurelia exclaimed. She would not make it easy for him by owning that falsehood. 'If you thought that us conversing meant I have feelings for him or was planning to leave you, you are very much mistaken. You did, didn't you?'

He nodded slowly.

'Well, I'm not going to be the one who instigates that. I've weathered one scandal and survived that, but I have no intention of risking another by leaving you,' she said. 'If you do not wish me to live with you, I shall ask Edward if I can live with him rather than return to Siddon Hall. He's growing weaker and may need assistance at some point. What is more natural than his greatest friend's wife taking the burden?'

They both glanced towards Edward who was standing where they had left him, trying to appear as if he was not burning to discover what they were discussing.

'You must do as you see fit. I will not prevent you if you wish to leave me,' Jonathan said stiffly. 'But I must ask for clarification on one point. Why would *I* not want *you* to live with me?' He seemed genuinely puzzled, his brow furrowed.

'Because you only married me for convenience and marriage to me is a trial.' Aurelia folded her arms and looked Jonathan in the eye. 'I know you wished to marry my sister. I'm sorry Cassandra refused you. I'm sorry I wasn't the choice you wanted.'

She looked away, discreetly wiping her eyes with her sleeve as finally admitting it out loud caused tears to spill.

'I never wanted to marry Cassandra,' Jonathan exclaimed. He ran his hands through his hair, ruffling the waves. 'Why ever would you think that?'

Aurelia folded her arms. Her eyes swam with tears now. 'I read your diary. I saw how you described her and your intent to ask for her hand. I can read Greek,' she admitted. 'I've been able to read it for years. *"Tomorrow evening I shall propose to Miss Cassandra Upford."* Do you deny they were your words?'

'I don't deny them,' Jonathan said. 'And I did intend—reluctantly—to ask for Cassandra's hand. I thought I should because she was the oldest so it seemed right. But I never wanted to and when it came down to the moment I couldn't bring myself to do it. I had spent the evening watching you across the table talking with Edward and I knew you were the wife I wanted.'

'You didn't want a wife at all,' she reminded him. 'You were careful to make sure I knew that from the start.'

'And I didn't,' Jonathan said. 'But of all the wives I didn't want, you were the one I didn't want the least. Oh, that's not what I mean at all!' Jonathan pounded his fist on the wall, making Aurelia jump. 'I mean as I had to have a wife I wanted it to be you.'

His eyes were bright with emotion. Aurelia's heart began to beat faster. He wanted her. Her, not Cassandra. She didn't know what to say and was saved from having to respond by Edward stepping close and coughing discreetly.

'Jonathan, I hate to interrupt what is clearly a very emotional conversation, but Viscount Turnott has returned with one of the friends he spoke of earlier. They would like to speak to you once again.'

Jonathan and Aurelia both followed Edward's outstretched hand. Aurelia had never heard of the Viscount, but he was standing by the furthest loom and Arthur was by his side. Aurelia looked at Jonathan and shook her head.

'I didn't know he would come here.'

'I believe you,' Jonathan said. He took her hands and squeezed them tightly. 'Will you excuse me for a moment? Please don't run away again.'

She nodded, heart in her mouth.

Jonathan strolled over to the two men and greeted the young Viscount warmly. Aurelia watched as the Viscount introduced Jonathan to Arthur. When Arthur held his hand out, Jonathan's arm remained rigid at his side.

'I understand you were once acquainted with my wife. I have heard the circumstances under which you parted and as such I decline to shake your hand.'

Aurelia's mouth dropped open, unable to believe what had just happened. 'He'll ruin everything for himself,' she whispered to Edward.

Edward shrugged. 'Perhaps he thinks it is worth the price. You must tell me some time how you know that man. I do enjoy a piece of new gossip, my dear.'

Arthur peered round Jonathan and saw Aurelia. She watched as his face fell. He bowed stiffly to Jonathan and left. Jonathan and Viscount Turnott spoke briefly. To Aurelia, watching anxiously, it seemed the parting was reasonably cordial. Jonathan returned to her side.

'What were you thinking?' Aurelia cried.

Jonathan looked at her gravely. 'I was thinking that the hand of a man who could behave so dishonourably towards a woman is not worth shaking and that he is not the sort of man I would like to do business with. You understand why I had no other choice?'

'I understand. You would have done it had he insulted any woman of your acquaintance,' Aurelia said, remembering his words on the riverbank.

Jonathan shook his head. 'No. I did it because he insulted *you*.'

He turned to Edward. 'I may have just put paid to the opportunity we thought we had. Can you forgive me?'

Edward turned the cane round in his hands. 'I'd like to hear the full story of why you did it, but, yes, when I hear how he has injured our dear Aurelia I expect I will wholly agree.'

Jonathan nodded. 'I must also beg your forgiveness for the way I've behaved towards you. I've been appalling.'

He held on to Edward's hand and squeezed it

tightly. Edward swallowed and squeezed it back. His lips moved wordlessly and he turned away, shaking his head. Aurelia could see the emotion in his eyes and stepped away to give the men some space.

'Do you forgive me for deceiving you?' Edward asked. 'Can you look past what sort of man I am?'

Jonathan raised his brows in surprise. 'Your tastes were never why I was angry,' he explained. 'I wish you had told me before about everything that happened between my parents. I shouldn't have discovered it in such a manner.'

'I know and I regret it, but I thought it was the best course of action,' Edward said. 'I am going to visit Christopher before he dies. You can come with me, if you wish.'

Jonathan shook his head. 'I have nothing to say to him. You've been a better father to me than he ever was.'

'I tried to be,' Edward said.

The two men embraced, clapping each other on the back. Aurelia wiped her eyes. Both men turned to her with smiles and eyes that were also a little misty.

'We were interrupted in the middle of something very important,' Jonathan said to her. 'There's something you need to understand. I asked for *your* hand that evening Aurelia. Yours, and only yours, because I wanted to marry you.

Every time we met you fascinated me. I couldn't shake you from my mind. I sat through dinner that night watching you and dreading the point at which I would have to ask for your sister's hand.'

He stepped closer and reached for Aurelia's hand. Warmth spread over her at his touch, causing her blood to race. Tears pricked her eyes, but this time they were tears of joy.

'You sparkled. You glowed. You were a flame I couldn't tear myself away from,' Jonathan said. 'I don't ever want to. I know we said our marriage was for the business of birthing an heir, but you mean so much more to me. More than I ever thought you could. Do you know what I'm trying to say?'

'I do.' Aurelia blinked away the tears. 'And I know what you feel because I feel it, too. I love you, Jonathan.'

'You love me?'

'I do.' She felt lightheaded. 'I didn't mean to. I didn't think I could break every promise we made to each other not to care, but break them I did.'

Jonathan laughed aloud. He cut off her words by seizing her in his arms and swinging her round. Aurelia squealed with joy as her feet skimmed the ground. Jonathan lowered her gently and wrapped his arms around her. His eyes burned with joy.

'I love you. I can't even remember when I started to. I love the way you frown when you're thinking. I love your passion and your kindness. I love it when…' He looked around and his lips twitched. 'Well, perhaps I won't go into everything I love about you in such a public place, but I intend to show you later on.'

'I very much look forward to that demonstration.' Aurelia laced her fingers through his and his eyes lit up.

'I didn't dare hope you felt the same as I did,' Jonathan said. 'I felt you were hiding something, but I never dreamed you were hiding that you loved me!'

'I have been keeping secrets,' Aurelia admitted. 'I didn't want to cause an argument because I wasn't sure if we were strong enough to make up, but now I think we need to be honest. If we have disagreements, we'll have to work together to overcome them. That's part of marriage, too.'

She looked him squarely in the eye. 'I know you don't think it is necessary, but I have been teaching the factory girls. Not just sewing or how to recite Bible passages, but the same things as the boys. Please don't be angry with me. They're learning well. I want to continue doing it.'

Jonathan cocked his head to one side. Then his face broke into a wide smile.

'But not to read Greek, I hope—which is something I look forward to discussing with you, by the way. I agree as I can see it means so much to you.'

'It does. Thank you,' she said. She put her arms around Jonathan's neck and kissed his cheek.

'I can't deny you anything,' Jonathan said, slipping his arms around her waist.

'I should hope not,' Aurelia said, laughing.

Jonathan kissed her. 'Now, you aren't the only one who can keep secrets, Aurelia. I have been making travel plans for us. After our stay in London, I thought we might travel on the Continent for a month or two. We never had a honeymoon, did we? How does Paris sound?'

She slid her arms around his neck and leaned against him. She felt him shiver and smiled. Her heart gave a pulse of pure happiness. Time together with no interruptions. Nights to revel in their newly discovered love and understanding.

'That sounds wonderful. Thank you.'

Jonathan dropped to one knee and reached for her left hand. He ran his thumb over the wedding band.

'Aurelia Harcourt, I've asked you this twice already, but now I'm asking you again. My heart belongs to you as fully as any man's belonged to any woman. Will you make me the happiest man on earth by living with me as my wife? To *love* and keep.'

'Jonathan, my darling, nothing in the world would give me greater pleasure.'

Jonathan pulled her to him and held her tightly, his head against hers.

'I don't care if you never conceive, or if it takes ten years.'

Aurelia put her finger to his lips, silencing him and looked into his eyes. 'Jonathan, about that. There's one last secret I've been keeping. I'm with child.'

Jonathan's face lit with joy. He clutched her hands and stepped away, looking her up and down. 'You're sure? And you feel well?'

'Very well,' Aurelia said. Her throat tightened to hear the concern in his voice. 'I didn't want to tell you until I was sure and until I was further than before. But, yes, I'm carrying your heir.'

'Our *child*,' Jonathan said. He bit his lip and Aurelia realised his eyes were filling with tears. 'Our family. I like the sound of that, don't you?'

Aurelia nodded.

'It sounds perfect,' she breathed as Jonathan enfolded her in an embrace.

She put her lips against the soft spot beneath his ear and kissed him gently.

'Completely perfect.'

* * * * *

COMING SOON!

We really hope you enjoyed reading this book.
If you're looking for more romance, be sure to
head to the shops when new books are
available on

Thursday 17th September

To see which titles are coming soon, please visit

millsandboon.co.uk/nextmonth

MILLS & BOON

Coming next month

CHRISTMAS AT COURT
Blythe Gifford

'You are to be betrothed on Christmas Day.'

Alice paused, struggling to understand. Her parents had told her this season at court would be important for her future. That was the reason they had allowed her to come alone. They must have known.

She lifted her chin. 'To whom?'

'To John Talbot, son and heir of the Earl of Stanson.'

Had she seen him at court? It did not matter. It was not her place to object.

'When do I meet him?'

The Queen raised her eyes and looked behind Alice. 'Now.'

There, at the door, stood the man she had taken for a messenger only a few hours ago.

He looked not at all pleased.

*

Sir John stepped into room, jaw clenched. Lady Alice stared at him and his impression remained the same as when he had seen her earlier.

Young. Naive. Pretty. Tawny hair. Gentle, innocent blue eyes...

But as he watched, her expression shifted. Not angry. Not yet. But bewildered ...

He stepped forward and bowed, a gracious gesture, he hoped.

Silence. Though he could see countless questions in her eyes.

She glanced back at Dame Elizabeth. 'Is this to be announced to the court, then?'

'The betrothal ceremony will be a private affair, though word will become known, of course. However, my involvement must remain secret.'

'And the King's approval?' she asked.

'Has been obtained.'

She did not look as if she believed that, he thought. Not a dull-witted woman, then. So it was as well she did not know the priest who would preside was a secret ally of Henry Tudor, who was gathering an army in exile to take England's throne.

Dame Elizabeth waved her hand, as if she still reigned and the audience was over. 'Sir John, please see that Lady Alice returns safely to the palace.'

One final bow and they left the hall.

The wind from the river whipped around them. Beside him, she shivered. He reached out his arm, sheltering her with his cloak, pulling her close.

He thought of her, suddenly, not as a pawn in this game, but as his *wife*. Married, he would be free to explore the soft warmth of her, to touch her hair and ...

Guilt prickled his spine.

They entered the Palace, suddenly engulfed by the scent of Yule greenery, and he let her go, wishing her a night of peace. There was still much she was not to know.

Not yet, at least.

Continue reading
CHRISTMAS AT COURT
Blythe Gifford

Available next month
www.millsandboon.co.uk

WE'RE LOOKING FOR NEW AUTHORS FOR THE MILLS & BOON HISTORICAL SERIES!

Whether you're a published author or an aspiring one, our editors would love to read your story.

You can submit the synopsis and first three chapters of your novel online, and find out more about the series, at **harlequin.submittable.com/submit**

We read all submissions and you do not need to have an agent to submit.

IF YOU'RE INTERESTED, WHY NOT HAVE A GO?

Submit your story at:
harlequin.submittable.com/submit

MILLS & BOON

LET'S TALK
Romance

For exclusive extracts, competitions
and special offers, find us online:

f facebook.com/millsandboon

🐦 @MillsandBoon

📷 @MillsandBoonUK

Get in touch on 01413 063232

G